WATER UNDER THE BRIDGE

Katie Stearns

D1715767

For the ones who are tired of trying

CHAPTER ONE

Mara

Two weeks have passed since I moved in. Everything is new and changed and different...except me.

Each day, living in this new house bleeds into the night and back again seamlessly. The blurry day-to-day of my new life has me settling into a strange sort of routine. I go to bed on the couch, I wake up on the couch, I make coffee, go back to the couch, pick at leftover takeout, zone out in a dreamless nap on the couch, pick at more leftovers, then fall asleep on the couch for the night.

My mother calls every two days. I never have anything new to report, but I appreciate that she's checking in on me. In the fall months, she relocates to Arizona to stay with her sister and doesn't return until June. Without her physical presence, I feel even more listless and unattached to anything.

It was her idea that I move here, into this little story and a half house in a family neighborhood. I have nothing bad to say about it, really. It's cute with white vinyl siding and concrete steps leading down to the sidewalk. The floors are hardwood, and the walls are painted a neutral light gray. The galley kitchen is a little small but more than enough for just me, especially since I haven't cooked anything since the divorce four months ago. It's a charming house inside and out that would feel homey if anyone else lived here.

But I don't feel like I fit here, or anywhere, now that the divorce is final. Heartache has led me here, and it's heartache that will be my only companion in this house. I hate that I no longer live in the house I was forced out of by my now ex-husband. It was my favorite place. It was the place I lived with Mason, the man I swore I would love for the rest of my life. My home with him was once filled with love and happiness, and now it still exists that way, just with another woman in my place.

Every ounce of life worth living was wrung out of me when he chose her over our marriage.

This is not what I wanted. I wanted to work things out, move past his indiscretion, and carry on with our lives. But he had no desire whatsoever to fix the damage he caused. He said no to marriage therapy, no to leaving Sarah, and no to staying with me. He threw away ten years of loving me for the shiny new thing that, to him, seemed like the next best thing.

It's been four months since the divorce became final, and every day I think about how badly I don't want to be single again. I don't want to start over at the age of twenty-six. I don't want this cute little house in a family neighborhood, but now that's all I have.

I haven't had the motivation to put the house in order like my mom demanded. The boxes are all where the movers left them. A few have been opened so I could grab a hand towel or a fork or a different sweatshirt. The bed upstairs has yet to be dressed. The kitchen cabinets are empty. My TV isn't even plugged in. When I moved in, all the boxes seemed claustrophobic, but now they make me feel less alone. The perpetual state of undone has become the familiar thing that makes me feel somewhat secure now.

I can't get myself to exist outside of these walls and that couch.

My breathing is the only thing that marks the passage of time because I haven't even hung the clock.

Everything is quiet and still, inside and out.

So, when a sudden knocking comes from the other side of the front door, I'm startled. There isn't a single person I know who would be coming over. Mom left for Arizona last week, and all the people I thought were my friends slowly began to slip away towards the end of my marriage, like they knew what was happening and wanted no part of it.

My eyes fix themselves on the wooden door in curiosity, and then I lift myself onto my feet and edge through the boxes. Without a peephole, I have no way of seeing my unexpected visitor, so I take a breath and turn the handle slowly. I swing the door open just enough for my head to appear in the space.

Blinking slightly against the September sun, I see a woman standing on the other side of the screen door wearing a bright, warm smile that generates from a place of welcoming and friendliness. She's past middle-aged, possibly older than my own mother, but she chooses to wear much more casual clothing than my mom. Just a yellow long-sleeved t-shirt and jeans with a pair of tennis shoes. Her hair is brown and speckled with gray, just long enough to tickle the tops of her shoulders. Her blue eyes glitter as she smiles at me.

"Can I help you?"

"Hi! I'm Linda; I live next door," she greets, gesturing to the house next to mine, the blue one to the west. "I just wanted to welcome you to the neighborhood." Linda grins genuinely and opens the screen door so she can thrust a tin-foil-covered plate that I didn't notice she was holding into my hands. "I made you some cookies. I figured chocolate chip was a pretty safe choice. Unless you're gluten-free?"

"Um...no, I'm not," I answer softly. This woman's presence is so starkly different from my own that I realize how far I've fallen in terms of keeping a social life or even some semblance of a life in general. It's a tiny little wake-up call that I wasn't expecting today.

"Oh, great! I hope you enjoy them."

I look down at the shiny tin foil, overwhelmed by her thoughtfulness. "Thank you." I look up again and offer her a small smile. "I'm Mara."

"What a beautiful name. Fitting for such a beautiful young woman."

Her kind words don't register, but I think to keep some bit of a smile on my face.

"It's so nice to meet you, Mara. I'm sure we'll be seeing you around soon. Don't be a stranger, okay?"

I nod, clutching the plate, and watch as Linda goes back down the concrete steps and over to the right, across my driveway and the lawn to her house.

I close the door, feeling a little shaken but also a little warmed, and investigate the cookies under the tinfoil. The smell of sugar and caramelized butter hits my nose and instantly makes my stomach growl. I haven't been that hungry lately, but when I have eaten, I've just ordered takeout. So these homemade cookies are hitting me on another level. I pick one up, studying the chocolate chips dotted throughout, and take a small bite.

I'm transported to a memory of making chocolate chip cookies with my grandmother when I was a child. She was a much softer woman than her daughter, who laughed easily and gave out hugs whether she thought I needed them or not. Linda seems to be similar in that regard—warm, inviting, thoughtful.

I make my way over to the living room window facing Linda's house and tug back the curtain. I haven't given even half a thought to my neighbors. The fact that Linda made these cookies for me and brought them over to say hello makes my insides glow a little. It's a strange sensation after dwelling in so much quiet pain.

I let the curtain fall back in place and go back to sit on the couch where I shamelessly eat the entire plate of cookies in one sitting.

I know I'm supposed to be moving on or starting over, but I just don't know how. My mother likes to present this new life of mine as something exciting and fun. *A blank page! A fresh start!* But it doesn't feel like that. It feels like these boxes contain the only pieces I have left of the life I loved, and everything else just exists outside of me.

I ache to find something that could glue those pieces back together again. The one thing that would work is silent and unpracticed in my throat. The voice I used to sing with, that gave me such purpose and meaning, has left me just as much as Mason did.

If anything, that's what makes this house feel so empty. I know my voice could fill it up with melodies and songs, but I can't get myself to rejuvenate that place inside of me.

Before all this, I used to be a singer. I used to play guitar and sing my own songs for crowded bars and coffee shops. Once I gained a following, I went on to play bigger venues and made more money. And once I jumped into YouTube and iTunes, nothing could've stopped me from being a success.

But then, I found out about Sarah. Mason stopped trying to pretend, and asked for a divorce. Losing him took away my passion for anything I used to love, and now I don't know how to get it back. I don't know how to put one foot in front of the other. I couldn't even get myself to go over and pack up my things from our house; my mom had to step in and hire movers. She was the one who took charge and decided on this house.

I know if the divorce had just happened, she wouldn't have gone to Arizona. But pushing me towards this house was her way of telling me it was time to suck it up. She's always been the tough love kind of mother, and though I usually dislike that about her, this time I see it as the helpful shove she intends it to be.

I can't wallow in this emptiness forever.

Maybe I can't sing, but I can still try to find something new to fill my time.

Unfortunately, the only thing I come up with is plugging in the Smart TV my mother moved over here from the guest room in her house where I was staying before this. Flipping mindlessly through the channels doesn't really do me any good, but it's better than just sitting on the couch staring up at the ceiling. At least it distracts me from missing Mason and rehashing all of the hurt he caused. The plate Linda gave me sits on my kitchen counter for the rest of the week. Every morning, I get up and look at it for a long moment, and then I go back to the couch where I resume my channel surfing.

I should return it.

I should take the white ceramic circle in my own two hands, walk out the front door, across the yard, knock on her door, and give it back to her.

Even though Linda is nice and did something sweet for me, I don't know how to return the favor. Before all this, I would've baked cookies or something of my own to put on that plate when I returned it to her, to show my gratitude. But I haven't cooked, much less baked, anything in months.

So, now I need to muster the motivation to walk that empty plate over there or risk Linda thinking I'm not going to give it back. I think I would die if she showed up at my door and asked for it. It's that thought that emboldens me enough to bring it as far as my front door.

But then I look down and take in the state of my clothes. I've been wearing this pair of gray sweatpants for at least four days, and the black t-shirt even longer. I touch my hair and immediately get my fingers tangled in the long strands. I guess I need to freshen up before I step out into the light of day. The very thought of taking a shower exhausts me, but I set the plate down on the coffee table and slog through a shower.

The hot water is nice, and I admit I smell better, but the wetness in my long auburn hair makes me feel like a drowned sewer rat, only cleaner. I grab jeans and a shirt from one of the boxes in my otherwise untouched bedroom upstairs, and then I find myself back at the front door with Linda's plate.

I take a deep breath, feeling stupid and foolish that somehow I've become such a shut-in that I can't even get myself to return my neighbor's plate without having a mental breakdown, and open the door. I gulp at the screen door handle and then open that, too.

I step out onto the small concrete landing, the sun beaming down on me from above. The brightness makes me squint my eyes. The screen door closes behind me with a sharp *snap*, and that's when the panic kicks in. Just sheer, confusing, unnecessary panic grips me by the lungs with an iron fist.

My knees wobble, and I sit with a plop on the top step, the plate clasped tightly in my sweaty hands. I close my eyes and focus my mind on each breath going in and going out.

It's just a plate, I tell myself. It's just your nice neighbor.

But it's more than just that. I haven't left my house since I moved in, not even for a walk or to check the mail. The broken pieces of me feel a little more contained inside those walls, and out here I just feel…exposed. Raw.

But after a few terrifying moments of intentional breathing, I start to notice the smell of the grass. I feel the light breeze moving over my damp hair. I feel how the sun warms the skin on my face.

The anxiety ebbs away as I let myself ease into those things. And when I open my eyes and look around my small front yard, I'm hit with a deep, moving sense of gratitude that beautiful things still exist even when I'm so lost. The world is waiting for me to return to it whenever I'm ready.

I hug the plate to my chest and take another breath. I'm reminded to be gentle with myself. If all I can handle this month is returning this plate, then that's okay. My best is my best no matter what my mother has to say about it.

Feeling a little encouraged, I get up and carefully step down to the grass. I walk across my driveway and into Linda's yard with my heart beating strong and fast. I come to a stop in front of the porch and look up at her home. It's a beautiful craftsman house, blue in color, with a white front door. There are a few kids' toys scattered around the porch, and a welcome sign hangs beneath the brass door knocker.

Gathering myself, I lift my hand to knock but freeze as my anxiety creeps up like before. I lower my hand, breathe, and lift it again. Nothing. My brain will not make my hand knock. I swallow hard, feeling foolish, and before I can think twice, I set the plate down on the welcome mat and sprint back to the safety of my unpacked house.

Be gentle, I tell myself as I lock myself inside and try not to cry.

I thought that would be the end of the plate, but I was wrong. I thought I would go back to quietly existing next to my nice neighbor, but the next day, Linda is on the other side of the door once again, that same plate in her hands, this time with blueberry muffins on it.

"Would you mind if I pawn these off on you? I made way too many," she says with that warm smile. I don't notice that she worded it like I'm doing her a favor by accepting them, but if I had, I would recognize how sweet that is.

"Oh...sure." I take the plate through the opening of the screen door.

"Excellent. Enjoy. Say, is it just you here, dear?" she asks, glancing curiously over my shoulder into the house. "Not to sound like a nosy neighbor, but I haven't seen anyone else here but you."

"Yes, it's just me," I answer quietly, not doing a good job of hiding how much it stings to say that out loud.

"Of course. If you're ever lonely, just stop over, sweetheart. You enjoy those muffins, and I'll see you around." She grins at me, and in a blink of an eye, she's on her way back to her house.

I close the door and look down at the plate full of delicious blueberry muffins. Without even a shred of self-respect, I also devour these in one sitting. Then I walk the plate to the kitchen, wash it, and find a clean towel to let it dry on.

I look at it for a long time, studying the little beads of water resting on the smooth surface and how the sun through the window glints on each drop. It's just a plate...but look what Linda does with it. Offering me kindness and calories and thoughtfulness. For the first time, I'm interested to know more about Linda. Does she have a husband? Kids? Is she retired?

I could spy on her. It wouldn't be hard to do. But I have a feeling that Linda would probably tell me her life's story if I showed up on her doorstep and did more than leave her plate on the mat.

Maybe a neighbor like Linda is what I need to slowly draw me back out into the world again. I just need to let her.

CHAPTER TWO

Mara

"Mara, are you listening?" my mother questions hotly in my ear.

"Yes, Mama," I answer softly.

There's a brief pause on the line because I called her an endearment. I haven't called her Mama in probably fifteen years. But I said it on purpose, because even though she was just hounding me about getting out of the house, I know she means well.

"I'm worried about you. Maybe I should fly back."

"I'll be okay, Mom. I'm just trying to find my feet again," I insist quietly.

She sighs. "I don't want to say this, but maybe you should see a...*therapist*." She says the word like it's dirty or scandalous. It reveals that she believes therapists are for crazy people, or that therapy is something to be hidden or ashamed of.

But between her words, I think she's trying to say that I could use someone to talk to. Someone to help me through my grief. I don't know that I could open my mouth and talk about what I'm feeling. It feels too deep for me to pull out with plain words. It's something a song could do, but I can't sing anymore.

"Have you gotten outside at all? A walk can do wonders," my mother suggests, clearly trying to think of all the other options short of therapy.

I shake my head, then remember I need to verbally respond. "No."

"You should. Tomorrow, have your coffee outside and then go for a walk. I bet you'll feel so much better."

"Sure, Mom."

A walk isn't going to heal my soul. A little extra vitamin D isn't going to make Mason love me again. But I do agree that I spend too much time inside, alone, in silence. All I do is lie on the couch and mindlessly watch cookie decorating videos on the TV. Sometimes I think, but most times, nothing is happening in my mind. I'm just...empty. Breathing. Existing. A comatose heart barely beating in my chest.

My mother and I say our goodbyes, and I realize my mom is right. I need to make some kind of effort. I can't just keep banking on Linda to bring me out of my comfort zone each time she brings me baked goods on that plate.

So, I force myself out onto the concrete landing and sit on the top step. To anyone else, it isn't loud out here. It's a relatively quiet neighborhood in the good part of town. But every car that passes shakes me up a little. A teenager on a bike whizzes by, and I feel my spine straighten. A dog barks, and I have the urge to cover my ears.

But the air smells sweet and clean. The concrete is rough and dry under my hand. To the right is a flower bed where I focus on a flower that has yet to bloom. The longer I stare at it, the more beautiful it is. It's a living, breathing thing, so green and so tenacious as to push up through the soil so it can become something beautiful. Born in darkness, it seeks the light.

A blue pickup truck rolls up and parks on the street in front of Linda's house. Printed on the side is *Sauk Rapids Tree Services*. A man about my age gets out of the driver's seat, and I shamelessly watch him stride up the walkway. Something about the roughness of his walk holds my attention. His boots hit the ground in almost a stomp as he walks, the gait of his steps swaying his muscular shoulders. The gray long-sleeved shirt he's wearing has the same logo as the one on his truck, and the fabric clings to his firm biceps in a way that Mason's shirts never did.

When he gets to the porch steps, he must feel my eyes on him, because he looks over at me. My heart gives one offbeat *thump* when those dark eyes meet mine. He frowns, probably because I'm staring at him like a creep, and then goes inside.

I haven't spared even a moment to look out the window towards Linda's house. I haven't paid any attention to her comings and goings, or those of other people like that man. He's probably her son, I realize, even though he didn't seem to exude the same friendly warmth of his mother.

I move my eyes back to the flower bud, and when I've had my fill, I head back into the house.

Sitting outside becomes my new thing. Instead of spending all day on the couch, I break up the day by sitting out here. My thoughts are minimal, but being outside of those walls feels like a tiny bit of progress. Like there's at least a small part of me that wants to edge forward into whatever my new life becomes. Just a peek into what could be.

Because I spend more time outside, I inevitably notice things about my neighbors. Mostly Linda, who waves at me with a smile every time she's outside, and the man whom I've decided is definitely her son. He leaves every morning and comes back in the evening, meaning he has a job and lives with her.

I've also caught a few glimpses of a little girl, probably no older than six, who likes to play with fallen sticks in Linda's front yard. I've caught her peeking at me from behind a porch support at least twice this week.

She has almost white-blonde hair, and even from all the way over here, I can see how blue her eyes are, looking absolutely nothing like her dark-haired and dark-eyed father. She isn't loud or silly or rambunctious like most kids. She seems shy except for when her dad comes home. On two separate occasions, I've witnessed the joyful way she bounds through the yard to greet him as he gets out of his blue truck in the evening.

He scoops her up like she weighs nothing and carries her into the house. It's the only time he doesn't frown at me. His daughter makes him oblivious to me then. It makes it easier for me to pick apart what it is that makes me so curious about him.

It isn't the fact that he seems unmarried that makes me curious, or the tone of his strong arms, or how much his face changes when he smiles at his daughter. I'm curious about him because he emits an energy completely unlike his mother. This man, I feel in my heart, is just as unhappy as I am.

There's something I recognize in the sullen way he walks. Something I understand in the exhaustion on his face when he gets home. But because he frowns at me whenever our eyes meet, it's fairly apparent that he doesn't like seeing me sitting outside like I do.

But that isn't something I'm going to give up, not when it's the only progress I've made in the nearly four weeks I've lived here. Sitting in the open air is the only thing that reminds me that time is still passing. It isn't my fault that it makes one of my neighbors uncomfortable.

I turn my gaze to the flower beside me, whose bud has changed color from green to lavender now. It looks so fragile and elegant, but it didn't start that way. It began much smaller and buried in darkness. It had to seek out the light all on its own, and even now, it continues to stretch upward.

After many moments of studying this little flower, I see something move beyond it. The little girl is back, her arms hugging the porch support across the yard, her blonde hair moving with the September breeze as her blue eyes stare at me.

But this time, when she realizes she's been spotted, she doesn't dart back behind the white column. Instead, she holds my blank gaze for a minute, and then she moves from behind the post and sits on the top step of the porch.

I look back at the flower.

She moves again, this time down the steps and to the boundary between my yard and Linda's. She pauses there, staring at me with a serious expression with her little hands clasped behind her back.

When I say nothing, she creeps closer still, across my driveway and the grass on the other side. She stops in front of my bottom step and looks up at me with those wide, light-blue eyes, and I stare right back.

We're just two people, silently taking each other in. I think she must be trying to figure me out, but doesn't seem to be succeeding because she inches closer, pausing on each step for a minute or longer until she eventually sits down next to me.

I turn my head to look at her, and it's then that she finally speaks.

"You always sit here a lot. What's wrong?" she asks in a small, timid voice.

I think for a moment about the best way to reply and decide to go with the simplest idea of what's wrong.

"I'm sad."

She blinks, thinking over my response. "I get sad sometimes, too."

I nod and take in the denim skirt she's wearing, which is paired with a pink t-shirt that says "Girls Can."

"Why are you sad?" she asks after another long moment.

I look down at my left hand resting on my thigh and feel the grief swell inside me from examining my bare ring finger. I wonder if he's proposed to Sarah yet.

"I love someone who doesn't love me back."

She nods solemnly, like she understands.

"My name is Rosie."

"It's nice to meet you, Rosie."

"Rosie isn't actually my name," she adds after a moment. "Rosalie is. Rosalie Ann Dunbar."

I inwardly enjoy the matter-of-fact way she speaks.

"I'm Mara." I omit a last name, mostly because I don't know which one to say. Neither one seems right to me anymore.

I watch her eyes unabashedly roam over my facial features.

"Your hair is pretty."

For the first time in months, I want to laugh. My hair is a mess, hanging limply over my shoulders, so I'm assuming she's referring to my hair color. Maybe she's never seen anyone with auburn hair before.

"So is yours."

"Daddy says it's the same color as my mommy's."

I give her a very slight smile. "Your mother must be very beautiful if you look anything like her."

"That's what he says."

We both fall silent. A few cars go by, and then Rosie pipes up again.

"Sometimes I help Grandma bake things for you."

The plate has been returned to Linda's doormat twice more this week, and each time, it returns to my hands with fresh baked goods the very next day. I've been living off cinnamon rolls and banana bread this week, and I'm not mad about it.

"I bet your grandma likes when you help her."

She nods vigorously like she's proud to be a good helper.

"Grandma likes you."

I tilt my head slightly at her. "You think so?" I guess she must; otherwise she wouldn't bake me things.

She nods again, even more vigorously, her eyes wide. "I like you, too."

A genuine, though small, smile creeps across my mouth.

"I like you, too, Rosie."

Across the yard, Linda's front door opens, and she steps out quickly, her gray flecked brown hair whirling back and forth as she looks all over her front yard and porch.

"Hi, Grandma!" Rosie calls and waves.

Linda places her palm on her chest in obvious relief when she spots us. "There you are!" she calls back and then starts down the porch steps and towards us with a smile. "Looks like you've made a new friend."

I'm not sure if she's addressing me or Rosie, but she's the one who replies anyway.

"Yeah! She's nice, just like you said!"

I give my new little friend a soft smile as Linda appears at the bottom of my concrete steps. She's wearing the same "Girls Can" shirt as Rosie, but in blue. She puts her hands on her well-rounded hips and gives her granddaughter a teasing look.

"What, did you think I was kidding? Grandma's always right." Linda winks at me, and I realize it's the first time I've interacted with her without that plate. For some reason, it's easier for me to talk to Rosie than it is for me to talk to Linda, even though she's been nothing but warm and friendly to me.

Rosie hops down the steps, and Linda catches her in a big hug, the kind of hug my mother has never been able to master.

"Come on, Rosie Posie; your daddy will be home soon," she says cheerfully.

"It's pizza night," Rosie tells me. "Do you like pizza?"

"Yes," I say quietly, already seeing where this is going.

"You can eat pizza with us," she tells me, like it's obvious that I'll be joining them.

I blankly scramble for a reason not to, but I really have nothing to keep me from going over other than that I don't feel like it. And that her dad doesn't seem to like me. When I hesitate and struggle with my answer, Linda thankfully saves me.

"You're welcome over if you like, Mara, but there's no pressure, okay?"

I try to smile, but I think it comes out like a grimace.

"Maybe next Friday then," Linda suggests, even though Rosie makes a disappointed sound in her throat and gives me puppy eyes. My heart smiles at that, and I realize I can't turn her down completely.

"Next Friday sounds great."

CHAPTER THREE

Sean

When I walk through the front door, I'm relieved in more ways than one. First, it's Friday. And even though there's always the possibility of an emergency, I can at least pretend that I have the weekend off. Second, it's pizza night. Getting excited about pizza might make me sound like a teenager, but I look forward to it every week because it's Rosie's favorite. And third, when I rolled up to my house tonight, the woman who lives next door wasn't sitting outside this time.

I don't know what she's doing, sitting there so often now. Sometimes I watch her from inside the house, just trying to figure out what the hell she's doing. At first, I thought maybe she was sitting there to spy on my mom and my kid, but she doesn't really look around. She doesn't pay the passing cars any mind or watch what the neighbors across the street are doing. She just sits there.

And when she sees me, she doesn't smile or even seem to realize that she's made eye contact with me. And those eyes...they look empty and hollow. It reminds me way too much of someone I used to know.

"Daddy!" Rosie shouts as I close the front door behind me. A grin breaks out on my face as she runs to me with her arms outstretched. I pick her up and hold her tight, savoring every time she does this because I know in probably a couple of years, she'll stop being so glad to see me. One day, I won't be her favorite person anymore.

"Hey, Rosiecakes," I greet warmly and kiss her blonde hair. She leans back in my arms to look at my face.

"It's pizza night," she tells me like I don't know. I slip my feet out of my sawdust-covered work boots and carry her through the toy-strewn living room towards the kitchen where Mom usually is. "I asked my new friend Mara to have pizza, too, but she was too shy."

"Your new friend Mara, huh?" I say as I enter the kitchen, thinking she must've made a friend at school. I'm grateful she's made a new friend actually because she isn't usually that kind of kid. She's quiet, shy, and nervous around kids and people she doesn't know.

My mom is leaning over the puzzle she's been working on all week at the small table by the window. At the sound of my voice, she looks up at me and Rosie with a wide smile.

"Don't worry, Rosie; she said she'll come next week, remember?"

I put Rosie down, and she squeezes her arms around my right leg. I give my mother a stern look because she better not be trying to arrange another playdate for Rosie that's really a cover for introducing me to single moms. It's been five years since Gabby died, but my mother knows better than anyone that I'm not interested in dating. Even so, she's attempted to introduce me to a few women she thinks would be good for me and Rosie.

My hands are already full with the two most important

women in my life, and with the tree trimming business I run with my best friend Rhys, a relationship isn't even on my radar.

"Doug on his way?" I ask as Rosie goes to join my mom at the table.

"He's visiting Josh this weekend," she tells me, a slight tinge of disappointment clouding her tone. "He said he'll call me when he gets there."

My mom's boyfriend is a good guy. He's a widower like me and has a couple of grown kids. Josh lives in South Dakota and Jana lives in the twin cities—I forget which suburb. They're all decent people, which is good since my mom and Doug are pretty serious.

She's happy again after losing my dad to an aneurysm seven years ago. Don't get me wrong—it pleases me that she's so happy. But her happiness just makes her think she's that much more justified in pushing me to date. It's just one more reason she wants me to settle down with someone.

The oven beeps twice, indicating it's done preheating, and I look over at a pan of brownie batter sitting on the stove, ready to be baked.

My mom gets up from the table and puts the pan in the oven, letting out a blast of hot air that warms my knees.

"Pizza *and* brownies," I comment, though I give my mother a suspicious side glance as she sits back down and returns to her puzzle.

She's been baking a lot lately. More than usual. I figured she was making treats for Doug because I never see her baked goods anywhere after she bakes them. But he's gone this weekend.

"They're not for *you*, Daddy," Rosie says, sounding way too much like a teenager.

"Who are they for then?" I step closer and rest my palms on the edge of the table, looking down at the scattered puzzle pieces.

"For my friend, Mara. I've been helping Grandma bake for her," she answers proudly.

"I thought she was your *new* friend."

My mother narrows her eyes at my daughter and leans toward her slightly. "That was a secret, remember, Rosalie?"

Rosie's face blanches, and then she sinks down in her chair sheepishly.

"Sorry, Grandma."

I heave out a heavy sigh and straighten up, crossing my arms. "Alright, out with it. Who's Mara?"

Rosie says nothing and avoids my eyes like she doesn't want to get in any more trouble with her grandma by saying anything else.

My mother picks up a puzzle piece and nonchalantly tries to fit it in place. "Mara lives next door," she says simply, and even throws in a shrug.

My spine goes rigid. They've been baking things for *her*? I scowl at my mother.

"I see. Any particular *reason* you're buttering up our new neighbor?"

She sighs and rolls her eyes. "Please, Sean. Not everything is about you."

"So, you're *not* trying to set her up with me?" A shiver runs through me at that thought.

"No," she replies firmly and looks up at me finally. I hold her gaze, not sure whether to believe her.

"We're just trying to cheer her up, Daddy," Rosie confesses with guilt all over her little face. "She's sad."

"That's right. And it's always nice to try to cheer up someone when they're sad, right, sweetie?" She says this to Rosie but gives me a very motherly glare as she speaks, like it's a childhood lesson I've forgotten.

Of course, I haven't forgotten basic kindness. And she knows I can't argue with her about what she's saying—not in front of Rosie.

I have no doubt that woman is sad. It oozes out of her. The right thing to do is the kind thing; I agree about that, but I'm more than a little wary when it comes to the reasons *why* Mara is so sad. And those reasons are none of my business, nor do I want them to become my business.

"You guys are just too sweet," I say to them both, and I mean it. They're being *too* kind to a perfect stranger who hasn't left her property since she moved in.

Rosie beams and goes back to finding more edge pieces. My mother shakes her head slightly at me, knowing exactly what I really mean.

"I'll call in the pizza and then I'm going to take a shower," I announce, and then stride out of the room.

Pizza has been consumed, jammies have been donned, teeth have been brushed, a book has been read. All that's left to do is tuck this kid in and turn off the light.

I'm reclined beside Rosie in her twin-sized bed, and this is usually when I kiss her forehead and leave her to sleep. But when I look over at her in her Peppa Pig pajama dress, she's looking up at the ceiling thoughtfully.

"Whatcha thinking about, Rosiecakes?" I ask quietly.

She lets out a little sigh that makes me smile.

"I'm not good at keeping secrets," she laments. She's clearly still upset that she let her grandma's secret slip, and if there's anything that makes me feel like a good parent, it's that. Typical five-year-olds don't feel the depth of remorse Rosie does whenever she messes up. When she hurts someone's feelings, she dwells on it for days before I can convince her to let it go.

"I don't think Grandma should have asked you to keep that secret. She didn't want me to know you made friends with Mara because she knows I don't like strangers."

She nods. "I don't like strangers either," she agrees, and I would say that statement is correct. It takes her a long time to warm up to people, which is why this school year has gotten off to an interesting start. She hasn't warmed up to her teacher, and I wouldn't be surprised if Rosie doesn't until after the new year.

Which is why I'm a little thrown off by her sudden friendship with the sad neighbor woman.

"You like Mara though, and she's a stranger," I remind her.

She thinks for a long moment, her light blue eyes still on the ceiling. It isn't lost on me that she's an old soul. She's always been like this. Serious and thoughtful. I can't decide if it's just her personality or if she feels the perpetual absence of a mother in her life.

"Yes, but I think she needs a friend, Daddy."

My heart softens a bit, and I turn toward her. I set my hand on her blonde head and smile at her.

"I think you're right, Rosie," I say gently. She looks at me solemnly through her long eyelashes, and I'm hit with how she looks more and more like her mother, Gabby, with each passing day.

They share the same blonde hair and blue eyes. Rosie has the same crinkle to her brow when she's hurt that Gabby did, and the same wide smile.

"And who better than you? Although I don't like the idea of sharing my best friend." I grin and tickle her side.

She cackles and wiggles until I ease up.

"Don't worry, Daddy. You'll always be my *best* best friend."

"Good. Now gimme a kiss, and then it's lights out."

She obliges, pushing her little pout briefly to my mouth, and then settles back into her pillow as I get up.

I flick off the light, revealing the glow-in-the-dark stars on the ceiling over her bed.

"Goodnight, sweet girl. I love you."

"Love you, Daddy."

I close the door behind me and head down the hall to the kitchen. My mother is cutting up the brownies for Mara and placing them on a white plate. I fold my arms over my chest and lean my shoulder into the fridge, watching her.

She glances at me once but keeps up with her task.

"You shouldn't have asked her to keep a secret from me," I say quietly.

My mom sighs. "I wasn't planning on it being a secret forever," she explains to the brownies. "I just wanted a little more time to get her to warm up to us."

"And then what?"

"I know you're suspicious, but I'm really not trying to set you up with her."

"Right. She's just a sad person who needs you to feed her sugar and carbs, and you need her to like you."

My mom turns quickly and brandishes the butter knife she's holding at me. "Don't you do that. Don't you make me feel bad for being nice." She turns back to the brownies. "Your daughter is right. Mara is sad, and the fact that Rosie has any interest in a new person at all is reason enough to keep reaching out to our new neighbor. It's the right thing for everyone."

I frown at her little speech as she finishes cutting and covers the plate with tinfoil. For a moment, I feel guilty for being so hard on my mom about this. But I realize she doesn't understand why our new neighbor in particular has my hackles rising. I don't want to say it out loud, but I should.

"She reminds me of Gabby."

My mom freezes, the plate of brownies still in her hands.

"She's more than sad, Mom. That woman is severely depressed. And more than anyone, I know what that looks like." I take in a gulp of air and swallow hard. "I don't like the idea of Rosie spending time with someone we don't know, someone whose mental health is apparently fragile."

Mom sniffs and nods sympathetically. She puts the plate down on the counter and turns toward me. "I'm sorry, Sean. I didn't think about it like that—that Mara would remind you of Gabby."

I nod. "It's okay. I know it sounds harsh, but I really don't want anything to do with her."

She sighs and chews her lip as she eyes me with concern. "We can't just turn a blind eye to someone who's struggling, Sean."

Her words feel like a hot knife in my back. "Is that what you think I did?" I blurt out angrily, and then immediately regret it when Mom's eyes widen.

"*Of course not,*" she hisses in shock.

I push off the fridge, my shoulders tight. "I know. I'm sorry." I shake my head slightly.

"She seems to be alone, and I'm worried about her."

"You don't even know her," I mutter.

Her eyebrows scrunch together, and I know I'm about to get chewed out.

"I don't *have* to know her to care about her wellbeing," Mom fires back indignantly. "It's called compassion, Sean, and apparently, I did a horrible job of teaching you what that is."

I don't appreciate the guilt trip, but her viewpoint is... honorable. I'll give her that.

"Mom, I know what compassion is, but we don't know this woman. I don't want Rosie around her."

We glare at each other for a silent moment, both of us knowing she's going to concede because I always have the last word when it comes to what's best for Rosie. Mom knows she isn't allowed to overstep that.

She crosses her arms. "I already invited her for pizza night next Friday. I'm not going to uninvite her."

I scowl at that but realize I'm not going to win that one. "Fine." It's anything but fine, really, because the idea of her being in my house makes me nauseous. Looks like I'll have to suck it up for a couple of hours.

"Fine."

My mom and I have always been close, so it doesn't feel good to fight with her or disappoint her.

"Come here," I sigh, opening one arm to her.

She hugs me tightly, despite my lack of compassion. "I love you."

"Love you, too." I release her, and we part ways.

I head upstairs to my bedroom, and she goes back to the puzzle on the table.

It may be harsh to set a boundary with someone I don't even know, but to me, it feels necessary. I tried to shoulder someone's mental health once before, and it left me a single father with an infant. I'm not in the market to reach out to help another person's struggle with depression. I have my own to deal with.

CHAPTER FOUR

Mara

I forgot how much I like chocolate. How did I forget that? How did the taste of food become so muted and secondary to the foods I put in my mouth?

Linda and Rosie brought me a plate of brownies yesterday, and I ate them for dinner. The only good thing about returning that plate days later is it keeps Linda from knowing that I eat everything she makes me in one sitting. I also haven't mentioned that to my mother, who would probably give me a lecture about nutrition and excess calories if she knew I was mostly eating butter and sugar and carbs.

Honestly, if it adds a bit to my waistline, I'm okay with that. I've recognized that I'm struggling, and I've come to terms with the fact that we make the best choices we can when we're just trying to survive each day. At some point, I'll visit the local grocery store and get myself something healthy to eat. Until then, I'm more than content to consume whatever Linda brings over.

It's been a month since I moved in. Part of me feels like I've been here for five years, and another part feels like I moved in this morning. I feel lost in a weird time loop where I'm stuck in the present. There's no feeling of past or future. Time doesn't really feel like it's passing. I'm just stuck in the same day, every day.

Sitting outside helps, but it's only meant to be a baby step, and I feel like there must be a next baby step to take. This is how I find myself at my front door, white plate in hand, determined that this time I won't leave it on Linda's doormat. This time, I will knock and give it back to her with gratitude. Like a normal person.

After a long and thorough mental pep talk, my mind goes blank until I'm standing on Linda's porch. The welcome sign stares back at me while I take a deep breath.

Just knock.

Lift your hand and knock.

It's not hard.

Why is it so hard?

This is dumb. You can do this, Mara. Just knock and say thank you. That's all it is, then you can go back to the couch.

I clear my froggy throat, hold up my fist, and force myself to bang it against the door.

My pulse skyrockets, and the blood rushes to my head instantly. I forgot about the waiting. I forgot that I have to wait for the door to open after I knock. What is probably only a few seconds feels to me like hours, and the anticipation is visceral. This was a bad idea. It feels like a bad idea.

I'm half bent over to set the plate down on the mat when the door opens. I look up and freeze. It isn't Linda or even Rosie standing there. It's her son, and he frowns at me more deeply than ever. I didn't think to see if his truck was parked out front.

It's the first time I've seen him close up. His brown eyes are lighter around the pupil, almost golden, and hooded by long black eyelashes. His dark hair is a little messy and so is the flannel shirt stretching across his chest. But his face, however handsome, is filled with deep dislike as he takes me in. He exudes such negative energy that I feel like a criminal, like I'm fessing up to stealing this plate and not returning it dutifully. Every tense bit of him is saying that I'm very clearly not welcome here.

I straighten up, panicking, and thrust the plate at him roughly.

"Uh, thanks for the brownies. Tell Linda, I mean. Tell her thank you for the brownies," I stammer out in a rush.

One side of his mouth morphs into a half-grimace as his knuckles go white from how tightly he's gripping the plate. Definitely, definitely not welcome here. "You're Mara," he states in a low voice.

I nod quickly and step back. "Um, I live—"

"Next door," he interrupts.

I nod again, my blood feeling like it's vibrating through my veins. He studies me with those golden-brown eyes, and I feel like I might die. He doesn't like me being here.

"Sean," he introduces in that same low voice. "Rosie's dad."

"Right," I gasp out. "She's—she's a sweet girl," I stammer.

He narrows his eyes at me then, and I panic.

"Uh, well, tell Linda thanks. Bye." Then I turn and run. Hair flying behind me, I run back to the security of my house.

I collapse face first onto the couch, a heap of embarrassment and self-deprecation.

That was just the *worst*.

I'm never doing that again. In fact, I'm never sitting on the stoop again either. Not if it means there's a chance of seeing him look at me like that. I may never leave the house again. It's brutal out there.

I never used to be like this with people. If someone was unwelcoming or even rude to me, I always found a way to respond with kindness and warmth. Like Linda. I wasn't the kind of person to back down or let people walk all over me. But now, all I can do is cower from anything even remotely uncomfortable or threatening.

All I can do is sleep and songlessly wander around this little house. I can't even bear the thought of picking up my guitar again. My calluses have long healed over. The kind of movement in my soul that always inclined my fingers to play and my voice to sing has been deathly still even before Mason asked for a divorce.

What used to be the thing I was put on this earth to do is no longer available for me to access.

I have nothing to put myself into now.

And what little headway I feel like I've made by sitting outside and knocking on Linda's door feels like it's been taken from me by that man's hostility. I don't want to open my front door to Linda and Rosie again. I just want to sleep and feel like I don't exist.

———

"Mara, you can't keep doing this," my mother says on the phone the next day. Her tone is weary and yet firm. "You can't let Mason take your life away from you like this."

I'm lying on my back on the couch, looking balefully up at the ceiling with my phone pressed to my ear.

"This is all his fault. You need to blame him and hate him and use it to push yourself forward," she continues, sounding equally exasperated at me and angry at Mason. "I know the house is paid for, but maybe a job would be good for you. Maybe you should apply for something, just to get yourself out of the house."

Her suggestions go over my head. She's trying to help, but nothing she says is particularly helpful. I can barely get off this couch, much less out in the working world.

"What about the woman next door?" my mother pipes up again when I say nothing. "You said she was nice. Maybe you could ask her to have coffee or something."

I close my eyes in embarrassment at the mention of Linda. She and Rosie were knocking on my door this morning with a plate full of homemade glazed donuts, and I had a mild panic attack. I didn't open the door; in fact, I made sure it was locked and curled up in a ball on the couch until they left.

"I think I just need more time," I say, my voice as small as I feel.

My mother scoffs loudly. "*More time*, Mara? How much time? Another month? Two? A year? You need to fight for yourself, Mara. Enough of this pity party you're throwing. This is your life. You need to stop hiding from it and live, even more than you did before Mason. Do you hear me?"

Tears pool in my eyes. Her words are meant to be inspirational, but all I can hear is her aggravated tone. My current state reflects poorly on her parenting skills. Her failure to get through to me makes her feel like a failure, and if there's anything she hates, it's failing. It stings to realize I'm letting her down.

"I'll try, Mama," I whisper, and then hang up.

The little voice that tells me to be gentle with myself speaks up again. It's a much more understanding voice than my mother's. I close my eyes and take in deep breaths, focusing on the fullness of my lungs, and then push the breath out slowly through my nose.

If all I can do is breathe today, that's okay. Tomorrow, I can always try again. Tomorrow I can try something else to get me out of the house. If all I have is the promise of tomorrow, I'm still blessed.

I do eat those donuts. Despite how they unfortunately remind me of Linda and her family, I feel very slightly boosted. Maybe it's the sugar.

Either way, I run with that little shift in my spirit. I force my feet to take me upstairs to the bedroom, where my lonely bed still sits bare.

I rifle through a couple of boxes to find the sheets, and by the time I've wrestled that tan fitted sheet onto the mattress, I'm worn out. I toss the flat sheet on top and call it a day. I still don't want to sleep there. But I'm one tiny step closer to the idea.

And this time, I make sure the blue truck is gone before I walk the plate over. I don't even think about trying to knock and put the plate on the doormat.

As I'm taking the porch steps down, the door opens behind me. I get the panicked urge to sprint back to my house, but Linda's kind voice keeps me rooted to the bottom step.

"Mara, hello!"

I slowly turn around, wincing slightly at being caught. Linda has picked up the plate and is smiling at me brightly like she always does.

"Thank you for bringing my plate back, dear. How did you like the donuts?"

I fidget with the hem of my dark purple hoodie. "Delicious as always," I answer quietly.

She smiles a little wider and comes closer, hovering at the edge of the porch. "I was hoping to catch you, actually. I was worried when you didn't open the door yesterday."

I nod slowly. "Uh, I was...in the shower," I lie.

"Oh, of course," she says lightheartedly and waves one hand at me. "I just wanted to make sure Sean didn't run you off. He didn't make you feel uncomfortable the other day, did he?"

She seems so concerned for me, and it's a different kind of concern than my mother's. Linda's is softer, sweeter.

I don't quite know how to respond, mostly because it would be more polite to deny her son's frown-laden behavior towards me.

So, I just settle on a strained smile and a shake of my head.

Linda examines me for a split second, clearly seeing through me like only a mother can, and then sighs quietly.

"You'll have to excuse my son. He doesn't mean to be so surly."

I think he does mean it, but I don't say that.

"It's okay," I assure her weakly and take the last step backwards.

"I've already told him he needs to straighten up and

be nice when you come for pizza night on Friday," she adds, halting my retreat any further.

Pizza night. I forgot all about it. The stunned expression on my face gives me away but Linda pretends not to notice.

"Come on over at five, okay, sweetheart? Rosie can't wait. She's been talking about it nonstop," she tells me, laughing.

She mentioned Rosie so I wouldn't back out, I'm sure of it. Nothing gets past her, and despite how she's trapping me into pizza night, I'm kind of impressed.

"If it's a family thing, I don't want to intrude," I say, even though I know Linda isn't going to let me off the hook.

"Oh, nonsense. We're happy to have you."

I resign myself to the fact that I'll be going, so I nod. "Thanks."

"Don't be a stranger!" she calls to me as I trudge back to my front door.

I give her a wave and go inside, feeling both relief and dread. Clearly, Linda doesn't want there to be any hard feelings, but I have no reason to believe Sean feels the same way. An apology from Linda on his behalf isn't the same as an apology from him.

Not that I really deserve an apology. Sean has every right to be as unfriendly as he wants. It isn't his fault that I'm fragile and sensitive.

Maybe it'll all get sorted out on Friday. If anything, he'll probably be a little less hostile to me in front of his mother and daughter. That's really the best hope I can muster about him at this point.

And I'll take any hope at all at this point.

CHAPTER FIVE

Sean

It's been a busy day. Rhys and I climbed into those treetops shortly after sunrise. Many of our customers are getting their trees trimmed or cut down before the cooler weather begins. Most people seem to have enough common sense to not risk the heavy Minnesota snow falls weighing down the branches of trees that hang over the roofs of their homes.

Fall comes only second to mid-summer when it comes to our busy season. There's usually half a dozen major windstorms that blow through the tri-county area and cause enough damage to require our services. Might as well be raining dollar bills instead of hail, to me and Rhys.

He and I had a lot on the schedule today, but I made sure to make it back in time to pick Rosie up from school. The plan was for my mom to be the one to pick up Rosie from school, but I'm worried about my little girl. Every day, she drags her feet when it's time to leave for school. As far as I can tell, she hasn't made any friends in her Kindergarten class.

So, now I'm waiting in my truck outside her school, anxious to know how the day was for her.

I love my daughter to pieces, and she knows all it would

take is one good sob from her to break my heart and make me consider asking my mom to home school her instead of making her go back to public school.

I'm an absolute pushover when it comes to my daughter hurting. It's probably why the first jerk who breaks her heart will end up with my fist in his face. But that's a ways' off. Right?

The school bell rings, jarring me out of my thoughts, and I lean forward in my seat, trying to pick out Rosie in the mass of children exiting the double glass doors.

When I spot her, I jump out of the truck and jog over to her. When she catches sight of me, her previously sullen face brightens instantly.

"Daddy!" she exclaims as I scoop her up.

"Hey, Rosiecakes."

She hugs me tightly, which is a good indication that she had at least a couple of stressful moments today.

"Did you have a good day?" I ask as I carry her to the truck.

"Yeah."

She says nothing else, not another word as I buckle her into her car seat. That doesn't bode well. I tighten up the shoulder straps and then study her little face.

When I look at her, I see all the ages she's ever been all at once. It's proof that she'll always be my baby girl, even when she's old enough to have a baby girl of her own.

"You okay, sweet pea?"

She sighs and nods, her blue eyes downcast. "I'm okay, Daddy."

I kiss her forehead and close the door before walking

around to the driver's side, wishing I knew how to draw her out of herself. Apparently, she's too much like her old man when it comes to expressing negative emotions.

Thank God we have my mother to coax things out of us.

I ask her a series of questions on the way home, all of which she answers with a subdued, "Mhm." I realize that even if I asked her if she had anchovies for lunch, she would respond the same way.

Mhm.

It's things like this that make me feel like I'm totally blowing it as a parent. Connecting with Rosie feels like more work than it should as she gets older. By the time she's a teenager, will she be a stranger to me? That thought churns my gut, and I turn up the radio to distract me from going down that rabbit hole.

When we get home, I notice Rosie perk up for just a moment when I get her out of the truck and place her on the grass. She stands tall for half a second as she looks over at Mara's house, and instantly deflates again when she realizes Mara isn't sitting outside.

I furrow my brow at the obvious disappointment my daughter feels about that and grab her hand as we walk towards the porch.

My mother chewed me out as soon as I brought her plate into the kitchen the other day.

"Why didn't you invite her in?" she had exclaimed. "That's the first time she's knocked on our door, and you had to scare her off!"

I just grumbled a halfhearted apology and dealt with the glares she sent my way all evening.

I don't get what my mother is up to. It's like Mara is a

stray cat she's trying to lure into being a house cat. The woman seems a little feral to me, if her running away from me is any indication.

And for whatever reason, my daughter has taken a liking to her. Of all people, Rosie has to like *her*.

I guess I'll have to figure out a way to be civil, being that my mom and daughter have decided to take her in.

Lucky me.

I know the minute I step into the house that Mara didn't flake on joining us for pizza night like I had secretly hoped.

I can hear Mom in the kitchen, chattering on about how she met Doug at the farmer's market when she forgot her wallet and he, being behind her in line, graciously offered to pay for her produce.

My tired shoulders sink at the realization that she's talking to Mara.

Then Doug's cheerful voice carries through the living room, and I spot him in the doorway to the kitchen. "It's all history from there, isn't it, Angelface?"

Part of me wants to gag at that term of endearment, but I know he loves my mom. He treats her with kindness and consideration in everything he does. He's a better boyfriend than I was a husband.

I take a deep breath and move through the living room. Doug looks over and smiles as I approach. I give him a nod.

"Here he is," Doug announces as I appear in the kitchen doorway. He pats me on the shoulder, causing a little puff of sawdust to exhale out of my shirt.

"Good to see you, Doug."

"Oh, Sean, I was just telling Mara about how Doug and I met," my mom tells me unnecessarily. Her blue eyes are bright and full of excitement, not just because she loves that story, but because she finally has her special guest inside the house.

Mara is sitting at the little table by the window, a puzzle piece in her hand. She's wearing a teal long-sleeved shirt that's mostly covered by her long, dark red hair. Her jean-clad thighs are pressed together beneath the table. When she looks over at me, I'm immediately sliced in the chest with those hollow blue eyes. Despite her wan complexion, the scattering of freckles across her nose gives her the appearance of a livelier expression. When she returned the plate the other day, I closed the door and couldn't get the beautiful rust color of her hair out of my head. It doesn't escape my notice that she's pretty, but I can't get past the gloom she emits. Like she's been to war and seen things she can't unsee.

"Mara is good at puzzles, Daddy," Rosie tells me, causing me to swing my gaze across the table to where my daughter is sitting, and I'm taken aback by the smile on her face. That's the first time I've seen her smile all week. I swallow hard and nod.

"Just like you, Rosie Posie," my mom says happily and kisses the top of Rosie's head.

My daughter hands Mara a puzzle piece, and watches with deep interest as she tries it out in a few different places before snapping it into where it belongs.

"Yay!" Rosie exclaims and gives her another piece.

I clear my throat, deeply uncomfortable that a sad stranger can make my daughter smile better than I can, and mumble something about taking a shower before the pizza gets here. I tell Doug to make the call and get the hell out of the kitchen.

I shuck off my clothes in the bathroom upstairs and quickly shower, my mind moving over the reasons why Rosie is so enamored with our new neighbor.

Am I not enough for her? Is my mom right in saying that Rosie needs a mother figure in her life? I can't bear to entertain that thought. I'd go to the ends of the earth for that little girl, but try to find a mom for her? No. I'm not even slightly on the market. Even if I found a nice girl who meshed well with my family, I still wouldn't go for it. Moving on with someone new just...doesn't feel right. Moving on would mean I have to leave Gabby behind.

I dry off and get dressed, wishing this evening was already over, and head back downstairs. As I'm about to enter the kitchen, I hear Rosie speaking, and I pause in the hallway, staying hidden in the shadow.

"You're my favorite friend," she says to Mara.

"You're my favorite friend, too," Mara replies quietly. Even though she's saying something warm to my daughter, her tone is still weighed down. Gabby spoke like that all the time in the months before she died.

"Do you have lots of friends?"

A moment of silence passes, and I realize my mom and Doug are in the living room, lightly bickering over some new show on Netflix. I feel my temper flare at that, because apparently my mom thinks it's perfectly okay to leave my daughter in the kitchen alone with a stranger.

"I used to," Mara answers, so softly I almost don't hear it over my mother in the next room.

"Were you not nice to them? Sometimes kids think I'm not nice to them, but I just don't like talking so much."

Rosie's little voice is clear and sweet, laden with her attempt to understand her new friend.

"I was always nice to them," says Mara. "They just wanted to be friends more with my husband."

Hmm.

She's married? My mom told me she's living in that house alone. Maybe they're separated. And her friends chose him? That's rough. A pinch of sympathy creeps into the back of my mind. Maybe her reasons for being sad aren't so scary.

"I mean my—my ex-husband," Mara corrects, her voice cracking.

"Because he doesn't love you anymore," Rosie adds matter-of-factly like they've talked about this before. "And that's why you're sad."

"Yes."

Well, that's cleared up then. She's recently divorced and friendless, which is why she's so morose. That's strangely comforting to me. Her life fell apart, and *that's* why she's struggling. That's understandable, and I feel for her.

There's a beat of silence then, and just as I'm gathering myself to walk in, Rosie continues.

"My teacher says I shouldn't feel sad. She says I should be happy I get to come to school and learn and play with other kids."

My heart breaks at the uncomfortable way she says that. Like her teacher has been making her feel bad for not being happy or energetic like her classmates.

"It isn't wrong to be sad, Rosie," Mara says gently. "It's okay to feel exactly whatever you're feeling. Sadness and depression are things a lot of people struggle with."

"What's depression?"

My stomach squirms, and I'm stunned that Mara's response isn't something even remotely kid friendly.

"Depression is when you're so sad and so empty that you don't want to do anything. You feel like you can't enjoy anything you used to, even if you try."

I feel a strange sort of tingling up and down my legs. She's describing exactly the way Gabby was, and it drags me right back there to that time when I felt so helpless to do anything for my tormented wife.

And here is this stranger, telling my daughter about all those same symptoms her own mother faced. How dare she? My hackles rise.

Is she really telling my kid about depression? She has some nerve to be having that conversation with a five-year-old. It's obvious Mara knows so much about depression because she has it. The last thing I need is for Rosie to think she has depression, too. So, before Rosie can say anything, I plow into the room.

Mara and Rosie are where I left them, both seated at the table. Mara looks up at me with those empty eyes, still holding a puzzle piece, and Rosie whips her blonde head towards me in surprise.

"That's enough of that," I say gruffly, glaring at Mara. "She's *five*," I growl. "What's the matter with you?"

Mara blanches and blinks a few times, remorse surging into her expression. "Oh—I—I'm sorry. You're right. I—I didn't mean to—" She stutters to a stop and seems to fold into herself on the chair so that she appears as small as Rosie.

"Daddy, why are you mad?"

"Nothing, Rosie. We'll talk about it later," I assert and quickly pick her up and carry her into the living room. My mother and Doug have apparently resolved their little tiff and are sitting on the couch together, his arm around her shoulders. When my mom turns her head and sees my angry face, she immediately stands up.

"What happened?"

I set Rosie down on the couch next to Doug and straighten up. "Forget it."

The doorbell rings then, and Doug goes to answer it. The pizza delivery guy is standing on the porch, holding two pizza boxes. As Doug pays, I scowl wordlessly at my mother.

She scowls back, her eyes flitting to the kitchen doorway and back to me, like she knows I said something mean to Mara. She shakes her head at me, like she's disappointed, and goes to comfort her poor little neighbor woman in the kitchen.

I swear, she cares more about Mara than she does about me. *I'm* the one who lost his wife and has to raise his daughter alone. *I'm* the one who has to live with her death every day of my life. But no, this stray cat she's trying to adopt is what matters the most right now.

All I know is, the second we're done eating pizza, that woman better be going back home.

CHAPTER SIX

Mara

The puzzle and its many pieces blur as Sean stalks out of the kitchen with his sweet daughter in tow. Her little face is utterly confused from over his shoulder, and then I'm alone in the kitchen. Just me and this puzzle of wildflowers.

I take a deep breath, crushed.

Before Sean got home, I was feeling better than I have in months. Linda and Doug are the cutest couple, and Rosie couldn't take her happy eyes off me. They made me feel so welcome and so at home. I almost cried a handful of times within the first ten minutes I was within these walls, simply because they all made me feel a warmth inside of my chest that I haven't felt in almost a year.

But then, Sean walked in, and I felt the cold permeate me all over again. And now my heart is back to being a useless lump, as frozen and as unyielding as his demeanor towards me. A distant part of me says I didn't do anything wrong, but it's just a tiny whisper without any conviction.

The doorbell rings from what sounds like a long way off, and then Linda enters my periphery. I look up slowly from the puzzle to find her looking back at me with an apology on her worried brow. Her presence reminds me that time hasn't stopped at all, and that I need to navigate what comes next.

I've angered Sean by having a conversation with his daughter that maybe should've included him or even been just between him and Rosie. I've handed him a tangible reason to dislike me.

So... I should probably just go.

I open my mouth to say as much, but Linda speaks first.

"No. You're staying," she instructs, pointing one finger downwards. "Rosie and I invited you over, and we were having a lovely time before Sean showed up. If anyone should leave, it's him."

I shake my head slightly. "He didn't do anything wrong," I defend him painfully because he really didn't. He was doing what he thought he should to protect his daughter.

"He made you feel like *this*," she reminds me, tapping her foot on the hardwood floor. It's clear to me that she's every bit his mother now as she was when he was a boy. She's still just as ready to reprimand him now as she was then.

"No," I whisper. "*I* made me feel like this."

I let Sean bowl me over. I let Mason do it, too. I don't have the inner strength to hold my own when someone is harsh or unrelentingly cold. The increasing emotional distance Mason put between us over the last year or so was something that cut me down at the knees when I should've stood my ground. I should've fought for him instead of grasping at anything I thought would make me a better wife. I should've fought for myself instead of pretending he wasn't falling in love with someone else. My mother has told me as much, many times, and I'm starting to see it, too.

Linda's face morphs into both concern and confusion, but before she can ask me what I mean, Doug comes in carrying pizza boxes.

"Let's eat up," he says excitedly and sets down the boxes on the counter next to the fridge.

She pays him no mind; in fact, she seems to focus in on me more, but then Sean and Rosie enter the kitchen as well, and she turns to glare at her son, despite me not blaming him.

He ignores my existence completely and keeps Rosie close to his side while we eat pizza in the living room. And when I get up to leave, shortly after finishing our food, I can see the protest in Linda's blue eyes already.

"Thank you for having me," I say quietly, pulling at the sleeve of my long-sleeved shirt as I face the room.

"You don't have to rush off," Doug says, and Linda squeezes his thigh appreciatively. I can see why Doug is a good fit for Linda. He's a lover of people, too. Kind, genuine, friendly, just like her. I've caught Linda admiring his clean-shaven face more than once tonight, especially when he smiles and his blue eyes nearly disappear because of how squinty his face gets.

"Absolutely. Why don't we watch a movie?" Linda suggests brightly.

"Yeah!" Rosie exclaimed, jumping to her feet on the couch cushions.

"Maybe another time," I answer, glancing at Sean, who's unabashedly staring at me with hard brown eyes. His disdain for me hasn't wavered in the slightest. I know he wants me to leave. He probably never wants me to set foot in this house again. It wouldn't surprise me if he forbade Rosie from seeing me ever again. So even though I actually wouldn't mind staying for a movie, I feel like I don't really have a choice.

"Please! Pretty please!" she begs me, even sticking out her bottom lip in a pout.

"She said no," Sean says sternly.

Sean tries to grab her and get her to sit down on the couch again, but she wriggles stubbornly out of his grasp and jumps down to the floor, then right over to me. She hugs my legs tightly, peering up at me.

"Tomorrow? Tomorrow, can you watch a movie with us?"

I chance a look at Sean's irritated face and know he would rather I didn't. "Um, maybe."

Rosie lets out a disappointed sound that crushes me a little. I squat down and hug her to me in consolation and squeeze my eyes closed. She flings her little arms around my neck.

"I want you to stay," she whines sadly.

Sean stares at me, but I take a deep breath and rub Rosie's back for a moment.

"I know you want me to stay, sweetheart," I murmur. She nods into my shoulder, her hands tangled in my hair. "It makes me feel really good that you want me to spend more time with you, but your daddy wants to spend his own time with you, too."

Her arms tighten a little more.

"You have so many people who love you, don't you? Sometimes we have to take turns 'cause there's so many of us." I pull back and look into her sad eyes. "And right now, it's your daddy's turn, okay? And we can see each other again soon."

Her bottom lip trembles as she thinks over my words,

her blue eyes roaming over my face. "You promise?"

I glance behind her to her father, not wanting to make a promise to her and then break it because he doesn't want me around his kid. But he says nothing to indicate that.

"I promise."

She smiles just a little and gives me one more hug. Then she releases me and sulks back over to her daddy.

I stand up, and glance around to each face, remembering just now that Doug and Linda are still sitting on the couch to the right. They're both looking at me with soft smiles, a note of appreciation in Linda's eyes.

I clear my throat and look back at Sean. His hands are placed gently on his daughter's shoulders as she gazes at me sadly. His dislike for me hasn't returned yet. It's been replaced by... puzzlement?

"Thank you again for having me."

"Of course, dear," Linda says warmly. "You're welcome anytime."

I nod at her, give Rosie a little smile, and then head for the front door.

The thing is, I'm not welcome. Sean has been pretty clear about that. But if I ever manage to get on his good side, I know it would be a blessing to be welcome in that house.

Their house feels like a home. They *live* in that house. Rosie told me they do movie nights and game nights in addition to pizza night, and sometimes in the summer, they all set up tents in the backyard and have a campfire and make s'mores. Rosie's drawings are taped up all over the house, not just on the fridge. And her toys and Linda's puzzle boxes can be found all over their cozy living room. Even their coffee-colored couches are well-loved and their end tables scattered with both children's and adult's books.

My mother was too busy to read books or do puzzles with me. She was a successful realtor who was sometimes off to show a house or meet a client without much notice. My father was even busier, and when they divorced shortly before my eighth birthday, I realized that my relationship with him didn't suffer because there wasn't one to begin with. I haven't spoken to him since his call to wish me a happy ninth birthday. I can't even remember what he did for a living or what color his eyes were.

And despite the very stern way Sean spoke to his daughter just now, I can tell that he loves her well. Somehow, I know he's doing his best, and to me, just showing any effort at all means a lot. He's protective of her because he loves her, and that's what I choose to hold onto as I walk back to my house.

My very crowded, lonely house. The difference between mine and the one next door couldn't be more pronounced. I don't live in my house. I survive in it. This is just four walls to shelter under. The only thing that isn't empty are the boxes.

But if I unpack these boxes, then I can't live in this strange middle ground where I'm no longer part of the past and not participating in the future. Unpacking would make my divorce reality. Unpacking would remind me that no matter how well I arrange my things here, it still won't be a home.

I spend most of the next day on the couch, watching the sun peek through the gap between the wall and the curtain. The light moves across the floor until it hits the opposite wall, and that's when my mother calls.

It's just before five, and she opens the conversation

with, "I hope I'm not interrupting your dinner," which is her fishing for whether I'm even eating dinner tonight. Which I'm not.

"Don't worry, mom," I reply with a sigh.

She replies with a sigh of her own. She's been doing that a lot during our phone calls. She's becoming more and more exasperated by my lack of action. My lack of anything.

"I don't even know what to say to you anymore," my mother tosses out impatiently. "What are you doing all day? How can you live like this, Mara?"

I close my eyes and rest my head back against the couch. She hasn't brought up seeking out a therapist again, which probably means it's what I should do.

"I'm about *this close* to getting on a plane so I can set you straight. You obviously can't do it yourself."

"No," I croak out. I don't want her coming here. Her kind of pushy, frustrated help isn't what I need. I need gentleness. Patience. Understanding. I need...*Linda*. "I'm okay, Mom. Just last night I had dinner with my neighbors."

"You did?" For the first time, I hear a bit of hope in my mom's voice. "Well, that's great! I'm glad you finally listened to me and reached out to someone."

A tiny bit of irritation spits some angry things in my ear.

Of course, Mother. Take all the credit so you feel like you helped.

I shake the thought away. "Yeah, they're really nice." It's mostly true. And even though I don't know where I stand with Rosie's dad, she and Linda really did lighten my spirit. "So, you don't have to come back, Mom. I'll be okay."

I hear almost a sigh of relief on the line, and I'm not sure whether it's relief that I'm okay or relief that she doesn't have to fly here to push me back into line.

"Okay, Mara. We'll talk soon."

"Later, Mom."

I hang up, glad that I managed to convince her not to come and disrupt my lonely routine. She's always been about saving face, even if it's unhealthy and unhelpful. After my parents got divorced, she made a show of being okay, and she expects me to do the same.

But I just can't. It takes too much energy to pretend to be anything other than what I am.

And yet, I hear her words in my head.

How can you live like this?

I glance around my cramped living room, noticing the words scrawled in black permanent marker on each one. Everything is compartmentalized like this, and I'm comfortable with it that way. But there's one word that stands out to me from across the room.

Photos.

I had picture frames hung all over my and Mason's house. In every room and hallway. Pictures of us at prom. Pictures of us at graduation. At the fair. Laughing. Hugging. Kissing. So many from our wedding day and with our families.

I know those pictures belong in that box. I know I should just walk that whole box unopened to the garbage can. But something pulls me off the couch and has me peeling back the clear tape. One flap gets folded open and then the other.

And there they are. Heaps of picture frames. Numerous pictures of a life that is over now. Was any of it real? Did he ever love me, or was I just enough to not warrant leaving until someone better came along?

I grapple at the flaps and fold them back down as the memories start speaking to me from those frames. Memories that are stained and tainted and marred by what Mason did. I back away from it like the box may sprout arms and legs and chase me.

And then suddenly, I find myself throwing open the front door and moving down my concrete sidewalk to where it connects to the city sidewalk. I turn around, my heart beating out of rhythm as I look up at the little house I don't know how to call mine. Boards and shingles and glass, inhaling and exhaling the staleness of my broken life. Its screws and nails and construction glue barely able to contain the mess of who I am.

I fold my arms around myself, fighting to breathe normally, and then I point myself down the block.

I take one step, and then another. Two more, and then three. There's the corner, just two houses down. I can walk that far. It's just as simple as not stopping.

The corner looms closer, the evening air sweet but with a tiny chill that keeps me aware of my task.

Just walk.

I feel the slightest breeze touch my hair. A red car drives by. Laughter filters out of the house on the corner. And then, I turn to the right, my feet lifting and my legs moving more than they have in months. The air feels different out here. My lungs feel different breathing it.

But then, I turn the second corner, and I realize that this is the farthest I've been from my couch since I moved in. My chest tightens and squeezes, making it harder to breathe through the panic. I walk quicker, my legs beginning to burn just enough to remind me how easily tired my body has become. I keep my eyes on the third corner and start to feel the tears sting my eyes.

I want to get back to the house. Now. I feel like at any moment I'm about to break into a million pieces.

But a small little flickering of satisfaction perks up—the satisfaction of moving my body in a way that is useful.

The third corner has me nearly sprinting, my long hair bouncing off my back. Each beat of my heart feels like a painful punch to the chest.

Then the last corner approaches, and the tears move down my face. The glimpse of my house down the street doesn't feel like sanctuary or peace or even relief. It feels like embracing a coffin. A place where I fit that no one can get inside of. A thing I can control. It feels like gravity, how you hate that it pulls you down but appreciate that you can always rely on it to be constant.

When I'm within twenty feet of my sidewalk, I run to it, embarrassed and ashamed at my anxious behavior and yet unable to stop it. It's when I'm climbing my familiar concrete steps to the door that I hear a truck door close. I glance to my left as I reach for the screen door handle and see the dim shape of Sean walking up the lawn to the porch next door.

Before I can decide for sure whether he's caught sight of me, I dart inside and bolt the door.

I lean my forehead on it, breathing raggedly.

I don't know what I've learned from walking around the block, but I do move that box full of photos into the closet of the spare room off the kitchen so that I never get the urge to look through it again.

CHAPTER SEVEN

Sean

The branch I'm tied to sways and bucks as the weight of the piece I sawed off falls to the ground below with a soft thud. This is the part that most people can't stand to watch. It seems like the most dangerous part of the job, but in reality, I'm perfectly safe as long as my tethers and hooks are secured correctly.

Years ago, when I first told my mom that Rhys and I were going into business together, I made her promise not to watch me work. That if she ever saw my truck somewhere, to just keep going, because I know without a doubt that she would pass out to see me up so high.

But I was that kid. I gave both my parents a run for their money. I was constantly climbing any tree I could get my hands on. When I was seven, I climbed the oak tree next to the house and got onto the roof. I got grounded for two weeks for that, but it was worth it.

Being on top of the world like this is my favorite place to be. If that wasn't good enough, I also have a chainsaw.

"Let's call it a day!" Rhys shouts up to me from the ground. "The weather's starting to turn!"

I look up and see the dark clouds rolling in from the south.

"Alright!" I call back, and then shimmy my way back down. I unclip my tether to each harness point on the tree until I'm about twenty feet from the grass, then I climb down the rest of the way.

Rhys pats me on the arm, his eyes pointed up at where I was just sawing. "The city won't like it that we're a day behind, but what can you do?"

We're at Smith Park today, cutting down five dead ash trees piece by piece.

"Yeah, I'm not risking my neck in a thunderstorm," I agree and undo my harness.

We stow away our gear in the cabs of our trucks, and it begins to rain just as I open the driver's side door to get in.

"Want a beer? Let's go to Drake's," Rhys suggests from over the hood of his truck which is parked next to mine.

I glance at my watch. Because of the weather, I have an extra hour and a half to kill.

"Meet you there," I call through the rain, and then pull my door shut and start it up.

I follow him through town, taking a left on John Street, and by the time we park outside the bar, the rain is coming down in sheets. We get out and make a run for the entrance, still managing to get fairly soaked.

Rhys shakes his brown hair off like a dog as we find seats at the counter. Barry, the owner, limps over with a smile. Barry Brown was our shop teacher back in the day. After he had an accident with a circ saw, he retired and took over the bar from his dad. There's a rumor that the chunk Barry cut out of his knee is hidden in a mason jar somewhere on the premises, but honestly, I don't want to find out for myself whether that's true.

"Hello, boys," he greets with a toothy smile. "What'll it be?"

"Whatever you have on tap," I say distractedly as I type out a quick text to my mom to let her know I'm not working outside in these conditions.

"Same," Rhys agrees, and I pocket my phone as Barry gets to filling our glasses.

The bar is a simple square room with your typical neon beer signs, but coupled with those are other pictures of the locals. Some of them are football team pictures or little league baseball photos, some of which are hung there because Barry's grandkids are in them somewhere. There's an old jukebox in the corner that doesn't work anymore (I think someone spilled an entire pitcher of beer on it), and a smattering of small bar height tables.

We're too early for happy hour, but the plus side of that is the bar is quieter. Back in my younger days, I was part of the rowdy crowd, but it's been a long time since I've had more than a few beers in one sitting. Becoming a husband and father changed that for me.

"How's Rosie girl doing? Is she warming up to her teacher at all?" Rhys asks as he accepts his glass from Barry, and I do the same.

I sigh. "Not really."

It's been almost a week since pizza night. My mother didn't speak to me for a solid twenty-four hours because I apparently "ruined the whole night." She can think what she wants. Mara shouldn't have been talking to Rosie about being sad and depressed. She should've told Rosie to ask me instead.

"She'll get there," Rhys assures me lightly. He runs a hand through his damp hair, which is cut closer to the sides of his head and longer on the top. I told him he looks like a douchebag with that haircut, but he just told me I was jealous.

A crack of thunder rumbles through the space from outside.

"Sounds like we might have a few more clients after this one," he comments with a little smirk.

I clink my glass against his and take a long sip, the cool ale chilling me from the inside out.

"What's up with you? You've been quiet lately," Rhys questions suspiciously.

I shrug. "Just this woman who moved in next door," I answer with a growl.

"A *woman*?"

I glare at him. "Don't go there, man. It's not like that." Not that she isn't beautiful, because she is, but there's more to a woman than how she looks.

"Mhm." He chuckles and takes another gulp of his beer. "So, what's it like then?"

I look down at my glass, the condensation wiggling down the side of it.

I've been wanting to talk about it with Rhys, but I wasn't sure how to bring it up. He was my best man at my wedding. He was friends with Gabby. He was there for me after she was gone. I know I can rely on him, but that doesn't mean it feels good to talk about what happened and why Mara reminds me of my wife.

"First off, my mother loves her and so does Rosie."

"Rosie does, too?" he asks in surprise.

"I know. It's so weird. Mostly because this woman is...strange."

I clear my throat as I recall the handful of times I've seen her out walking this week. The first time, I thought someone was chasing her by the panicked look on her face. But then I realized she was just scared to be outside of her house. It made me feel bad for her. Not bad enough to let my mom invite her over for pizza night again tomorrow, however.

"How so?"

"She barely says anything, but when she does open her mouth, she tells my daughter what depression is like in one breath and then calms her like a pro the next."

"She's a better parent then you are, dude," he jokes like an idiot.

I roll my eyes and sip my beer.

"There's no doubt in my mind that she's depressed. Like severely depressed. Just like Gabby was."

Rhys's upper body stiffens when I say my wife's name. "What do you mean? You think she's suicidal?"

"Wouldn't surprise me," I mutter to my glass. I can feel my friend's gaze on me as he stews over what I've said.

All I can think about is coming home from work that day and finding out my mom had taken Rosie for the afternoon. Later she told me that Gabby had said she just needed a break, so my mom gladly came over and picked up baby Rosie. She said Gabby seemed tired, but nothing seemed off.

I walked into our little apartment, everything eerily quiet. Baby clothes strewn all over, like usual, the dishes unwashed in the sink, like usual. I didn't mind stepping up with the chores after Rosie was born. Gabby had the most important job, and the most taxing, so I gladly did dishes and cleaned up every night when I got home. I wanted her to feel less pressure to be doing everything, and to be doing everything *perfectly*. I thought it was helping, but I had noticed her becoming less responsive to me and to Rosie in the last couple weeks. I didn't think too much of it, but when I walked into the bathroom, I realized much too late that I should've dragged her to the doctor if I had to. Maybe if I had, she would still be alive.

The image of her floating in the bathtub still fully clothed with blue lips will haunt for me as long as I live.

"If you think she's suicidal, you need to do something." Rhys's firm voice snaps me out of the worst moment of my life, and I look over at him. "If she's struggling that much, you need to get her help, Sean."

"Yeah," is all I can muster. His words remind me of what Mom said about having compassion.

He grips me by the shoulder and turns me toward him slightly. "Hey. Talk to me, man."

I clear my throat, fighting my rising emotions. "I just wish Gabby was still here. I wish I could've—"

He squeezes my shoulder. "I know. I know how much it kills you that you couldn't save her. But...she's gone. Your neighbor is still here. Get her the help you couldn't get Gabby."

I stare at him for a long moment. I hadn't thought about it like that. I've viewed her through the same lens as Gabby, but only in how she reminds me of the worst. The woman doesn't mean a damn thing to me, but if I imagined something bad happening to her that I could've prevented, I know it would bother me. Just because I don't know her doesn't mean

I shouldn't care about her mental health, especially when she very well could be suicidal. She doesn't need my judgment. She needs my help.

"You're right," I rasp out. "Thanks."

He gives me a sympathetic smile and releases my shoulder.

We sit in silence for a while after that, both of us lost in thought. It's one of the reasons we're such good friends. Not only has Rhys seen me at my worst, he sits with me when my mind is stuck in the past. He understands what it's like to mourn and regret. He has his own ghosts from the past that haunt him, and even though he barely talks about the family he escaped from in high school, I know it still affects him every day.

On the way home, my mind goes to a place I don't often let it go. It never does me any good to dwell on the what-ifs and whys. But Rhys's advice has me stumbling back into them.

There's so much I didn't do for Gabby. In the hospital after Rosie was born, the doctor mentioned postpartum depression. So did her doctor at her six-week check-up. But I didn't realize Gabby's symptoms were as bad as they were. I thought she was just exhausted and overwhelmed by our new little addition.

But it was much more than that. Her disinterest in anything to do with Rosie was stubborn and unmoving. The first time Rosie smiled, Gabby had no reaction. That should've been my first clue that something was wrong. Instead, I just did more chores and gave her more hugs. I trusted her to know when to ask for help when I should've realized the marked change in her personality post-birth was a cry for help in and of itself.

I could've saved her. All of that could've been remedied.

As I pull up in front of my house and park, I glance in the rearview mirror at Mara's house. In my gut, I know she's as lost as Gabby was. And I know that's why my mom has been so welcoming. She lost a daughter as much as I lost a wife. Maybe she's thinking the same thing—that Mara needs someone to help her out of the pit she's living in.

I get out of the truck and sink my hands into the pockets of my work jeans as I walk up the wet grass to the porch.

I go inside and find my mom in the kitchen, doing a puzzle at the table as usual. Before Rosie can run over to hug me, I lean down and wrap my arms around my mom's shoulders from behind, squeezing tightly.

"Oh," she says in pleasant surprise. "What's this for?"

I sigh. "Nothing. I just love you."

She rubs the back of forearm. "I love you, too, Sean."

I release her and go give Rosie a tight hug, too, then I set her back down on her chair.

"It's okay if Mara comes over tomorrow for pizza night," I say softly to them, and then leave the room.

CHAPTER EIGHT

Mara

I t's torture to keep up the walking. I usually enjoy the first block, taking in how each tree I pass is a little more yellow or orange every day. The air is beginning to cool, proof that September is marching on even if I feel like I'm standing still. But moving my body feels good, even if every walk I force myself to go on results in a small panic attack.

I know it's good for me—the fresh air and the movement—but I dread leaving the confines of my house. It's painful to see how the world is going about its usual orbit. People drive their cars to work and shuffle through their grass to get the paper or the mail. The sun goes down, and it comes up. And all I can do is berate myself into walking around the block.

But my mother was pleased to hear that I've started walking. She mentioned me getting a job again, but I know I wouldn't be a good employee. I don't think I could be reliable in showing up on time or even at all, and there's no way I could be cheerful and friendly. She doesn't want to hear that I need more time, but I do.

A few nights ago, I chanced a repeat of pizza night with

my neighbors. When Rosie and Linda came over to invite me, and insisted it was because Sean said I should come, I wasn't sure whether to believe them. If he did say that, it's likely he was trying to be polite or maybe didn't want to start a fight with his mother.

But then I went over, and he didn't glare or frown at me. His golden-brown eyes made me feel warm, but I assumed it was because I'm not used to a man looking at me. Mason barely did towards the end of our marriage. Even before that, I can't recall a time when his eyes on me made me feel the way Sean's eyes felt on me. He...*studied* me. I felt him taking me in all through dinner. Not like he was scrutinizing me, but more like he was observing. Taking notes. It was odd, but it was an improvement from his previous attitude toward me. Either he changed his mind about me, or he was doing a good job of concealing his dislike. Whatever the reason, I decided to go with it and hope he really didn't mind me being around.

It's a relief to feel even a little welcome, especially after being pushed out of my marriage. I try not to think about Mason and Sarah. I try not to wonder how they are or picture them in my old house, living my old life. I try to keep my mind on more tangible things.

Things like the sound the front door makes when I open it. The scent of baked goods from Linda that are still feeding both my body and my soul. The unyielding concrete beneath each foot as I walk away from my house and then nearly sprint back to it. The breeze and the leaves and the sparrows. Those things keep me from backing myself into the corner of the couch and into the little corner of my heart where it hurts the most.

I'm currently facing my front door, psyching myself up to go on my daily afternoon walk when my phone rings. My first thought is that it's my mother because literally no one else calls me, but she and I just spoke yesterday. I pick it up off the couch, and my stomach rolls.

Mason is calling.

My hands shake and tremble so violently, I almost drop my phone.

Why is he calling me? Now? Did things with Sarah not work out after all? Does he regret what he did? Does he wish he had stayed?

The last time I spoke to him was in his lawyer's office when we signed the divorce papers. *Hurry up already,* he said to me as I tried to get my hand to move the pen over the paper.

Without giving even a thought to whether I should answer or not, I accept the call and lift my phone to my ear.

"Hello?" my voice is small, as small as it was the last time I saw him.

"Mara, I forgot the password for the internet company login," Mason says in that familiar deep, casual voice like we're just friends who talk about things like these. Like he isn't my ex-husband. Like hearing his familiar voice speak my name doesn't shatter me all over again.

The little, tiny voice that thought he was calling for something else goes quiet and still as death.

I clear my throat, trying to keep the wave of embarrassment from affecting my voice as I answer him.

"It's the last four digits of your phone number and then your first name," I murmur, feeling my tattered heart break. Because he doesn't need me. He *never* needed me. He's moved on.

"I knew you'd remember. Thanks." He hangs up then, leaving me teetering on the edge of my sanity.

I drop my phone on the couch and move away from it

until my back hits the front door.

Was I nothing to him at all? Just another brain to store useless information like that? Will he call me again next month and ask for the account number for the cable?

I'm a bigger fool than I thought.

I close my eyes and rest my head back against the wood as the tears burn my eyes. Something strange fills me up from the inside out—some bitter, painful, burning thing that pushes every hurt he's ever caused me to the surface. The walls around me tremble as the tears come, threatening to wash me away entirely.

And then, I turn, open the door, and walk down to the city sidewalk, feeling everything and nothing. Deaf to anything else, I walk. My feet don't feel like they're touching anything. The cars passing on my left don't make a sound. I don't notice when I pass the street corner, going straight instead of turning right like I usually do.

Then, the black, sludgy contents of my deepest pain oozes out from my chest and into each limb, weighing me down with truths I can't handle.

Mason's life is better without me.

He's *happier* without me.

I was holding him back.

The scenery changes around me as I walk on, unbeknownst to me. I don't know that I'm far from my house. I can't see past the thoughts in my head.

Mason, holding her hand. Smiling at her. Raising a child with her. Never mentioning my name again because I was so insignificant to him.

A strange sort of buzzing fills my ears, loud enough for

me to pay attention to it. It isn't buzzing, I realize, but the sound of water. Rushing water beneath me.

I look to my right and see the wide Mississippi river, covered by the Sauk Rapids bridge. I realize I've walked for probably forty minutes to get to this bridge from where I live. I reach out one shaky hand to touch the cold concrete, and then the other. The cement is scratchy and rough, and something about that pleases me. I drag my fingertips over it so that it grates against my soft skin, causing it to redden in protest without my dear calluses to protect them.

The sound of the water below me is powerful and strangely inviting. I could lose myself in that sound. That thundering, splashing, crashing sound. So reckless and churning, like me. I step closer and look down over the edge. A damp spray wafts up from the surface of the river sixty feet below.

I feel a deep pull that I can't explain.

What would happen if I jumped?

Would I survive? Would everything stop the second I hit the water? Or would I wake up in a hospital bed with injuries and regret?

No, Mara. You can't.

I swallow hard. I can't. I have to keep going. I have to turn my feet around and walk back. Back to my little house next to the only thing I have that gives me a bit of hope that my life is somehow changing for the better, even if every bit of progress hurts.

I take a deep breath, and just when I'm about to step back, I hear a somewhat familiar voice call out behind me.

"Mara!"

I turn and spot Sean standing about fifteen feet away

from me, his truck parked on the bridge with the driver's side door wide open, like he got out in a hurry. He's breathless, standing there with panic in his dark eyes.

"Hi," I whisper out in surprise.

"What are you doing?" He glances out over the bridge and back at me quickly, concern indenting his forehead.

"I...I was just...thinking."

About jumping.

He hears what I don't say. It's clear in the way he takes a slow, tentative step towards me. When he sees that I don't shrink back from him or dart towards the ledge, he takes another and another until he's five feet from me.

"Did you walk here?"

I nod. He studies me for a moment and then reaches out his hand.

"Come on; I'll give you a ride back."

I stare at his outstretched hand, realizing that he's offering it like a lifeline. I lift my hand and place my scratched fingers into his warm palm, which he instantly clasps. He tugs me back from the bridge's ledge, keeping his eyes on mine like if he looks away, I might change my mind. He doesn't let go of my hand until I'm seated in the passenger seat of his truck. He buckles me in, still looking worried, and then closes the door.

The cab of the truck is silent as he quickly walks around the hood.

And the silence is good. That hypnotizing sound of rushing water is abruptly cut off, and I can hear my own heart beating in my ears. That strong, steady thing pumping life through my body despite my turmoil. I close my eyes for a moment, just marveling at it, and when I open them again,

Sean is getting into the truck.

He starts up the engine without a word and puts it in drive. After an anxious glance in my direction, he pulls out onto the road that goes over the bridge. I clutch my seat tightly as he makes a U-turn, going back the way I so thoughtlessly, subconsciously came.

I scared him, I realize. He jumped out of his truck because he thought I was going to…

I close my eyes again, mortified that he saw me in such a vulnerable state. I don't know how I'll ever be able to look him in the eyes ever again.

But in a way, I'm grateful I stared down into the depths of my pain, because it made me realize that I'm not ready to give up my life yet. Part of me may want it all to stop, but there's another part that wants to see what's around the corner for me. Part of me doesn't want this to be the end.

"Are you okay?" he asks with a slight shake to his soft voice.

I nod, clenching my hands together in my lap. I'm shaken, I'll admit. Scared by the kind of thought I had on the bridge. But I'm also relieved to have found my will to live, to *really* live, and not just exist like I've been doing since the divorce.

Sean signals to turn onto our street. The clicking sound feels loud to me in the silence between us.

He pulls into my driveway instead of parking on the street like usual, which is nice of him. I reach for the door handle to get out, ready to disappear into my house and try to pretend this never happened.

"Mara, wait a second," Sean demands quietly.

I pause, wanting to ignore him, but I return my hand to

my lap. I don't want to talk about what I was really doing on the bridge, but what else could he be stopping me for? I take a steadying breath and turn my head towards him. He's staring at me intently, and it instantly causes goosebumps to rise all over my skin. I've never met a man who has this kind of effect on me, just from looking.

"Are you alright?" he asks. "Be honest with me."

A blush of embarrassment creeps up the front of my neck. "I'm okay."

He keeps staring at me, one wrist rested on the steering wheel. His mouth twists to one side like he's deciding something, and I can't stop my eyes from dropping to his bottom lip.

"Is there..." he trails off and then awkwardly clears his throat. "Is there someone you can talk to? It's pretty clear you're going through some stuff."

Some stuff.

How gracious he is to call my mental crisis moment *some stuff.*

"Um, I...don't. Not really," I answer truthfully, feeling more pathetic by the second. "But I'm okay," I repeat. He ignores that.

"I know that sometimes things feel really bad, but... everything can be fixed."

I nod awkwardly, looking away as the blush spreads from my neck to my face, too.

He sighs, and I see him thread his free hand through his hair out of the corner of my eye. "What I'm saying is, life can really suck sometimes, but that doesn't mean it always will."

My throat feels tight with humiliation.

"And, you know, it's okay to ask for help."

I nod, pressing my lips together, and continue avoiding eye contact.

He sighs again, this time heavier. "Will you look at me please?"

My shoulders flinch at his directness, and I instantly do as he says. His expression has a shadow of contrition over the concerned expression he's wearing.

"This is all probably none of my business, and I get that. But...I don't want the fact that I've been a jerk be the thing that keeps you from reaching out. You said you don't have many people in your life, but I know my mom and my daughter would be heartbroken if something happened to you."

I blink in surprise at his words and how he seems to be leveling with me.

"I'm sorry for making you feel like you aren't welcome over. I just..." He shakes his head slightly. "I'm protective of my family."

"Of course, you are," I agree gently. His apology means a lot, actually. I wasn't expecting that.

He nods and then the silence returns. An explanation for the bridge is creeping slowly up my throat, and with it comes a sense of panic.

"I wasn't going to—" I blurt out and then stop myself, my heart pounding. "I—I know what it looked like, but I'm not...I was just looking at the water under the bridge."

Sean studies my hot face for a quiet moment, his chocolate caramel eyes seeing through me.

"It's dangerous to look at the water under the bridge," he says slowly, purposely, hinting at a deeper meaning.

I nod. "I won't do it again."

After one long look in which I know he's trying to figure out whether I'm being truthful, I give him a microscopic smile.

"Thanks for the ride." I get out of his truck then and am surprised when he does, too. I stop my pursuit of the concrete steps, and he stands in front of his truck.

He clears his throat, and I can feel him hesitating over what he wants to say next. "Do you mind if we exchange numbers? I'd like us to be able to contact each other, especially in the case of an emergency."

"Oh," I say surprised, but I guess I shouldn't be. We're neighbors, after all. "Okay. Let me go grab my phone." I climb the steps to the front door.

"Wait, what?" he blurts out, and I look over my shoulder at him with my hand on the screen door handle. "You were out walking without your phone on you?" He's equal parts exasperated and terrified, I think.

I blush slightly, feeling like a kid caught with her hand in the cookie jar, because the fact I was on the bridge without a way for anyone to contact me just makes everything look worse.

But then his expression changes to something softer, something that looks more like...grief. Or fear. He sighs and comes up the steps behind me.

"Go on; get your phone," he commands gently.

I open the screen door and then the house door, and to my astonishment, he follows me into my unpacked living room. Feeling self-conscious, I grab my phone from the couch, and when I turn around, he's staring at the state of my house. The first person, besides the movers and my mother, to ever set foot inside.

"You haven't unpacked yet?" he asks, puzzled and incredulous, as he looks around at all the sealed boxes.

I bite my lip, feeling my anxiety ratchet up at him seeing the way I live. The small, empty, cramped, minimal way in which I live.

"It's...it's just a lot, and I don't know where to start," I explain lamely. It's not a lie. Unpacking everything is absolutely a big job, so big that when I look around, I feel overwhelmed by it. It's a tidal wave of cardboard and packing tape and reality.

Sean brings his eyes back to me, sympathy inching across his brow. He takes out his phone from his pocket and comes closer, opening up the contacts for me to enter in my number. I do the same, and when our phones are returned to their rightful owners, he looks around again.

"This might be weird, but my mom is really good at organizing. She's one of those people who thinks it's fun. So, if you want some help unpacking, I'm sure she would be more than happy to help. Actually, me and Rosie could help, too," he says softly.

I hug myself as I consider it.

I can't live this way forever. It's been nearly two months since I moved in, and I've only managed to "put away" one box, if that box of photos even counts. He's offering me help, and what I feel like is very non-judgmental help, so I feel a bit obligated to accept. Even if the idea of them rifling through these boxes makes me uncomfortable.

"We could just do the kitchen and bathroom stuff at least," he adds, like he's belatedly realized he doesn't want to intrude on my privacy.

I take a breath and nod. "Okay. That would be nice."

He nods, too, looking into my eyes for a brief moment before he takes a step backward toward the door.

"We'll come over tomorrow, then. And just...think about what I said before, okay?"

I give him an uncomfortable nod.

One side of his mouth lifts into a small smile, the first one I've ever seen directed at me, and then he opens the front door to leave.

This time when the door closes, the silence around me feels different. It feels warmer. Because Sean looked around the inside of my mess and offered to help. He didn't get mad at me like my mother would have and chastise me for waiting so long.

I hear his truck start up and peek through the curtain as he moves it to the street where he usually parks. He seems tired as he walks up to the porch and goes inside.

I'm tired, too, after all that. But for now, I'm remembering that I'm glad to be alive.

CHAPTER NINE

Sean

I stare down the coffee maker in front of me, my hands anchored to the edge of the countertop as the machine gurgles. When just enough coffee for a cup's worth collects in the carafe, I immediately pour it into a mug and attempt to swallow down some of the searing, caffeine-giving liquid.

I usually get up early for work, but this morning, I'm awake an hour earlier than needed.

I barely slept last night. I tossed and turned, worried over, and thought about Mara on that bridge. When I did manage to drift off, I dreamt about it. Except at the last second before Mara jumped, she suddenly turned into Gabby, her hand just out of my reach before she leapt over the edge and disappeared from view.

I woke up with a panicked jolt each time. And now, I'm exhausted and plagued more than ever by losing my wife.

If I had just come home an hour earlier...

I refill my cup and take it outside to the front porch, making sure to close the door quietly so I don't wake up Rosie or my mother.

The morning air is cold, biting the exposed skin of my neck, hands, and face. The coffee keeps me warm as I sit on the wooden bench my dad built when I was a kid. I look over to Mara's house, noticing the windows are dark.

How many times has she walked to that bridge? Was that just the first time I saw her, or was it the first time she's stood there and contemplated the distance down to the water?

I've never slammed on the brakes so hard in my life. And when she turned and looked at me, it was like I had shaken her awake, like she had been sleep-walking. I'll never forget the moment she put her hand in mine, and she let me move her away from the edge.

Rhys is right. I need to keep an eye on her. She may not be anything to me, but she's someone to somebody. She has a family who loves her, I assume. And even if she doesn't, that's all the more reason for me to get on board with my mom's and Rosie's efforts.

I heave out a sigh into the pre-sun morning air. I can't let Mara fall any further into her depression. She might never make it out if I do nothing.

I didn't tell my mom about finding Mara on the bridge. I don't want her to worry about the woman any more than she already is. The bridge will be an unspoken secret between me and Mara.

I take my cup back inside to refill, stepping over stuffed animals and kids' books in the living room. I've long given up on getting Rosie to clean up at the end of the night. She likes to leave things where they are so she can go right back to what she was doing when she wakes up.

As I pass the fridge, a drawing on the fridge catches my attention. It's another of Rosie's green crayon masterpieces, but this one is stick figures. She always draws people with huge heads and little bodies, though this one is slightly more proportionate than usual, like maybe she worked extra hard on it. I see my mom's handwriting labeling each person.

Daddy. Rosie. Grandma. Mara.

My heart skips a beat. Mara? *Mara* is in our family drawing? I look closer at the figure Rosie drew of her, only recognizing it as Mara because of the scribbles that resemble her long hair.

I rub at the ache permeating my chest. That should be Gabby drawn there. But Rosie doesn't know her. I've shown her pictures, and I do answer her questions as age appropriately as I can. But Gabby is more of a stranger to her than Mara is.

I close my tired eyes for a moment. Rosie will never know the woman I loved. She'll only ever know that Gabby loved her because I've told her. She'll never experience her mother's love herself.

I hate that there will always be a hole in her life where Gabby left it. And in mine, too.

The coffee only got me so far today. By the time I get home, I'm exhausted. But Rosie is already waiting on the front porch to go over to Mara's. My mom told her this morning that when I got home, we were going to help Mara unpack, which I'm sure tested her five-year-old patience while she was at school all day.

Her excitement to help isn't lost on me, and the smile on her little face stays there both before and after I shower and get dressed. She definitely gets that from my mother. Linda Dunbar has always been a helper, a reacher-outer. I wasn't surprised the first time she took over baked goods for the new neighbor because that's what she does. I just didn't expect my mom to try and adopt her into the family.

I won't lie; I'm a little nervous to unpack Mara's house. But I was so shocked to see all those boxes last night that the offer was out of my mouth before I could think better of it. There's definitely no backing out now, even if I'm exhausted and anxious to spend time with Mara.

"Alright, you ready, Rosiecakes?" I ask as I come into the kitchen. She's sitting at the table with my mom, looking disinterested in the puzzle on the table. When she hears my voice, she lights up and immediately hops to her feet.

"Yes! Let's go!"

I chuckle and grab her, throwing her over my shoulder as I stride to the front door, my mother laughing from behind me as she follows.

We walk over to the house next door, and Rosie squirms down as we reach the concrete steps. I've noticed Mara doesn't sit out here as much these days, but then again, she's been walking more.

I swallow down the memory of last night, and it feels like acid burning down the middle of my chest.

Rosie bangs her little fist on the screen door glass gleefully, and a minute later, the interior door opens. Mara's expression is a little sheepish and nervous when she opens the screen door and looks out at us.

"Mara!" Rosie exclaims, and rushes forward to hug her legs, nearly knocking her over.

"Easy, Rosie," I warn lightly, and follow her in, my mom bringing up the rear.

"Oh, what a beautiful house," Mom comments warmly as she looks around, seemingly unbothered by the state of

Mara's life. To be fair, she was forewarned. I wasn't.

Mara stands by the couch, her hands fidgeting with the hem of her purple sweatshirt. I can tell by her nerves that maybe she's already regretting accepting our help. She doesn't look anyone in the eyes, except for Rosie, who is standing as close to her as possible.

"You know, the couple who lived here before you did a good deal of renovating before they put it up for sale," my mom continues, looking around at the different features around the living room. New baseboards and refinished hardwood floors, to name a couple. "I'm so glad you get to benefit from all their hard work, dear."

Mara gives her a tight smile and a nod. She chews on her pink bottom lip and continues to avoid eye contact. There are more shadows under her blue eyes than usual, and I assume she didn't sleep the best either.

My mom takes the reins with just one clap of her hands. "Well! Let's get to work, shall we? Let's start in the kitchen." She goes on ahead without needing Mara to lead her, and we file in behind her.

I get out my utility knife and cut the tape on all the boxes. Mom chatters on about this and that, oohing and ahhing about this dish or that pan, mostly to fill the silence, I think.

Only one box has been opened before we showed up, and if I had to guess, there are only a couple more throughout the whole house that aren't still sealed shut. How has she lived so primitively? Her cupboards are bare and so is the small pantry next to the fridge. She's been living out of just a few boxes.

It occurs to me that she needs more help than I thought. She needs someone to take care of her because she's barely taking care of herself. My eyes find her dark red hair as she and Rosie put away some gray colored plates. What was she like before this? Without the depression hampering her spirit, is she usually cheerful? Or funny? Outgoing?

I know what it's like to watch depression steal someone from you one tiny change at a time. Gabby went from being a loving and attentive wife, someone I could laugh with and swap stories, to someone who would barely look up if I said her name. And watching the small, quiet ways Mara interacts with my family makes me feel a sense of grief and loss for her. It's a loss of *self* that not everyone understands.

The kitchen takes an hour to situate, and then my mother chooses to tackle the bathroom next. Rosie is more interested in playing with the empty boxes in the kitchen at this point, so me and Mara put away towels and random cleaning supplies in the empty bathroom cabinets while my mom keeps an eye on Rosie.

She's loosened up a little by now, so even though we're alone, I choose not to bring up last night. Maybe it's better if we don't. Maybe that was her rock bottom, and things will only get better from here on out.

"Mara!" my mom calls from another room. "I didn't know you played guitar!"

Mara's eyes widen just slightly, and she darts out of the bathroom. I follow, feeling like she might need my help in telling my mom to mind her own business.

I find them in the spare room off the kitchen, which has a few random boxes here and there, my mom holding up a black hard shell guitar case and grinning at Mara.

Her back is to me, that long red hair falling down almost to her waist, so I can't make out her expression, but from the tense way she's holding her shoulders, I can guess she didn't intend for my mom to bring up this part of her life.

"I...I used to," Mara answers so quietly I almost can't hear her. She touches her thumb across the tips of the fingers on her left hand, like she's remembering the bite of a guitar string on them.

"Oh, dear. I'd love to hear you play sometime," Mom gushes excitedly. "Grant used to play piano, and I miss hearing music in the house."

Both of my parents tried to get me to do piano lessons as a child, but I was never interested. I was content, the way my mom was, just to hear my dad playing from anywhere in the house.

Mara clears her throat awkwardly, and I step further into the room, coming to her side. There's a deep sorrow on her face as she looks at the guitar case in my mom's hands, like the guitar inside is a ghost of something she once loved.

Then my mom gasps, causing my eyes to swing over to her. "Oh my gosh! *Mara!*" she exclaims in recognition. "Mara Matthews! I saw you perform at the State Fair two years ago! I *thought* you looked familiar!"

Mara blushes an overpowering shade of crimson, so different from her usual pale complexion.

To say I'm surprised at this information would be an understatement. It's hard to imagine this quiet, empty person being a performer. I feel like if she opened her mouth to sing, nothing at all would come out.

"Remember, Sean? Cheryl and I went together, and I came home just raving about her," Mom reminds me expectantly, like I log that kind of random and useless information away.

"*Mom*," I snap quietly, glancing between her and Mara

with my eyebrows up, hoping she reads the room and notices that Mara seems less than comfortable with this topic.

"Oh, it was just *magical*. You have such a rare, beautiful talent, my dear," Mom continues glowingly, hugging the case to her chest, oblivious and a little star struck.

"Sheesh, Mom, why don't you ask for her autograph?" I growl and roll my eyes.

My mom stiffens, seeming to remember herself, and quickly thrusts the case at Mara.

"I'm so sorry! I totally lost my head," she laughs, but still looks fondly at Mara, who's holding the guitar case almost awkwardly, like she's forgotten the weight and feel of it.

"Come on, Mom. I thought you were keeping tabs on Rosie." I gesture for her to leave the room, and she goes, slightly confused. I turn back to Mara. "Sorry about that. She's a menace sometimes."

Mara carefully leans the case against a box near the corner, and then slowly faces me again. She averts her eyes, as she usually does with me, and I prepare to give her a minute to herself when she speaks.

"I haven't sung in a long time," she murmurs to the floor. "It used to bubble up out of me without even a thought...and now I..." She trails off and then shakes her head slightly.

I swallow hard, her distress pulling down on my lungs. Not only did she lose her husband and her friends, she lost her voice, too. She lost everything.

"It'll come back."

I don't know why I say it, or how I know it's true. If the presence of this much pain exists, it must mean that the joy she felt singing was just as strong. Something like that can't disappear forever.

She looks up at me, blue eyes fully connected with mine, like they were on the bridge last night. Except this time there's just a flicker of hope sparking to life behind those irises.

"It will?" she whispers hopefully.

"Yes. One day you'll sing again, when you're past all this."

Past all this hurt, is what I mean.

Mara's eyes lower thoughtfully for a moment, taking my words in, and when she meets my eyes again, she gives me a small, appreciative smile that cuts me deeper than her hollow eyes do.

Just that much of a genuine smile out of her makes me positive that Mara has a stunning smile. For the first time, I find myself hoping I'm still around when she can smile wholeheartedly again.

And then I wonder if she thinks the same thing about me.

CHAPTER TEN

Mara

He hasn't looked at me like this before, not even last night on the bridge. Like I'm not someone he just tolerates. Like he really sees me.

I don't remember Mason ever looking at me with this much understanding and warmth.

And his words trigger the first time I've even wanted to believe that one day I'll sing again. The first time I've really felt like it's possible.

Sean is mostly a stranger to me, but I can see that he has more faith in me than I do in myself to get through this. And I'm realizing that he and his amazing family aren't going to let me go it alone anymore. That's why they're here tonight, to gently help me forward.

The squeeze I've been feeling in my chest since they arrived to help unpack finally begins to loosen.

I feel gratitude move through me for these people who are here to walk alongside me until I can see the light again, rather than hearing my mother on the phone every other night scolding me to just turn the light on.

"Thank you," I say to Sean, wishing belatedly that I had thought to really speak up.

He nods once, just a single dip of his scruffy chin, and then he takes a step back.

"Are you hungry? Let's order some food."

The sudden change of topic snaps me out of our heartfelt moment, but I realize he may have done it on purpose. It seems he's attempting to keep me at arm's length. I don't take offense to that. I can respect that he likes his space. I know a lot about that.

"Sure."

I follow him into the kitchen, where Rosie is curled up at the bottom of an empty cardboard box in the little dining room. Sean goes over and peers down into the box.

"Whatcha doing?"

"I'm a sleepy kitty," her little voice says.

"Are you a hungry kitty, too?"

Rosie's blonde head pops straight up, her eyes big. "Yes! Hungry kitty!"

Sean chuckles and pulls out his phone to order food.

My eyes move to Linda, who's leaning her hip against the counter next to the sink, just staring at me like I'm suddenly a whole different person.

I wasn't actively hiding my former profession from her. She just never asked, and I never offered up that information, mostly because I didn't want to have to explain that I haven't done anything music-related since before the divorce. I put it all aside so I could focus on giving Mason as many reasons to stay as I could think of.

Instead, I just ended up losing the two things that I loved the most in my life.

And I'm ashamed of that, ashamed that I gave so much of myself away, and it wasn't enough to convince him to stay.

I'm not the person I was. I'm not the singer who could pour my heart into the microphone in front of anyone and everyone. So even though Linda may suddenly see me in a new light, I know that I'll never sing the way I used to. Whenever I'm able to sing again, it will be nothing like it was before. It can't be. Not when so much has changed, and I've splintered and fractured and crumbled through it.

Rekindling it again will be a delicate thing, and it isn't something I can do yet.

"Oh, Mara," Linda whispers with a wistful sigh. "There's so much I want to know about you."

I blink, not expecting her to say that and instantly worried that she's about to ask me dozens of questions I won't want to answer.

Sean looks up from his phone at his mother, his brow furrowing in her direction.

"I hope you know how dear you are to us," Linda adds before Sean can chastise her.

My heart squeezes, her soft tone so maternal and warm that I wish this woman was my mother, too. I look past her, catching Sean's uncertain expression, like he isn't sure how I'll react to that statement.

I look back at Linda and nod. "Thank you." I'm not sure what the proper response is, but I am thankful.

Linda smiles and moves toward me. In one motion, she hugs me tight in a hug so familial and warm that I close my eyes and let myself hug her back. Then, I hear a cardboard scuffle, quick little footsteps, and then Rosie's arms around my legs. Over Linda's shoulder, a shadow of pain crosses Sean's features that I don't understand, and then he turns away and brings the phone to his ear.

Sean orders in Chinese food for dinner, and we settle in the living room to eat. Because I only have the couch, Sean sits on the floor with Rosie as we eat around my coffee table.

While we waited for the food to arrive, Sean took a handful of boxes upstairs to the bedroom where I'm sure he noticed my not-slept-in bed. I'm uncomfortable with them discovering what a mess I am. But Linda and Sean haven't slid me any judgmental glances or made any comments about how I'm very obviously sleeping on the couch and rotating through a few sweatshirts.

The idea of my neighbors being inside my house had me up most of the night. Because Sean and I exchanged numbers, I almost texted him to cancel this morning at least a dozen times. But I was sure Linda would show up anyway, so I languished in anxiety all day.

The absence of boxes along some of the living room walls is strange to me, and I'm not sure I like how much bigger the room feels. I've gotten so used to being hedged in that now I feel exposed, especially with them sitting here with me.

But allowing them to help me do something I haven't been able to do myself is good. Accepting help is good, even if it's uncomfortable. Even if unpacking is causing me to deal with the fact that I can't go back to my life before. That *this* is my life now.

At least with the Dunbars next door, I know I won't be alone.

———————————

When my neighbors leave, I feel the loss of them. They were here for a few hours, and with each passing minute, it seemed warmer and homier inside these walls. I turned down Sean's offer to hang pictures, opting not to explain that the only ones I have are pictures of me and Mason. So, my walls are still blank, and they press in on me a little more now that they're less covered up by boxes.

I wander around the kitchen, opening drawers and cabinets to memorize their contents. Seeing each pot and pan in its new place has my mind reeling back to all the meals I made Mason and how hard I worked to have it all ready by the time he got home from work. Then, he started getting home later and later, oftentimes not even hungry because he said he had already eaten. What he hadn't said was that he had already eaten dinner with Sarah.

I look over the bathroom as well, almost catching the faint sawdust scent of Sean in that space. A blue towel hangs on the towel rod next to the shower, a matching one hung on the hook next to the mirror. My face looks the same as it has all these months. Pale. Deflated. Lost.

And then I climb the stairs, knowing that this room is the one I've avoided the most since I moved in.

I find the boxes Sean moved up here, settled near the closet door. The tape has been cut, but the boxes remain closed, like he was hinting I shouldn't let them sit here for another month. But then I see the bed and am stunned to find that it's been made. Pillows at the head, covered by the light green comforter my mother purchased for me. Seeing the bed made up has an effect on the room that I wasn't expecting.

For the first time, I notice the soft white curtains hung on the window behind the simple wooden headboard. The downy comforter layered over the sheets has transformed this hollow room into something that seems much more inviting and much less intimidating.

There's also a small end table with a lamp on the right side of the bed, adding to the idea that this room has a function other than a catch-all room. I move forward and flip on the lamp, and then go back to switch off the overhead light.

The warm glow of the lamp has my shoulders relaxing a little. Something about it makes the room feel like mine, and only mine. Even though I loved sharing a bed with Mason, this bed doesn't remind me that I sleep alone. It just reminds me of comfort and rest.

Maybe I can do this. It feels better in here. I should at least try. The whole point of unpacking is to be able to use each room as it was intended. I need to let myself settle here because it's all I have now.

I tiptoe closer, run my hand over the comforter, and then slowly pull back the corner. I ease myself under the covers and burrow in, immediately recalling how cozy it is to be buried in a big blanket. I let out a contented sigh and close my tired eyes, choosing to keep the lamp on, and fall asleep quickly.

It feels lonelier here than before. My footsteps echo more on the floors. I hum of the fridge seems a little louder. It makes my mind wander, especially to the spare room where my guitar is. Seeing it in Linda's hands last night felt like she was holding my heart instead.

I find myself standing in the doorway of that little room, gazing at the black case. I don't know how long I stand there, just looking, before I inch my way towards it and run my unpracticed fingers over the cool, smooth exterior.

I learned to play guitar at a young age. It was something to fill my time with, really, because I was alone a lot after my grandmother died. My mother was glad for me to be interested in something she didn't have to attend a performance or function for, so she encouraged it. It kept her from feeling guilty about working so much, I'm sure. Music gave my mind a place to go, and then when I realized I could carry a tune and stay on pitch, my heart quickly found its home.

Thinking about it now is an aching agony.

How did I so willingly cast this aside? Something so important and vital to my own sense of self... abandoned so that maybe my husband would remember that he loved me. I close my eyes, ashamed of how easy it was for me to choose him when he could only choose himself.

I swallow hard, open my eyes, and lift one latch with a sharp *snap* that fills the room. I do the next latch, and then the last one, and tenderly open the lid. Tears fill my eyes as I look at my instrument. Acoustic, electric blue in color, with the capo still clipped on the headstock. I can smell the strings, a metallic, sweaty sort of scent that brings me back to the last time I performed in public.

It was a short set at a coffee shop in St. Cloud. I was there for maybe forty-five minutes before I packed it up and quickly went home to see Mason. The small crowd listened so raptly as I sang and played, seeming to be part of the song itself.

I miss that.

I sniff, my cheeks wet, and close the lid.

Mason didn't take it from me. He didn't have to. I gave it away, just as much as the rest of me, in my desperate attempt to keep him.

It all feels foolish now. And pointless. And unfair.

Because I lost him anyway.

And for the first time, I feel a surge of anger burn through me.

Anger at what I've lost. Anger at myself and at him. Anger at the woman who played a role in breaking my marriage.

I didn't deserve for him to change his mind about what he wanted. It wasn't my fault that he realized too late how young we got married.

But it *is* my fault for leaving myself behind...for choosing him, even when he told me he was in love with Sarah and wanted out. He didn't ask me to do what I did. He just wanted me to let go.

I take a deep slow breath and blow it out slowly.

It'll come back, Sean's voice whispers in my head.

It'll all come back again. My voice, my passion, my ability to be a functioning member of society. I'll get it back. One step at a time. One walk around the block at a time. One plate of baked goods at a time.

My life *will* be good again.

Just keep going.

CHAPTER ELEVEN

Sean

I immediately catch the sweet scent of sugar and butter in the air when I step inside my house after work. I shake my head slightly, knowing that whatever my mom is baking will be put on a plate and walked over to Mara sometime tomorrow. After kicking off my work boots, I head into the kitchen where my mom and Rosie are mixing something on the counter, Rosie standing on a stool so she can reach.

"Smells good, ladies," I say, and move closer to kiss Rosie's head.

"Grandma said we get to keep some for us, too," she informs me happily.

I smile and look over her little blonde ponytail to see a bowl of vanilla batter and flour dusting the countertops.

Mom chuckles and turns to kiss my cheek in greeting. "I don't think Mara could eat all these cookies, do you?"

"I bet *I* could," I tease, poking Rosie in the side.

She pops her hip and puts a floury fist on it. "No, Daddy; you'd get a tummy ache."

"Not him," my mom says with a laugh. "Your daddy is a cookie monster!"

Rosie giggles and turns back to her sloppy mixing.

She's been perkier lately. She still has her quiet moments, and my mom tells me she still hasn't warmed up to her teacher, but she's been much easier to make smile and laugh these days.

I don't really want to acknowledge why, but it's obvious. Mara is the only change in our lives that I can pin Rosie's improved mood on. I glance over at her drawing on the fridge again and tell myself not to worry about it.

When we came home from Mara's last night, my mother would not stop talking about her. How she used to be this amazing singer—a rising star in central Minnesota. I leaned against the kitchen doorway as she spouted off question after question about Mara.

"Why do you think she stopped singing? I wonder if she plays any other instruments? Does she come from a musical family? Does she even *have* any family? I've never heard her mention anyone; have you? Oh, the poor dear. She must be on her own. I'm so glad we went over to help unpack."

And on and on without needing any input from me.

I do wonder about Mara, to be honest. But the details aren't that important to me. I don't need to know her life story. Not if all I'm interested in doing is making sure she doesn't end up floating in a bathtub like my wife.

"Daddy?" Rosie asks, drawing my attention from her artwork.

"Hmm?"

"Can Mara come over for pizza night again?"

My mother grins at me over her shoulder and then goes back to portioning out cookie batter on the parchment lined baking sheet next to her.

"If she wants to," is my unenthusiastic response.

"Oh, she will, Daddy. I know she will," Rosie says with confidence, nodding at me.

"And how do you know that?"

"Because she's my *friend*, silly."

"Yeah, Dad," Mom chimes in, giggling.

I roll my eyes at them in good humor. "Oh, right. Of course. Silly me."

They go back to their task, and I gaze at them for a moment, remembering how they both hugged Mara last night, like she was family. Like she was someone they loved. It was bittersweet for me to see. That should've been Gabby sandwiched between them. But she chose something else, forcing the two most important people in my life to love around that hole she left.

I don't want it to be Mara who fills that hole. After seeing her on the bridge, I know I'll never be able to trust her not to make the same choice Gabby did, especially if she doesn't get help. The parent part of me thinks it's a horrible idea to let my daughter get attached to someone like Mara, but it's too late for that. The best I can do now is keep trying to offer Mara whatever help she needs.

I head upstairs to shower, and when I get out and am dressed, I shoot off a text to Mara.

Sean: *Might as well save my mother a walk over there tomorrow and just come over now for some cookies.*

My stomach squirms a little after I hit send. Rhys and

my mom are really the only people I text or call. It's weird to be texting a woman, especially a woman I don't know that well. The unfamiliarity of communicating with someone new has that same squirm in my stomach moving up my chest. As I step down the stairs, my phone beeps in my hand. I'm surprised Mara has responded so quickly.

Mara: *Is that okay?*

Her timid nature makes more work for me. Maybe that's why my mom is so curious about her and has so many questions. You have to draw her out of herself with gentle reassurance. My guess is that's due to her divorce, but who knows?

Sean: *I wouldn't have invited you over if it wasn't.*

I kick myself at how harsh that probably comes off in a text message. As I walk back into the kitchen, I try again.

Sean: *Come over, please. If you want.*

That's a little better, I think. I said please.

My mother takes a sheet pan bearing a dozen sugar cookies out of the oven and places it on the stove, humming to herself. She already has a plate ready to put them on once they cool, the same plate Mara handed me when I answered the door that time. She looked terrified, but I know I didn't exactly give her a welcoming smile, so I guess that reaction was warranted. Back then, I was glad to scare her off, but now, I realize I need to keep doing the opposite.

I glance towards the living room, and then stride through the kitchen doorway to look out the window facing Mara's house. The lights are on, illuminating a couple squares of grass and the front steps, even with the curtains drawn. A shadow moves across one window, and after a long moment, the front door opens.

The shape of Mara appears on the stoop, and then she moves down the steps like at any moment, she might turn back.

What did he do to her? I wonder out of nowhere. Did he break her down, make her feel like nothing? Did he cheat? Did he beat her?

My blood boils at that thought.

I don't know her story, and she's just my neighbor, but the thought of anyone raising a hand to her fills my body with tension and anger.

Mara finishes the steps and keeps going until she reaches the other side of her driveway. Here, she hesitates, and I feel what my mother must feel like. Hoping this little stray thing decides we're a safe place. That we won't hurt her. That, if anything, we want to take care of her.

After a moment, Mara moves forward again, and I abandon my post by the window so I can meet her at the door. But she doesn't knock. I peek through the peephole to see her standing on the other side of the door, the porch light revealing how nervous she is to knock and come inside. I watch her close her eyes and take a couple of deep breaths, and I feel something soften inside me.

She really is trying, isn't she?

That's all I wanted Gabby to do. Just keep trying. I think she tried for as long as she could, but the end came because she was tired of trying.

I step back from the door. Will Mara get tired of trying, too?

Three knocks sound out, and I know that I have to make sure she keeps trying.

I open the door, making a conscious effort to keep a friendly expression on my face, but it doesn't seem to matter.

When Mara sees me, her eyes get just a bit wider, and I catch a trace of a blush move across her freckled cheeks. She's wearing a light pink long-sleeved t-shirt and jeans, her long hair draped over her shoulders as usual.

"Come on in," I say, stepping back and gesturing her through the doorway with one arm. "They're in the kitchen."

Mara's face relaxes slightly, and she nods at me before coming inside. She waits for me to close the door and then quietly follows me to the kitchen.

Mom is putting a new tray of cookie dough into the oven as we enter, and when she closes the oven door and glances my way to say something, she does a surprised double take that makes me chuckle.

"Rosie, look who it is!"

Rosie whips it around on her stool so quickly I have a mild heart attack, but then she jumps down and grins all the way to Mara's legs, which she hugs tightly.

"Hello there, Rosie," Mara says gently, bent down over my daughter's head so I can't see her face. But I swear I can hear a smile hidden behind her dark red hair that is engulfing Rosie's upper body.

"Mara! We're making cookies for you!" Rosie announces, stepping back through the curtain of Mara's hair and looking up at her excitedly.

Mara gives her a little smile and then shoots one at my mom as well.

"Well, this is a surprise," Mom says, folding her arms and giving me an amused, though slightly suspicious, smile.

"You're welcome," I say, smirking back at her.

She rolls her eyes.

"Have you ever made cookies, Mara?" Rosie asks, and grabs Mara's hand to pull her over to her stool.

"I have, but not for a long time."

"That's okay! I can show you."

And Rosie very confidently does show Mara how to mix and use the scooper to put the cookie dough on the trays. I just take a seat at the table and watch as my daughter immerses Mara into the process, both of them getting flour on their shirts and faces by the time they're finished.

My mother flits here and there, cleaning up after them and adding in her two cents, and all I can think is how easily Mara fits into this picture.

She so naturally interacts with Rosie, more so than she does with me or even my mom. And Rosie blossoms like a flower beneath her attention.

"I used to make cookies with my grandma when I was a little girl." Mara's soft admission perks up my ears. "I miss her. She was my favorite person."

"Now *I'm* your favorite, right?"

My mom laughs at that and shakes her head at me. I just smile back at her.

I expect Mara to just say an appeasing "of course, you are" and leave it at that, so I'm completely caught off guard when she squats down in front of my daughter and looks her square in the eyes.

"Rosie, you absolutely *are* my favorite person."

My sweet girl takes in just how genuine Mara is being

and then beams like the sun and throws her arms around Mara's neck.

Mara hugs her back, and when I hear a sniff coming from the other side of the kitchen, I look over and see my mother wiping a tear from one eye.

I clear my throat as Mara stands up again.

"So, you showed Mara how to make cookies, but have you showed her how to *eat* them?" I ask Rosie. "That's the best part, in my opinion."

Mara gives me a friendly glance that makes my stomach flip. It's hard to ignore how much of a stunner she is. Just one little glance at me, and I feel it down to my toes.

"Cookies for dinner!" my daughter exclaims, and I laugh.

"I didn't know we were calling dessert 'dinner' now," I tease warmly.

"*Da-ad*," Rosie draws out in a low whine.

"Nice try," my mom says to me.

"What? You're on Team Cookies For Dinner, too?"

"I didn't say that."

I sigh and get to my feet. "You can have *one* cookie, and then we'll have dinner," I explain sternly to my daughter, who gives me a frowny face for a split second before she brightens back up again.

"Can Mara stay for dinner?"

I look over at Mara, pleased to see her mouth form a little smile.

"If she'd like to, that's fine."

Rosie turns on her heel so she's facing our neighbor.

"Please, please will you stay for dinner?"

Mara swipes a bit of flour off my daughter's cheek. "Of course."

———————————

They make dinner together, too. Mom insisted on not making our guest cook, but Rosie's insistence on Mara helping was louder. And cuter.

I watched something change in Mara as she cut up vegetables with my mom and Rosie. Her shoulders relaxed and her expression did, too, like she was settling into an old groove that she had missed.

My girls are good for her. They bring her out of whatever fog she's lost in. It gives me hope for her. Maybe this is what she needs—to not be alone.

"You're a natural in the kitchen, Mara," my mom says as she brings the pan of steaming chicken and vegetables to the little table by the window. The delicious scent of garlic and alfredo makes my mouth water.

Instead of cleaning up Mom's puzzle, I just threw a teal tablecloth over it and set the table with Rosie.

The cookies have been put away in a container, although I did spy my mom putting some on a plate for Mara to take home with her later.

"Yeah," she replies to Mom as she glances at the counter behind her. "I used to cook a lot." Her voice has gone dark again, as has her face, and she sits down next to me without looking up from the empty plate in front of her.

"Why did you stop?" Rosie pipes up curiously, sitting next to Mara and across from me. I notice she scooted her chair a little closer to our guest.

"I guess because the food I made wasn't being eaten," Mara explains carefully.

"Because it was bad?"

I try to cover my laugh with a cough, but my mother still sends me a glare.

"No, it wasn't bad," Mara answers, looking at my daughter thoughtfully. "The food I made just wasn't wanted. Most of what I made got thrown away."

I frown at that. I'm about to ask why it wasn't wanted, because I have a feeling it's more complicated than that, but she speaks again.

"I forgot how much I like it. Thank you for reminding me." She smiles slightly at my mom and then reaches for the wooden spoon. She serves Rosie first, and then herself, before passing the spoon to me.

The questions on my face must show, because when her gaze flicks towards me, those blue eyes snag on mine. I manage to smile.

"Well, we're always hungry over here," I say. "Feel free to spoil us."

Mara smiles back at me, just a little upward tilt of her mouth that hints even more at how beautiful she is.

"Like you aren't spoiled enough," my mom tosses out with a laugh as I fill my plate with chicken, carrots, and broccoli. "Your mother lives with you."

"Hey, don't act like you do everything for me around here. You may cook more often, but you and I both know it's usually me who does the dishes." I stab a piece of chicken and bring it to my mouth.

My mom rolls her eyes as I chew. "That is the one thing your father did a good job teaching you." She leans forward a little across the table in Mara's direction. "They say the way to a man's heart is through his stomach, but the way to a woman's heart is by washing the dishes."

I shake my head slightly as my mom laughs heartily at her own wit.

I shovel a couple more forkfuls into my mouth and then look up to see how Rosie's doing across the table. She's already eaten half of what Mara put on her plate, and I notice her mimicking Mara with each bite. Mara eats a bite of chicken; Rosie eats a bite of chicken. Mara eats a carrot; Rosie eats a carrot.

"Your dad was the one who played piano?" Mara asks me gently, oblivious to my daughter's mimicry.

"Yeah. He wanted me to follow in his footsteps and become a music teacher, too, but I was too busy climbing trees to care about piano lessons."

"Was he *ever*," my mom chimes in, gesturing with a forkful of carrot. "One day I came home to find him up on the roof! Can you believe that? I almost had a heart attack."

Rosie's mouth gapes open in surprise. "On the *roof*, Daddy? That's not safe at all," she informs me seriously.

I chuckle and shrug. "I lived, didn't I?"

"Only because your father stopped me from wringing your neck." Mom pins me with a glare, like she still hasn't forgiven me for that stunt.

"Good thing prison stripes aren't your style." I wink at her and take a sip of water.

Mom narrows her eyes at me, but I can see her fighting a

smile. She opens her mouth to say something to Mara, but then her previously snarky expression drops away into concern.

I follow her gaze and find Mara's eyes rimmed with red, a saddened pinch to her brow.

"Mara? What's wrong, dear?"

"Nothing," she answers my mother with a little sniff. "I'm just not used to being around so much...*love*." She wipes at her eyes, blushing a little as Rosie gets off her chair and hugs her.

I know I come from good people, but I forgot that some people don't come from a loving family who would do anything for each other. My mom dropped everything to move in with me and Rosie. And even though she hasn't said anything to me, I know she and Doug want to get married. I have a feeling the only reason he hasn't popped the question is because my mom doesn't feel like she can move out and leave me alone in the house.

Does Mara have anybody like that?

She pats Rosie on the cheek and helps her back into her chair before sitting down again.

"Do you have any family, Mara?" I ask, and immediately regret it. But she doesn't shy away from my personal question like I expect.

"Just my mom. She's in Arizona until spring." She picks up her fork and goes back to her food.

"What about friends?" I blurt out, hating myself but needing to know the answer.

"Daddy, *we're* her friends," Rosie says with emphasis on me being an oblivious weirdo.

I smile at how she raises both eyebrows at me, the way

her mother used to when I said something ridiculous. It makes my heart ache for a second, but then the conversation goes on, and I forget all about it.

"And I really am glad to have you all as friends." Mara looks over at me tentatively. "Because no, I don't really have anyone else." A bit of shame flickers over her expression. "It's been a difficult time for me, so I appreciate your kindness so much." She makes meaningful eye contact with me. "I know I'm just getting to know all of you, but I can already tell that I'm lucky to have moved in next door."

Mom's smile turns watery as she reaches across the table to squeeze Mara's hand. "You're exactly where you're meant to be, dear."

Her words bounce around in my head as the conversation goes on, trying to decide whether my mom is right. I've never been a huge believer of anything really, so the idea that fate is involved somehow just seems…lame. I don't believe Mara was meant to wind up living next to us, but the fact is that she *does*. And while her depression triggers me, I think that we can help her. I don't think it's too late for Mara to turn things around and love her life again.

I don't consider myself Mara's friend, but I do feel a strange sort of platonic need to look out for her. I want to get her the help I didn't get Gabby.

CHAPTER TWELVE

Mara

This shouldn't be so nerve wracking. It's just grocery shopping. Why does everything feel just slightly too loud? The brand names and prices are hard for me to focus on. Everything on these shelves are blurring together, giving me a headache and an impending sense of doom.

I quickly wheel my cart out of the aisle and move over to the produce section.

The foods are colorful and textural here, but in a more natural way that seems less intimidating.

After cooking with Linda and Rosie last night, I thought I was ready to start cooking for myself again. It felt good to create something with my hands. It felt good to be busy with something.

But walking through this grocery store is overwhelming and far away from the safety of my house and the warmth of the Dunbar family.

Making dinner and eating with them last night made me feel like I was part of a family again. It made me *long* to be part of a family again. My neighbors have allowed me into their lives, even Sean. And I desperately want to get to the point where I can invite them over to my house for dinner, too. I want to be able to give them as much as they give me.

Step one towards that goal is me standing right here in front of the root vegetables, making decisions I wouldn't have been capable of making two months ago, and putting myself out into the world; also something I couldn't do two months ago.

I place a small bag of sweet potatoes into my cart, take a moment to revel in my choice, and then move my cart along.

As my eyes and fingers take in the details of things grown by another's labor, I feel myself relax just enough to forget about the other things I need in this store. I just keep my mind here, on this task, and when I'm finished in produce, I take things one item at a time.

And when I get into my car forty minutes later with my purchases, I do feel overwhelmed, but it's in a good way. Maybe it's pathetic to get emotional at how I managed my anxiety inside a grocery store, but I'm proud that I got a hold of myself and didn't abandon my task because I was uncomfortable.

This is good.

And now I can go home and teach myself how to cook for just me. To cook in order to take care of my body. To rewrite my connotations with cooking so that I don't think about all the food I made Mason that he didn't want and didn't ask for.

It's a miserable process to undo what I've done, to let go of the memories that tie me to him, even simple memories like him glancing at the full meal I spent two hours preparing and then keep walking down the hall. Or being in the middle of a conversation and him picking up his phone and smiling at it. Or reaching for him in the night and feeling him scoot away from me.

None of that matters now because it can't be changed. His coldness towards me isn't something I could change then, and I can't change it now either.

So, I'll keep trying to gravitate toward the things that warm me up inside and keep me moving forward. And right now, those things are cooking and spending time with my sweet neighbors.

But by the time I get home, I'm exhausted from my first excursion out into the world. I bring the groceries in and put things in the fridge still in the bags. I leave the pantry items on the counter and go lie down on my couch.

I try not to chide myself too much for this. I know that most people can handle going grocery shopping without completely shutting down when they get home.

But I'm trying to be gentle with myself in a way my mother can't seem to do. She's let up some lately, now that I've been having interactions with my neighbors, but I know it won't be long before she's getting on my case about dating again.

I've only ever been with Mason. I can't even fathom what holding someone else's hand would be like. It will take me a long time to feel like I can move on with someone new. It's such a foreign concept to me because Mason was my whole world.

Maybe that was part of the problem. He was my everything, and I was his good enough. I emptied myself into hands that didn't want to hold me. The more I slipped through the cracks between his fingers, the more I tried to fill them with attention and smiles and chores. Now, I'm trying to scoop up what's left off the floor, all the pieces of me just cast aside that I now have to decide whether I want back.

Desperation can stay there. Unrequited love can, too.

Loneliness and lack of self-esteem need to be left where they are.

I'll work on putting the good things back. Patience. Faith in love. Companionship and self-respect need to have room to grow inside me, and they won't if I try to plug up the holes with unhealthy things.

Mason doesn't love me anymore. So, I have to do it myself.

The weather is getting decidedly cooler these days, but I don't mind. The autumn season feels appropriate for the changing season in my own life. And the cooler temperatures just make me bundle myself up even more in cozy fabrics and fuzzy socks.

The little purple flower next to my front door has started to shrivel and gray, and the leaves of the maple tree in my front yard have already started to turn a stunning, fiery red.

As October marches on, I spend most afternoons and evenings with my neighbors. In the past week, I've cooked something every day and taken it to their house for dinner.

It's satisfying to be able to contribute, and I can feel my appetite for food returning a little more with each passing day.

I brought over mashed sweet potatoes earlier this evening to go with the chicken wings Sean made on the grill, and it was the first time he ate something I made and let out an audible "mmm." I blushed, pleased that he isn't just being polite when he says he likes the things I bring over.

That little "mmm" still has a strange warmth glowing

in my chest, even an hour later as I settle myself over a puzzle Linda loaned me.

It's a picture of a red barn and a meadow with yellow flowers. I'm picking through all the red pieces when my phone rings.

I'm deeply surprised to see Sean's name on the caller ID.

"Hello?"

I'm immediately hit in the ear with high pitched background noise. After a second, I realize it's Rosie wailing. My stomach drops. Is she hurt? Is something wrong?

"Hey, Mara, it's me," Sean says tensely. "Rosie is beside herself, and I can't get her to go to bed. She says she just wants you. I hate to ask, but could you come over?"

Oh, sweet Rosie. I noticed she was a little down at dinner. She seemed tired, I thought, but maybe it was more than that.

She lets out another cry that breaks my heart.

"Of course; I'll be right there."

"Thank you," Sean says wearily and then hangs up.

I toss on my shoes and a sweatshirt and hurry my way over to their porch, worried for my little friend.

Linda was telling me a couple days ago how she doesn't like her Kindergarten teacher, and how her teacher doesn't like her either. I don't know how *anyone* could not like Rosie. She's a sweetheart. Maybe she had a bad day at school.

I knock twice and then go inside, something I've gotten accustomed to doing lately. Linda tells me I don't need to knock at all and to just come in, but that seems like a privilege I'm not quite deserving of just yet.

As soon as the door closes behind me, I hear Rosie crying from the other side of the house. I rush through the living room and into the kitchen, but it's empty.

I peer down the hallway off the kitchen to see Sean and Linda standing on either side of Rosie's bedroom door where she's crying loudly from inside.

Linda looks up and sees me, bringing an instant look of relief to her previously concerned face.

"Oh, she's here," she says to Sean, who turns to see for himself.

I move toward them, thrown off by the fact that they're both completely stymied over how to get Rosie to calm down.

"She won't let either of us close to her," Linda tells me, wringing her hands.

I look at Sean, whose face is lined and weary. Without a word, he nods me toward the doorway, and I peek around him into Rosie's dimly lit room. There's a Hello Kitty lamp illuminated on a white dresser to the left, and to the right is Rosie's twin bed, the light pink comforter twisted and half hanging off the bed. There are other toys strewn about the room, likely things that were offered to her for comfort that she refused.

I step inside and find her face down on her bed, blonde hair a messy halo around her head. She lets out a low wail that sounds similar to my name.

I glance over my shoulder at Sean, take a deep breath, and go to my friend. I gently touch her back, and she jerks away.

"I want Mara!" she shouts tearfully.

"I'm here, Rosie girl."

Rosie instantly scrambles to her knees, staring at me with puffy red eyes like she can't believe I'm really here. Then she throws herself at me without a word and cries into the hair covering my shoulder.

"I got you," I murmur, and sit on the edge of her bed. Instinctively, I rock back and forth with her curled around me.

I just let her cry for a while, allowing her to get all of her big emotions out, and then begin to stroke one hand through her soft hair. She quiets then, still clinging to me, and even though I want to ask her what has her so upset, I don't think she's interested in telling me. She just needs to feel safe.

My grandmother was so good at that. If I was frustrated or upset as a child, she was the only one who could calm me down. And it was by doing exactly this, just sitting with me and loving me. She didn't try to fix me or tell me how I should feel like my mom would. My grandma would hold me tight and sing to me, the slight vibrations of her chest against my ear soothing enough to make me forget what was wrong.

That's what Rosie needs right now.

I swallow hard and close my eyes.

You can do this.

I clear my throat and feel a wave of nerves hit me as I open my mouth to sing for the first time in almost ten months.

The sound is unfamiliar, like I'm hearing my own voice through a clogged filter. But singing *You Are My Sunshine*, as unpracticed as I am, bonds me even more to this little girl. She's the first reason I've had to sing in a long time.

She's my favorite reason.

I sing the song twice more, and then I hear her tiny little voice mix with mine. She's perfectly off key, going a slightly different tempo than me, but there's nothing in this world that I love the sound of more.

Then she looks up at me, strands of my hair stuck to her wet cheek, those innocent blue eyes seeing further into me than any other person ever has.

"I love you, Mara," she murmurs miserably.

I smile softly and hug her tight. "I love you, too, Rosie."

CHAPTER THIRTEEN

Sean

I watch as Mara comforts my little girl in exactly the way she wouldn't allow me to. It feels like a kick to the crotch. I don't want Rosie to need Mara. I want her to need me. I want to be the one to calm my kid.

While I typically land on the heavy-handed side of discipline, I realized quickly tonight that Rosie wasn't going to respond to threats or punishments for not wanting to go to bed. So, my mom tried, which usually works, but no matter what she tried to say to Rosie, my daughter pushed back.

Rosie has a more subdued personality, and that applies to when she's upset, too. She may cry or whine, but I've never heard her scream like that. My mom hasn't either.

I didn't want to set a precedent by giving into her request for Mara, but I didn't know what to do, and I was more than frustrated and ready to give up.

But now I understand why she wanted Mara and why she likes Mara so much.

Mara doesn't ask anything of her. She doesn't try to make Rosie be someone she isn't. She knows how to just *be* with Rosie, without expecting anything from her.

I look over at my mom, who's still leaning on the other side of the door frame, and open my mouth to whisper my little revelation, but then I hear singing.

Soft, quiet, vulnerable singing.

Mom's breath catches in her throat, and she stares at me. "She's *singing*," she whispers in wonder, tears springing into her eyes.

I look back at Mara, who's rocking Rosie gently, and feel my chest tighten.

She's singing to my daughter. The woman who doesn't sing anymore is singing because my daughter needed her to.

And then comes Rosie's voice, too, mixing with Mara's raspy tones and filling the room.

"They need each other, don't they?" I whisper to my mom.

She reaches out and squeezes my forearm, smiling knowingly.

Rosie and Mara settle down into her bed then, facing each other, and they speak so quietly to each other that I can't hear what they're saying.

My mother nods me towards the kitchen, and I take the hint. We both sit down at the table and take a deep breath.

"She's really something," my mom says with a soft smile. She looks as tired as I feel. Rosie's out of the ordinary behavior tonight has exhausted us both.

I nod, my eyes down the hall.

"I know you don't want to hear this, Sean, but tonight is proof that Rosie needs a mother in her life."

"No. She has us," I argue quietly, my eyes still on the hallway. "Tonight is just proof that she needs a friend."

I can feel her gaze on me still, trying to decide if I'm right. After a moment, she leans forward to speak.

"And it's okay with you if that friend is Mara?"

"I don't exactly have a choice in the matter, not if I don't want to break my daughter's heart."

My mom nods, and I watch her hesitate in whatever she wants to say. It isn't like my mom to hesitate, so I brace myself.

"Does she still remind you of Gabby?"

Her question stabs at my heart, and I hang my head forward with a sigh.

I don't want to tell my mom about the bridge. I don't want to tell her that Mara had a moment where I believe she was contemplating suicide. In that regard, Mara absolutely reminds me of my wife.

But this week she's been...different. She's been around more. Allowed herself to be welcome here. It makes me wonder if she reached her rock bottom and is trying to tunnel out. That's something Gabby never did.

"Sometimes," is the answer I go with because it's the most truthful without requiring me to explain.

Mom puts her hand on mine. "She's been doing better. I think she wants to open up to us, but maybe she just doesn't know how."

"She has no trouble talking to Rosie," I point out, the image of them talking together in Rosie's bed swimming in my mind's eye.

"And likewise," my mom agrees with a smile. "I don't

know exactly what she's been through, but I think we're both on the same page about being there for her, right? It seems like you've kind of come around."

"Right."

Movement in the hallway draws my attention away from my mom and to Mara, who appears in the kitchen doorway.

"She's out. I covered her up and turned out the light. Is there anything else she needs?"

The calm expression on her face makes me surer than ever that she needs my daughter as much as Rosie needs her.

I shake my head. "No, she should be good. Thanks, Mara."

She nods, one side of her mouth lifting up in a half-smile.

I jerk my head at the chair next to me. "Sit, if you'd like."

Mara eases into the chair and folds her hands demurely in her lap. "She told me she doesn't like her teacher."

I just nod, this being old news to me.

"She said her teacher yelled at her today to 'speak up.'"

"Mrs. Jacobson needs to retire," my mom says bitterly.

Mara's eyebrows dip in concern. "Could she switch to a different class?"

"Maybe," I answer with a shrug. It's already October; I don't know if they'd let her switch to the other Kindergarten teacher this late into the school year.

The three of us fall silent, each lost in thought over my Rosiecakes.

"I—I don't want to overstep," Mara says nervously after

a long moment, "but, I just want to say that if Rosie has another bad night, please don't hesitate to call me." Her nerves drop enough for a softer expression to show through. "She really is my favorite person."

My mother beams at her.

"Thanks," I mutter, trying to stuff down the bile I feel in my daughter needing someone besides me. Besides my mom, I've had her to myself all these years. She had no choice in being a daddy's girl, but I've always felt pride in how close we are. And now she prefers our sad neighbor over me when she's hurt.

I don't think my mom is right in assuming Rosie needs a mother. I think my daughter is lonely and feels like she can be herself around Mara in a way she isn't allowed to at school. And despite how the closeness Mara and Rosie share makes me jealous, I know I would have to be heartless to try and get in the way of it.

"Well, I'll let you guys get back to your evening." Mara stands up, her chair rubbing slightly across the floor. I get up, too.

"I'll walk you back."

Mara gives me a curious look, and she should, because I've never offered to walk her back to her house. But if my daughter is this attached to her, then we need to get some things straight.

I follow her to the front door, and we step out onto the porch. The air is cold, and Mara shivers even though she's wearing a sweatshirt.

Silently, we walk side by side across the yard and into Mara's. She seems anxious by the way she pulls at the cuff of her sweatshirt.

When we reach the concrete steps, I pause and take a deep breath.

"Listen, I know you and my daughter have this sort of connection or whatever, and honestly, I'm grateful for it," I begin, my hands deep in my pockets. "But I barely know anything about you. I can count on one hand the things I know about you."

Mara's brow quivers almost imperceptibly in the warm sconce light. "I could say the same about you."

I stiffen slightly, not expecting her to say that but realizing instantly that she's exactly right. She isn't the only one who's been quiet about their life. I frown for a moment and look down at the grass.

"That's fair," I respond quietly. I sigh, resigning myself, and look up at her again. "I'm her parent, and I'm protective of her. So, I want to know that you're someone I can trust," I growl out.

Mara stares at me almost blankly for a moment, and then her eyes lower thoughtfully a fraction. She clears her throat and meets my eyes again. "I understand."

"And in order to trust you, I need to know who you are."

She instantly tenses with so much nervous energy that it makes my stomach squirm. Apparently, I'm asking a lot of her. Knowing her is not something she feels comfortable with. Though to be honest, I feel the same about her knowing me.

"So, please," I say gently, "tell me."

Mara's blue eyes stay on mine for what feels like five whole minutes. I don't know what she's thinking. She just searches my eyes for something I can't name. She's guarded; I know that. I am, too.

"I... don't really know who I am." Her voice is small and broken, like she's speaking from a place far within herself, from a dark place no one is allowed to go. From the bottom of her obviously shaken heart.

"But I can give you the facts," she offers instead.

"Alright."

I let her have a moment to gather herself and then listen raptly as she tells me the story of herself.

"My parents divorced when I was eight, and I haven't spoken to my father since my ninth birthday." She pauses to take a deep breath and then presses on. "I met Mason in high school, and we got married a couple years after I graduated. He..." Her mouth squirms shut then, but she continues, forcing the words out painfully. "He divorced me because he fell in love with someone else."

I grimace at that. So, he cheated on her. What a dick. Her high school sweetheart ditched her for someone new. No wonder she's a mess.

"I'm sorry," I offer weakly.

She nods tearfully. "My mother picked this house for me and then left for Arizona where she stays in the winter. She calls every two days to harass me into moving on with my life. And—" Her voice breaks. "And I used to be a singer, as you know, but I'm not anymore and I... I feel lost." She looks down at her feet as she shuffles them. "That's what I am," she whispers, almost to herself, "lost."

I absorb that information, appreciative to get a fuller picture of what Mara's life is like. But it's that last word that has me contemplating.

She and I aren't that different.

After Gabby, I haven't been able to right the ship. Rosie kept my focus on what was most important, but all these years, I've been drifting aimlessly around the same harbor.

"My dad died from an aneurysm seven years ago," I say, and I feel the depth of Mara's attention as she looks up at me. "My best friend is Rhys. He and I own a tree trimming business. I met my wife Gabby on a double date with him and his girlfriend at the time. We were married two years later, and three years after that, she...died." I clear my suddenly scratchy throat. "Rosie was only five months old."

She gasps, her hands over her mouth. "Sean...I am so sorry." She moves her hands from her face to wipe at the tears welling in her eyes.

I just nod, not sure what more to say.

"She's never known her mother," Mara murmurs mournfully, like her heart is breaking right in front of me. She glances behind me towards the house and then back to me. "I'm so sorry. You've all been through so much..." She shakes her head slightly and sniffs. "You must miss her."

I feel my shoulders slowly squeezing upwards as her words hit me.

The short answer is yes. The long answer is that I miss her, love her, resent her, and blame myself for her death. Suicide does that...it takes who you love and leaves you with nothing but what-ifs.

"Yes," I whisper. "Every day."

Mara nods sympathetically, tears still in her eyes. "Of course, you do. You have so much more to grieve than I do —I'm so sorry for my behavior," she spits out quickly, almost in a panic of remorse. "I shouldn't be like this; I know that, especially when there are people like you who've lost a spouse to death and not divorce."

"No," I admonish. "Don't do that. You have just as much right to mourn and grieve as I do." My words don't seem to make her feel any better by the way she wipes at her cheeks. "We may have lost a spouse for different reasons and in different ways, but there isn't a competition when it comes to loss and grief," I continue slowly. "I learned that in grief counseling years ago. Everyone is entitled to their own grief, and no one else has the right to tell you if or how you're doing it wrong."

She seems taken aback at my little speech, but eventually, she nods thoughtfully, her teary face still a little scrunched up with emotion.

"You're right," she whispers finally.

"You don't need to apologize for anything, Mara. You're doing your best."

"I'm...trying."

My heart beats out of rhythm for a moment. Emotion wells up inside me as I think of all the times I wanted to hear Gabby say that. I take a step closer to Mara that makes her eyes widen. When I grip her chin between my thumb and pointer finger, she gasps and holds her breath.

"Promise me," I whisper, holding her surprised gaze and marveling at the softness of her skin, "promise me you'll keep trying."

Her beautiful blues stare back into my browns, so innocent and pure.

"I promise," she whispers back.

I check her expression for earnestness, and when I find it, my gaze falls to where I'm still touching her chin. Her cheeks heat and redden. I swallow hard, and then release her and step back.

Mara exhales, looking shaken, and yet, her eyes are brighter than I've ever seen them. That's a bad sign that I've exhilarated her by touching her, even just on her chin, though I can't deny how it exhilarated me, too.

I give her a nod and turn back towards the house.

"Good night, Mara," I toss over my shoulder as I go.

CHAPTER FOURTEEN

Mara

I press the heel of my hands into the yeasty lump of bread dough on the counter and bear my weight down on it. I fold it in half and turn it, then do it again. The repetition is soothing and allows me to explore the thing that's been on my mind for the last three days.

Promise me you'll keep trying.

The words stay with me, lodged in my brain no matter what I'm doing.

That unspoken secret between us makes me feel inexplicably bound to Sean. He knows my worst moment, and he nearly burned holes into my eyes with how fervently he needed me to promise him to never let myself get to that place again.

Despite the distance he's kept from me, for some reason, it matters to him that I don't give up. Maybe it's just for Rosie's sake, but there's a part of me that wonders if he's in the same place I am. On his own proverbial bridge, trying not to jump.

My heart hurts for him. For the death of his wife and Rosie's mother. His tragedy is a churning loss that I can do nothing about, but I wish—I *wish* I could.

And now that he's told me the bare facts of his life, I just want to know more. I want to know how I can help. I want to know how to be a friend to these amazing people who lost so much.

So, I'm taking a page out of Linda's book. I'm baking them a loaf of bread. And I'm going to bring it over on a plate that Linda will wash and bring back to me with that warm smile of hers that eases back my defenses.

I know it isn't the world served on a silver platter. But it's a loving thought wrapped in carbs, and that's something.

I'm coming around to that idea, that not every effort has to be mammoth or even perfect. If this bread turns out a little dense, it was still good for me to make and a nice thing to do for my neighbors.

That doesn't mean I'm not nervous when I take it over a few hours later though.

My little loaf of kindness smells delicious and is still just a little warm as I carry it over on a gray dinner plate. The crunch of yellow leaves under my shoes has me pausing to look down at them. I'm feeling less like a discarded, dead leaf these days. I'm feeling more like the yeast that made this bread rise, ready to thrive under the right circumstances. And my current circumstances are feeling better than my old ones.

I feel a little vulnerable as I knock on the door and then open it to go inside. It feels like I'm holding a little piece of my heart in my hands, hoping someone is happy to have it.

Rosie is sitting on the floor in front of the couch, coloring on a sheet of paper on the coffee table. She looks up when I come in, and her little face lights up. She has no idea how good that feels.

"Mara!" she exclaims and is halfway to me before I think to brace myself, so I don't drop the plate in my hand when she hugs me.

"Hi, Rosie girl," I greet her happily, hugging her, too. She's wearing a long-sleeved dress with hearts on it and leggings. Her blonde hair is pulled back into two adorable pigtails.

"Well, hello!" Linda calls from the kitchen, appearing a second later with a big smile. But she gasps when she sees what I'm holding. "What is that?"

"I made some bread," I say, and Rosie holds my hand as I bring it through the living room to where Linda is still standing by the doorway to the kitchen. I extend the plate to her, and her eyes stay on mine, seeing the elation I feel in being able to give her something, for all the times she's fed me when I couldn't feed myself. It isn't lost on her that what started as something truly one-sided has come full circle.

She takes the plate gently, smiling at my loaf, and then up at me. "Thank you, dear. It looks delicious."

I follow her into the kitchen, where she puts my offering on the counter. I glance to the left, expecting to see Sean sitting there, but the table is vacant. Then I question whether his truck was parked outside and remember I was focused on the leaves.

"He's out with Rhys," Linda answers my unspoken question. "He'll be back soon, I think."

I just give her a nod.

The memory of Sean's fingers on my chin is still branded into my brain. It was an innocent touch, nothing at all that meant anything more than him trying to convey how deeply he felt in that moment. But even so, my heart, that lately has been slowly warming again, beat like it never has before. I felt alive. Truly alive. Just from one small touch.

I don't know exactly what I should do with that, but I know I can't forget his gentle touch even if I wanted to.

Rosie takes my hand. "Come color with me," she demands, and pulls me back into the living room where I gladly sit beside her on the floor and color.

"I'm making tea; would you like some?" Linda calls from the kitchen.

"Sure. Thank you," I call back.

"Daddy says mommy hated tea," Rosie informs me casually.

I watch her sweet face carefully for a moment, feeling a grief that I can't explain to her. It must be so confusing to know facts about a person you'll never know, a person who is supposed to be such a big part of your life.

"Do you like tea?" I ask her.

She shakes her head. "I like coffee."

I raise my eyebrows at her. "Coffee? Really?"

"Grandma calls it her happy juice."

I crack a smile and go back to drawing. A minute later, Linda brings me a mug of hot tea, and I accept it with thanks. She sits down on the opposite couch with her own mug.

"So, Rosie, did you tell Mara about school?" Linda prompts.

"Oh," Rosie says, and looks over at me. "I'm going to have a new teacher tomorrow."

"You are? Wow. That's exciting."

She nods enthusiastically. "I don't like Mrs. Jacobson,"

she states even though we talked about this the other night when she was so upset.

"Mrs. Klein is so much nicer, Rosie. I promise," her grandma says warmly to her, and then looks over at me. "She's much younger and has a far better attitude about how different children learn in different ways."

"Oh, good." And I mean it. Hearing how her teacher has made Rosie feel so disliked and uncomfortable made me so sad for my little friend.

"Yes. It isn't bad to be different, is it, Rosie? Mrs. Jacobson just didn't want to work harder to give you what you needed."

Rosie nods, more interested in the forest of stick-like trees she's drawing.

Linda's words give me pause. They sound strangely familiar and yet altered somehow, like the words have been rearranged just enough to remind me of a feeling I've had once but can't name.

"Are you alright, dear?" comes Linda's curious voice, noticing that my blue crayon is frozen above my paper.

I bite my lip and look up at her, knowing in my bones that if I opened up to Linda, my feelings would be received in a way I've always wished my mother could do, but can't.

"Just...thinking." I shake my head slightly, anxiety sloshing my stomach around like a washing machine. "I guess I know how that feels. To need something from someone who doesn't want to work at it to make it better."

I don't quite know who I'm referring to. I realize it could apply to Mason as well as both of my parents. Mason, who didn't want to make things right with me. My mom, who couldn't be bothered to be a real parent when I needed one, so my grandma did it for her. And my dad, who didn't want to put in the extra effort it took to make sure I knew I mattered to him.

"I can safely say, Mara, that whoever made you feel like you aren't worth it is an idiot," Linda says, sounding perturbed, and sips her tea.

I guess Sean didn't relay our conversation to his mother. I thought maybe he would. I didn't tell him to keep it a secret. But part of me values that he didn't share what I told him. Though I can't see him being a gossip or loose lipped in any way. He seems deliberate in everything he does and says.

"What's an idiot?" Rosie asks, cocking her head slightly at her grandmother.

"A very stupid person," she explains sourly.

"Stupid is not a nice word, Grandma."

I smile down at my drawing of purple and blue flowers.

"I know. But some people aren't nice either." Linda's eyebrows are knit together, and I'm warmed by how indignant she is about someone treating me poorly. "And when people aren't nice to the people I care about, I get upset."

"Don't be upset, Grandma," Rosie says in concern, and gets up and gives her a hug.

Linda's face relaxes as she squeezes her granddaughter tight. "What would I do without you, hmm? I love you, sweet girl." She kisses Rosie's cheek.

"Love you, too, Grandma. You can let go now."

I giggle at Rosie's bluntness, and Linda releases her.

"Of course. Back to your drawing."

Rosie sits down next to me again and picks up where

she left off.

"Anyway," Linda says, waving one hand as she takes a sip of tea, "I hope you can find someone who happily goes the extra mile for you, Mara. You deserve it."

I smile softly at her to conceal the truth. I thought I had that with Mason. I thought he was the one I would grow old with. We made promises to each other...but he didn't mean them like I did. And as much as I appreciate Linda's hopes for me, I can't even begin to imagine what it would be like to love someone else. Mason is all I've ever known in terms of love and the opposite sex.

"Someone like Doug?" I say to change the subject.

Linda's blue eyes sparkle. "Yes. Someone sweet and funny and warm. Someone who makes every day better."

"How long have you two been together?" I ask, putting down my blue crayon and picking up a green one.

"Almost three years," she answers wistfully, smiling to herself as she looks out the front window.

"You two seem so happy together. And it seems like Sean likes him."

She nods, her smile straightening out a bit. "He wasn't sure about me dating at first, but he came around when he realized that Doug is a good man who makes me happy. I think it was just weird for him to see me with someone other than his father, you know?"

"I'm sure."

"What about your mom? Is she married?"

I shake my head. "She hasn't even dated since she got divorced, and that was seventeen years ago. At least not that she's told me."

"Hmm," Linda says thoughtfully. "Are you close with your mom?"

I'm not sure how to answer that question, and she seems to sense it by the way she waits quietly for me to come to my conclusions.

"I...don't know. I think she tries, but...we're very different. I get along a lot better with you."

Linda smiles brightly at me, and as she's about to reply, heavy footfalls sound on the porch, and then the door opens.

Sean walks in wearing jeans and a blue flannel shirt, and I can't fight the blush that heats my face when he sees that I'm in his house with his family and smiles.

"Hi, Daddy! I'm drawing a whole forest," Rosie tells him, waving her paper at him from next to me.

"Looks good, Rosiecakes. Hey, Mara."

"Hi." It comes out much shyer than I meant it to, but he doesn't seem to notice.

He closes the door and steps out of his boots.

"How's Rhys? I never see him anymore," Linda says disapprovingly from the couch.

"I know. He's the son you never had," Sean teases, making his mother chuckle. "He's good."

She shakes her head, scoffing. "Typical man. 'He's good.' Care to *elaborate*?"

Sean plops back onto the couch next to his mother. "About what? I see him almost every day of the week. It's not like there's anything new to report."

Linda rolls her eyes. "Because all you two talk about is work."

"Not true."

I love listening to them bicker back and forth. The way they tease each other—it's so different from the way I grew up. My mom isn't one of those people who jokes around. After my grandmother passed, the joy in my life decreased so much that I realized my mom doesn't know how to have fun or loosen up. Not like these people. It fills me up sitting here, observing the affectionate way they interact.

"Yeah? When's the last time you talked about something personal?" Linda challenges, turning towards her son on the couch.

"I don't know, like last week maybe? You want an exact time and date?"

She laughs at him, leaning her head back against the couch. "You're ridiculous."

My back pocket vibrates, startling me, and I take it out.

Mom calling

Her ears must've been burning. I swipe to accept the call and excuse myself to the other side of the room.

"Hey, Mom, can I call you back later? I'm at my neighbor's," I say, my eyes on my favorite family. Sean's eyes meet mine, watching me as I speak.

"Oh, you are?" she blurts excitedly. "Of course." She sighs in almost relief. "I just love how much you're getting out of the house these days, Mara." She sounds truly happy about it, and for just a second, I feel like she really cares, but then she keeps speaking. "I was so worried you would bury yourself in that guitar and never see the light of day. But you haven't even picked it up, have you? Good for you. Singing was never a steady job anyway."

With every word she says, I feel my eyebrows pull lower and lower into a deep scowl.

"Anyway, I'll let you be with your friends. Talk to you later." She hangs up without waiting for me to say anything, and I lower my phone and stare at it angrily.

Suddenly, Sean is standing in front of me, his flannel shirt blocking my view of the living room behind him. "You're scowling. I've never seen you scowl," he says to me in both surprise and concern. "Are you okay? Who was that?"

Acidic anger spreads through me like a chemical fire.

Good for you.

Good for me? *Good for me* that I can't do what I was made to do? *Good for me* that I'm so broken I can't get myself to do the thing I love most? *Good for me* that I can't tap into the deepest, most important place in my heart?

I feel myself start to shake with unquenchable ire, such an unfamiliar sensation that I feel out of control, like I could ricochet off these walls with no way of stopping.

"Mara," he says, trying to get my attention. The warm pressure of his hands on my upper arms just makes me feel even more radioactive.

I step back, out of his grasp, breathless and ready to blow. I don't realize I'm crying until I wrench open the door and the cool October air touches my tears. I run, no mental space for crunchy leaves this time, and throw myself inside my house.

The door is closed for only a second before it opens again, and Sean is there, wide-eyed and worried as I feel that anger clawing its way up my throat. I pull the neck of my sweatshirt over my face, pressing the fabric against my mouth with my hands, and let out a long, trembling scream that swirls through the empty silence of my living room.

And then my knees hurt from hitting the floor. My breath is hitching and catching as I force it in and out.

Warm fingers tug my hands away so my sweatshirt drops back down. My eyes focus on the blue plaid pattern of his shirt instead of his eyes.

"She's...*happy*," I whisper through clenched teeth. "She's *happy* that I can't play anymore."

"Who, Mara?" Sean asks, his voice quiet and edged with fear as he searches my face.

"My mother." I sniff and meet his brown eyes then. "How...*dare* she?"

Every negative thing she's ever said to me about my music plays through my mind. She never believed I was good enough to make any real money at it. She never thought music was worth my time or hers. If she came to a show, she had a list of things I messed up on afterwards. Never a word of encouragement or pride or support for the thing that makes me feel whole.

Sean swallows hard. "Mara," he murmurs firmly, touching my shaking shoulders, "you *will* play again. You will. And when you do, I swear, I'll be the first one to say I told you so."

His fearless brown eyes, so sincere and so steadily peering into mine, coupled with his words, break through the chainmail threatening to resurrect itself around my heart.

The suffocating haze of anger recedes enough for me to realize what he just saw. My usually calm demeanor was swallowed up by an anger so strong that I screamed out loud in front of him.

And...he's still here, on his knees in front of me, looking

at me like he's just as upset at my mother as I am and more certain than I am that my dreams are as valid as reality.

The breath rushes in deeper, my tense muscles relax, and in anger's place comes weariness and hurt and embarrassment.

"I'm...sorry," I whisper, covering my wet face with my hands.

"There's nothing to be sorry about," he whispers back. "Come here, I got you." He pulls me forward against him, and I allow him to. He's the first man to hold me since Mason. I close my eyes and breathe in the clean scent of his shirt as he smoothes one hand up and down my back. The vibrating anger has gone now, and so has the embarrassment. All that's left now is a soothing stillness being pressed into me with every selfless pass of his hand.

"Thank you," I whisper into his warm chest. He seems calmer now, too, his heart beating slower against my cheek.

"I got you," he repeats, and instantly, his words become my favorite three words in the entire English language.

CHAPTER FIFTEEN

Sean

It was hard to convince my mom and Rosie that Mara was okay. I told them she got an unexpected phone call, and her mom said some not nice things. Rosie, of course, wanted to go over and be with Mara, "because that's what friends do" but I convinced her the best way she could cheer Mara up was by coloring her a nice picture and bringing it over to her tomorrow.

But even as I got her ready for bed and tucked her in, her little face was scrunched up with concern. I love that about her. She has such a caring heart for the people that mean the most to her, just like my mom. And their concern for Mara has me surer than ever that they've adopted her into their lives.

After I slipped out of Rosie's room, my mom basically demanded I tell her exactly what happened. But it didn't feel right to share it with Mom when I wasn't sure if Mara wanted me to. What her mom said isn't even *my* business, so keeping it to myself seemed like the right thing to do. I kept it brief, to my mom's dissatisfaction, and escaped upstairs to my room.

It's been an hour, at least, since I sat down on the edge of my bed. The TV isn't on, nor is the light. I haven't changed my clothes or scrolled through my phone.

I've just been sitting here, waiting for the feeling to go away. The feeling of her snuggled up against me. Her soft hair under my chin. Her cheek on my chest. The warmth of her slightly shaking body in my hands as I comforted her.

I don't want to admit it. I don't want to admit just how unbelievably good she felt in my arms. This woman I barely know felt so...*perfect* being that close to me. Maybe I'm lonelier than I thought. Maybe I'm just having a big reaction because it's been five years since I held a woman like that. Maybe this is just all in my head.

Even so, it was much too hard to let go when she calmed down enough to pull back. I felt far too incomplete when my arms released her. There was a part of me that *woke up* and wanted nothing more than to take care of her to the best of my ability.

For her mother to heartlessly elicit that kind of reaction out of Mara made me incredibly angry. Isn't it bad enough that the woman has lost everything? No, her mom had to basically kick her while she was down. I've never seen her or anyone get that explosively angry. Maybe it should've scared me, but instead I feel...*relieved*. I'm relieved that Mara just let it out and felt it all instead of burying it and letting it fester into a reason for her to walk back to the bridge.

I wish Gabby had done that. I wish she had felt *something*. Even if it was anger or panic or grief. But she was just quiet. Unresponsive. It hurts to look back now and realize she was gone long before she ran that bath. There was no life left in her.

And that's how Mara was when I first met her. Lifeless. But seeing her scream tonight reassured me that she's still kicking. Still fighting. Still in there, trying to get herself out of the dark place she's been in.

Maybe that's why it felt so good to console her. Because I knew that I *could*. Because she was *letting* me. Because she allowed me to witness the incinerating power of the flame inside of her, even if it was vulnerable and massive and it hurt.

My little fire-breather.

The thought cracks a warm smile across my mouth, but then it instantly evaporates when I catch myself thinking such fond thoughts about Mara.

No.

She isn't my little fire-breather.

She isn't my *anything*.

I can't let her climb inside my ribcage and make a home there.

But the feeling doesn't go away, even as I crawl into bed and close my eyes. Even as I fall asleep, I can still feel her tucked in close to my chest.

And then I slip into a dream that feels remarkably real. Me in my bed, waking up surprised that Mara isn't in bed beside me. I get up and look for her, and as soon as I pass through the bedroom doorway, the hallway that should be there *isn't*. In its place is Gabby's and my apartment. Everything is ominously quiet and still as I walk through it looking for Gabby like I did all those years ago. I open the bathroom door and see the fully clothed body floating in the tub. But this time I see long dark red hair slowly swirling and concealing most of Mara's lifeless face.

I wake with a soul-shaking jolt, breathless and drenched in sweat. My heart slams against my ribcage as I stagger out of bed and across the hall to the bathroom. I lean over the sink and splash my face with cold water to shock myself fully awake.

"Sean?" comes my mom's gentle voice from my left.

I look down at my shaking palms, covered in water and darkness.

"Just a bad dream," I say weakly, my breathing just beginning to slow down. "I'm alright. Go back to bed."

Because she's my mother, she doesn't move. She's been startled awake many times before by my terrified shouts. But it's been at least four years since I've had that dream about Gabby. And this time it wasn't even Gabby in that tub.

I straighten up enough to anchor my hands to the cool countertop, but I don't look up. I don't want to see how pale and shaken I am in the mirror.

"When you were a little boy, I used to be able to comfort you after you had a nightmare," Mom murmurs sadly. "But I know that face. And that nightmare is the only one I can't do anything about because it really happened."

There's a gentle tremor in her voice that makes my eyes sting. I push off the counter and turn to face her where she's standing in the bathroom doorway. Her pale pink pajama bottoms and matching shirt stand out against the dark hallway behind her, but her face is dimmer. Just the whites of her eyes give me a reference for any feature on her face.

"Sorry I woke you," I say brokenly and move toward her in the dark. I hug her, and she returns it tightly. I can feel her squeezing me like she did when I was a scared little boy in the middle of the night. Tonight, I feel like I still am that scared little boy.

"There's nothing you could've done," she whispers into my shoulder.

The stinging intensifies into tears that well up in my eyes. Mara's dark red hair hovering just below the surface of the water flashes through my mind.

My heartbeat picks up again, thudding hard and fast in my ears.

I can barely live with myself after Gabby took her own life. I know if Mara did the same, I would never recover. I need to help her keep trying to move forward, for both her benefit and the protection of my daughter and mother who already love her like she's family.

I feel the need to text Mara right this second, to tell her...*something*. Something that will keep her here. But instead, I reassure Mom that I'm okay, and we both go back to our rooms.

I get back under the covers, but I know it's going to be a long night.

Rosie's little hand is like a vice on mine as we walk towards the school the next morning. We're meeting with Mrs. Klein a half hour before school starts, so there are no kids running around and no chatter or laughter as we go inside to see her new classroom.

I've had at least three cups of coffee after my mostly sleepless night, and despite how things always seem better in the morning than they do in the middle of the night, I can't shake off the nightmare I had. But before we left for school, Rosie and I walked over to give Mara the picture she drew. Just seeing Mara's face, however distant and tired, was something I needed. I needed to see her, just to know without a shadow of a doubt that she was okay and still here.

I think Rosie needed to see her, too. Even though Mrs. Klein is supposedly much nicer than Mrs. Jacobson, I know she still feels unsure and nervous. But Mara made her forget about it, at least for a few minutes, and she promised to be there when Rosie gets home from school this afternoon.

We approach the end of the hallway and pass Mrs. Jacobson's room to reach the last door on the left. The door is open, and I pause here to let Rosie peek inside.

She glances around, and I see her shift forward slightly when she spots the craft and coloring supplies on a bookshelf near the window.

I follow her lead and bring her into the room. A woman is writing something on the whiteboard with a blue marker, and when I read the words, I feel a bit of relief.

Welcome, Rosalie!

"Hello," I say, and the woman turns with a big smile. She's short with brown hair twisted into a knot on the top of her head, with pink and white polka dotted glasses in front of friendly brown eyes. She's wearing a simple dress with the alphabet printed all over it in different colors. I instantly get the impression that this woman is fun and cares about making school fun.

"Well, hi there!" she greets happily. "I'm Mrs. Klein! You must be Rosalie." She comes forward as she speaks, a smile staying on her face. She squats down in front of my daughter, who despite her new teacher's friendliness, is gripping my leg and hiding behind it.

"I'm Sean. And you can call her Rosie," I say, placing my hand affectionately on my daughter's head.

"What a sweet name," Mrs. Klein replies, still staying at Rosie's level. "Well, Rosie, I just want to say how happy I am that you're in my class now!"

Rosie remains where she is and says nothing.

"I know it can be a little scary to do something new, but no matter what, I want you to feel safe, okay? Together we're going to figure out how you learn best. And if something makes you sad or nervous, just tell me, and we'll make it better."

I breathe easier as she says these things to my shy daughter. This is exactly the teacher she needs to thrive.

"Do you want to come check out our classroom? It would make me so happy if you could find something you really love doing." Mrs. Klein gestures behind her and explains to Rosie all the different areas of the room. Reading corner, play kitchen, circle time rug, and the tables where she'll be coloring and doing crafts.

Rosie tentatively steps out from behind my leg and glances up at me. I smile at her in encouragement, and she awkwardly moves around the room, looking at everything.

Mrs. Klein straightens up, barely reaching my shoulder and wears an easy, genuine smile as she watches Rosie settle herself at the table and pull some paper and colored pencils toward her.

"She's so sweet," she says to me, and then turns to look me in the eyes. "Is there anything you have concerns about? The first day might be a little rough, but I have all the confidence in the world that she'll do great."

I nod. "Yeah, I already can tell she's going to do better in your class. Thanks for being so flexible."

"Of course; I'm happy to have her. If you'd like, I can send you updates via the school's app so you won't have to worry all day about how she's doing?"

"Yes, that would be amazing. Thank you."

"Absolutely. And feel free to contact me as well through

the app if you have questions or anything I might need to know, okay?"

"Thanks, I'll do that."

I step over to my daughter and lean down to kiss her forehead. I glance at the paper she's coloring on and recognize another family picture in progress.

"Okay, Rosiecakes, I have to go now. I'll pick you up after school."

Rosie's blue eyes look up at me nervously, but she nods.

"You good?"

She nods again, this time a little more vigorously.

I smile at her and kiss her forehead again. "Love you, Rosie. See you after school."

"Love you, Daddy."

I back away towards the door as Mrs. Klein joins my daughter at the table and asks if she can draw a picture, too.

I feel like I'm leaving my heart in that room as I turn away and head back down the hallway. My mom tells me it never goes away, no matter how old your kid gets. I'm sure one day when I walk her down the aisle, I'll feel the same way.

"Excuse me!" comes a woman's voice from behind me. I glance over my shoulder to figure out if she's talking to me, and I find a blonde woman walking toward me. The sway of her hips is accentuated by her tight black pencil skirt as her heels click across the floors.

"Uh, yeah?" I say, wondering if maybe this is the principal or something.

"Hi! I'm Sarah Callahan, the new school nurse." Her blonde hair is perfectly styled in messy waves framing her jaw, the kind that make it look like she didn't spend an hour on it.

She's smiling at me in a way that makes me uncomfortable. With too much teeth. Like I'm a gazelle, and she's a lion.

"This is my first school year, so I try to make it a point to meet as many parents as possible," she informs me, that smile staying wide and toothy even as she speaks.

"Oh," I say awkwardly. "I'm Sean Dunbar. My daughter is Rosie. She's in Kindergarten this year."

"Such a magical time, isn't it? How are you and your wife handling the change at home?"

My stomach clenches.

She wants to talk about my *wife*, huh? I could tell her. Make her feel ashamed and stupid for asking a question like that. But all she really wants to know is whether I'm a single dad. A red blush creeps up my neck, but it isn't from embarrassment or shyness.

"I'm handling it fine," I answer curtly.

She nods, her perfect hair unmoving. "Well, if you ever need help, um, *handling* it, just let me know. My number is in the school directory." Then, she winks at me suggestively and bites her lip as she looks me up and down.

Wow. Could she be any more obvious?

I nod at her with a grimace-like smile and make for the exit as quickly as I can without breaking out into a run.

I get into my truck and pull out of the school parking lot. Once I'm on the road, I finally relax.

It isn't the first time a woman has blatantly hit on me since Gabby died. But this time, something didn't sit right. Maybe because it was in a professional setting and this smiley woman could look up my contact information without anyone stopping her. Maybe because she has access to my daughter.

I try my best to shake off the disgusted feeling in my stomach. Maybe other men would've responded to Sarah Callahan's interest, but it doesn't feel right to trust a woman who smiles that much.

Or maybe I'm just used to being around Mara, whose smiles are small and used sparingly. Despite the fact that she's just barely my friend, I could really use one of those little smiles right now.

CHAPTER SIXTEEN

Mara

It was a fitful night of sleep. My mother's thoughtless words were only one reason. The other was that I felt something last night. Yes, something angry and acrid. But then...I felt something move inside my chest that hasn't moved in more than a year. I felt it when I was close to Sean, when my breathing steadied and matched his, when my heartbeat slowed and synced with his.

It was like a little...*nudge*.

Different than the nudge to play my guitar or sing, which I desperately wish I had. It was a little wordless whisper, issuing from the lonely, scared place in my heart that has frozen over since the divorce became final. For just one second with Sean, I felt my broken spirit take a breath.

I swear I felt it again when I saw him this morning. With him looking at me with an expression on his face that puzzled me. Like he wasn't sure I was actually standing there in front of him. He looked tired, I thought, though I did, too.

But Rosie was the thing that made me look at my mother's words differently. She brought over a picture of the two of us she had drawn in pink crayon. It made me think of the first time she came over and spoke to me, and how nervous and uncertain she was as she crept closer and closer, like she wasn't sure if I was a rabid animal or a tame house pet. And now, she's accepted me into her little world and fearlessly engages with me and includes me in her life. I'm positive that Rosie can do anything she sets her mind to, because she set out to befriend me, and despite my distance and fear, she succeeded.

I need to be that sure of what I want. I need to persist, the way Rosie did with me. And Linda.

I need to finally take my mother's advice and return to the things I loved doing, even if those things are not what she wants me to be doing, even if my love for music isn't something she understands about me.

She's right. This is my life. And I get to live it as I want to. Regardless of whether that includes her support or even her blessing.

So, I go into the spare room and get as far as unlatching and opening the lid. I stare at it for a long minute, admiring my instrument while prickling inside. It takes all my will power to lift my guitar out of its case and settle down on the floor with it in my lap.

The neck is smooth on the palm of my left hand, just like it used to be. The strings grab at my fingertips with little metal teeth.

It hits me like a freight train, then. The grief and the regret.

I cut my heart out and tried to shove it at someone who didn't want it.

I abandoned myself.

And this guitar in my unpracticed hands was once a

huge piece of me. It was the thing that brought me purpose and joy. I take a deep breath and strum. The sound is offkey and strange, so I work to tune each string until the strum sounds right.

Even in that rightness, there's a bittersweet quality lingering between the notes, too. The sound is a reminder of how much I hate the way I cast this aside, and yet also a reminder to my soul that I still love the feel of the strings indenting my soft fingertips.

Promise me you'll keep trying.

The chord finger placements feel awkward, mostly because there's nothing stirring inside me except the pain I caused myself. The pain that far exceeds the pain Mason inflicted. In the end, he was unfaithful. But he didn't pull every last effort out of me before he left. I did that.

And as I look down at the beautiful blue color of the guitar body, I make myself a promise. I will *never* give myself away to keep a man ever again. I will choose to keep the things I love. I will choose me. I will choose to love myself.

With that, I stagger through a few chord progressions that only make me long for the way it was before, when it was as effortless as breathing, as much a part of me as my own thoughts. I miss the friend I had in this guitar, these strings, those calluses.

"It'll come back," I whisper.

The cool wind sends shivers down the length of my body as I walk over to my neighbor's house. Leaves are falling steadily now, covering my fading green lawn with crimson and mustard. The dying leaves and cooler temperatures remind me that the holidays are coming up. My first holiday season without Mason. My mother has already booked me a flight out for Thanksgiving next month, without saying a word about it. Just forwarded me the airline information.

After my little flare up with her last night, I honestly don't know if I want to see her. I don't know that my Thanksgiving would be happier with her in it. I step up onto the porch and pause, sighing at the front door. Linda has put out pumpkins and corn shocks, making their front door feel warm and autumnal.

I'd much rather be *here* in this house for Thanksgiving. Linda would love that, I'm sure of it, but as welcoming as she and her family have been, they aren't *my* family. But the family I thought I was building with Mason has been taken from me, which just leaves my mother.

As I knock on the door and go inside, I have a strangely satisfying thought that I could stay and have my own quiet Thanksgiving in my own house. And if the Dunbars don't have other plans, maybe I could invite them over. The thought warms me as I close the door behind me, shutting out the chill.

I'm about to call out a hello to Linda, who I assume is in the kitchen, but then I hear Doug's voice.

"But Rosie is in Kindergarten now."

I can't see either of them from here, but their voices carry easily into the living room from the kitchen, where I imagine they're sitting at the table together.

"I know, but—"

"Sean doesn't need you as much now," Doug argues gently, but firmly. "It's the perfect time for us to—"

"He *does* need me, Doug. Just last night he had a nightmare about Gabby. He hasn't had one in years. I need to be here for him."

My heart clenches. Sean has *nightmares* about his wife? What kind of woman was she that she still gives her widower nightmares after all this time? I can't imagine Sean connected to anyone with ill intentions, or Rosie being from someone insidious.

I know the right thing to do is back out of the house as quietly as I can. This isn't my business, and Linda and Doug are clearly having a very personal argument. But some part of it fascinates me. The way they deal with their disagreement without calling names or saying awful things.

"For how long? The rest of his life? You've taken such good care of them all these years. Please let me take care of you now."

"That's not how it works when you're a mother." Linda's profile passes the kitchen doorway as she moves away from the table to the other side of the kitchen.

"Linda...I love you. I want to spend the rest of my life with you." Doug follows her, his hands reaching for her as he slips out of view again. "I want to wake up next to you every morning and—"

"That's what I want, too. I do. But now isn't the right time. Please try to understand."

There's a beat of silence that has me holding my breath. In some ways, silence can be good. It means that they're both thinking before speaking. But silence for me has only been hurtful. The quieter it was in our house, the more I felt Mason disappearing.

Even when I was a child, the quiet reminded me that my mother had other things to do. And despite her many offers to fly back to "help me," I know that if she had flown here, she wouldn't have let me forget it. That she had to come all the way up here to put my life in order for me. The silence between us now is more pleasant and preferred to me than the short conversations we have every couple of days.

"I'm sorry, Angelface," he says softly. "I don't want you to feel like it's me or them. It isn't like that, okay? I just...want more of you."

"I do, too."

Oh, my heart.

They love each other so much.

Linda is so different from my mother...she's so much more giving and selfless. Linda is putting her personal life on hold so she can be there as much as possible for Sean and Rosie. And Doug loves her enough to wait. I've never experienced a love like that. Even when I thought I had it with Mason, our arguments were never like this. He was never understanding or conceding. And towards the end, I didn't even put up a fight or try to argue about anything because I didn't want to push him away even further.

Poor Doug just wants to make an honest woman out of her, but she can't allow herself to let that happen when she knows her son is hurting.

When I hear their footsteps moving across the kitchen floor, I quickly turn, open the door, and then shut it again loudly. I turn back to see them entering the living room, holding hands and both wearing heartbroken expressions.

"Hi," I greet, trying to keep my face neutral so they don't figure out I heard their conversation.

"Hello, dear," Linda says with a smile that doesn't reach her eyes.

"I promised Rosie I'd be here when she gets home from school," I explain, even though I don't need to. I just need them to understand that I would be willing to let them spend time alone together if I hadn't promised Rosie.

"Oh, that's so sweet. I bet she can't wait to see you."

I step into the room after removing my shoes and join them on the couches. "How do you think it went today?"

"I'm sure she did fine," Doug says, pulling Linda close against his side as she sits down next to him.

Both of them seem subdued, and I hate to see it. "I can wait outside on the porch for her, if you guys want some alone time," I offer then, willing to face the cold out there if need be.

"Don't be silly. They'll be home any minute."

I nod and fold my hands in my lap.

"How are you, Mara? Sean told me last night that you had an upsetting phone call from your mom, but he wouldn't say exactly what happened," Linda says, leaning forward towards me a little with concerned blue eyes.

"Uh, yeah, she…she said something that upset me. It doesn't matter; I'm okay." My explanation isn't what she's looking for, but I'd rather not get into it again when I know that Linda is dealing with her own problems.

"*Of course,* it matters that she upset you," she argues, reaching over and putting her hand on my knee. "Did she apologize?"

I feel a bit of heat rush up the back of my neck. "Um, no, she didn't," I murmur back. "I don't think she even understood that what she said was hurtful."

Linda scowls and sits back into Doug's one-armed embrace with a loud huff. One side of his mouth pulls into a little smile at that, like he loves how much of a firecracker she is.

"Well, if I—"

Before she can finish her sentence, which I have no doubt would've very colorfully vilified my mother, the front door opens, and my favorite little girl comes inside, followed by Sean.

His golden-brown eyes find mine instantly, and though he studies my face like he's trying to figure out how I'm feeling today, I also notice just a flash of warmth light up his stubbly face.

I feel that little nudge again.

Before he can say hello, Rosie sets down her backpack and skitters toward me. She climbs up into my lap and snuggles in close.

"Hi, Rosie," I say to her happily, and wrap her up with my arms.

She gives a little sigh, which sounds like it comes from a place of contentment.

"How was your day, Rosie Posie?" Linda asks from the couch. "Was Mrs. Klein nice?"

She nods, strands of my hair tangling together where her cheek is resting.

"She's tired," Sean explains as he takes off his boots and steps closer to his daughter and me. "But I talked to Mrs. Klein about how things went, and she said Rosie did really well."

"Mrs. Climb lets me play alone if I need to," Rosie pipes up. "And she didn't make me feel bad for not being as loud as all the other kids."

Each of us chuckle at the inaccuracy of her teacher's name.

"I'm so glad to hear that, sweetie," says Linda. This time, her smile includes her eyes. "I knew you'd like her much better than your old teacher."

Rosie nods again.

Something about how she so unabashedly sits with me makes me incredibly sentimental. I've always known I wanted to be a mother, and Mason had agreed about us having a family. But when I brought it up, he always made an excuse to wait. Usually work related or stress related. Now I wonder if he ever really did want what I wanted, or if he just thought he was supposed to want to be a dad. So, when it actually came down to it, he felt trapped.

I wish he just would've been honest with me. God knows I still would've stayed with him if he had admitted to changing his mind about wanting kids. It's very clear I would've stayed with him no matter what he did, including cheat on me.

What a waste. Of everything. Time, energy, love.

But here, cuddling this little girl who has captured my heart, I feel just the slightest little stirring of hope that I could still have my own kids someday. That maternal instinct that I inherited from my grandmother and not my actual mother is still alive and well within me.

"I'm proud of you, Rosie," I murmur to her. She tilts her face up to look at me with those innocent blue eyes. "Change is scary, but sometimes it can bring us good things, too."

The room is still around me as Rosie and I study each other.

"Like how you moved in next door?"

I smile softly at her. "Exactly. I didn't know then that I was going to meet you and your dad and your grandma and

Doug. I was scared to be on my own, but you all make me feel less alone."

I give her a friendly squeeze, letting my own words reverberate through my brain.

For all the change that's happened in the last year, I can honestly say that this cozy family has been the best thing that's happened to me. If Mason hadn't divorced me, I never would've met the Dunbars. And just the thought of missing out on these people makes my heart lurch painfully.

"You're *not* alone," Sean says, surprising me.

I look up at him and wonder what he must see when he looks at me. This messy person just trying to learn how to breathe again, holding in my arms the most important thing in his life. *Trusting me* to hold the most important thing in his life. The only thing he has left of his wife.

And something makes me want to tell him that he isn't alone either.

Because when I look at him, I see a man bearing the weight of the world on his shoulders. I see a man who misses his wife and who loves his daughter so much, it hurts. I see a man who works hard, possibly too hard, so that he has a few hours of the day when he doesn't think about what he's lost.

I wish I could move mountains for him. Do the impossible for him. I wish I could be the one to help him hold his pain in a different way, the way his family is helping me to hold mine.

"That's right. We all have each other," Linda agrees, giving Doug a meaningful look. He kisses her temple to let her know he understands. He isn't just committing to Linda; he's committing to Sean and Rosie, too.

I bring my eyes back to Sean, who is looking at me like

I'm quietly drowning at his feet but don't know how to swim. It reminds me that I can swim. And even if I can only manage to tread water right now, for the first time, I feel like I'm more than just keeping my head above the water.

CHAPTER SEVENTEEN

Sean

I can tell my mom and Doug got into an argument. I can always tell. My mom is not one of those people who can hide how she's feeling. So even though she's smiling and seems to be having a good time making dinner with Mara and Rosie, I know something's bothering her. I can tell in between her words that something isn't quite right.

I'm having a hard time focusing on it though, I'll admit, because I can't keep my eyes off of Mara. She looks exactly like she always does today. Her long dark red hair cascades down her back, and she's wearing a black shirt paired with jeans. But after last night, seeing her lose her composure, I find myself studying her trying to see that fire permeating through her complexion and body language. After my dream last night, I keep staring at her like at any moment, she might evaporate into thin air and leave us forever.

I don't like the feeling of having another woman in our lives who would leave a hole behind if she left. But I also can't help but feel my chest loosen when I see her participating in our family life.

"Something on your mind, Son?" Doug asks me from across the table, keeping his voice down like he's offering me a chance to talk without involving my mother.

I clear my throat and forcibly turn my head away from Mara to look at Doug. "I could ask you the same," I reply. "Everything okay with you and Mom?"

An uncomfortable expression wrinkles his graying eyebrows. He nods, though he looks worried. I'm not sure whether to press him on it, considering it isn't any of my business, and ultimately decide not to say anything else. It's probably best if I stay out of their relationship.

"I don't see Mara as much as you all do, but she seems like she's finding her stride here," he says when my gaze inevitably returns to our unassuming guest.

I just nod, having nothing to add.

What she said about change earlier is stuck in my head.

Change is scary, but sometimes it can bring us good things, too.

When Mara moved in next door, I would not have said it was a good thing. But with each passing day, whether she's trying to or not, she's seeping into the cracks and corners of this house and filling them in. She's become more and more of a house cat, and less and less like the stray I used to see her as. And I'm starting to want her to stay. I'm starting to hope she doesn't get spooked by something and run away.

I'm uncomfortable with that, but it isn't something I can talk myself out of anymore.

Something about Mara is good. For Rosie. For Mom. For me. And if the relaxed expression on her pretty face is any indication, it's clear that we're good for her, too.

"Alright, you fellas ready to eat?" Mom announces, bringing a pan of homemade mac and cheese to the table, followed by Mara, who bears another pan with roasted chicken. As she leans forward to put it down on the table, I feel an impulse so strong that my arm actually moves toward her, but I quickly catch myself from reaching out to move her long hair back over her shoulder.

Thankfully, she notices nothing, and everyone sits down and helps themselves. I keep my eyes on my plate as I eat, not okay with how close I came to touching her.

If I close my eyes and think hard enough, I can still feel her close to me. Part of me is hungry to feel the real thing again, but I know it won't happen. I won't let it. At least not just for the hell of it. Not just because I liked how it felt.

"So, Rosie, did you decide what you want to be for Halloween?" Doug asks warmly.

My daughter shakes her head, avoiding his gaze. Even though she's known Doug for years, she can still be pretty shy around him. I think if he was around as often as Mara, maybe that would change.

"Do you have plans for Halloween, Mara?" Mom asks her, eliciting a surprised lift of her eyebrows.

"Oh—uh, honestly I forgot all about Halloween," she admits quietly, her cheeks a little pink.

"I don't like Halloween that much," Rosie says, almost like she's consoling Mara. "It's scary."

She's always been scared of the other kids all dressed up like something else, mostly the ones who dress up like monsters or mummies or whatever. Last year, we only went around the block, and even though she got candy out of it, she didn't want to go outside for a week after that.

"But that's the fun of it," Doug insists. "My kids used to love dressing up and trick or treating." He shovels a forkful of mac and cheese into his mouth, his eyes drifting towards the ceiling like he's lost in memories.

"It doesn't have to be scary," Mara reassures my daughter gently. "Sometimes it's fun to pretend to be someone else for a little while."

Hmm. I never thought about it that way. I study her, wondering who she would pretend to be.

"It is?" Rosie cocks her blonde head slightly, making me chuckle as I chew my chicken.

"Well, sure. It's the one night of the year when you can be anything you want," she answers sweetly. "You might not feel like a superhero every day, but on Halloween, you can be."

"Yeah, Rosie Posie," my mom jumps in. "You could be a superhero, or a ballerina, or a unicorn—"

"Or a puppy?" Rosie inquires, her light blue eyes open wide as she looks at me from across the table.

I narrow my eyes at her slightly. "Yes, you could be a puppy if you wanted," I say, knowing what she's about to say next.

"I love puppies. Maybe if I'm a puppy for Halloween, Santa will see how much I really want a puppy for Christmas."

My mom glances at me as she stifles her laughter with the back of her hand and then turns her head toward Doug so Rosie doesn't notice.

She's been asking to get a puppy since last Christmas. I don't have anything against dogs, honestly, but I have enough on my plate without adding a puppy that needs to be housebroken and babysat so it doesn't gnaw off chair legs or eat my work boots for a snack.

"That's a great idea," my mom says as she collects herself.

I shake my head at her, fighting a smirk, and take a sip of water. She knows how much I hate the idea of getting a puppy.

"What about you, Mara?" Doug asks.

"You could be Ariel, for sure, with your hair," Linda chimes in warmly.

"Oooh," Rosie says in approval.

Mara touches her long tendrils and blushes again, not sure how to respond.

"And your dad could be Prince Eric," Doug adds with a grin in my direction.

"Nope. Lumberjack," I tell my plate.

"Again? That's three years in a row," my mom complains. "Don't be so boring."

I roll my eyes. "It's easy. I have a flannel shirt and a plastic axe. It's perfect." I catch Mara glancing at me like she's imagining my low-budget costume.

"But it's hardly a costume. You basically *are* a lumberjack every day," Mom argues, pointing her fork at me.

"Exactly."

She huffs and goes back to her food. "You're just no fun."

I shrug.

"I think you'd make a handsome Prince Eric," Mara says to me with a little smile, and I assume she said it to join my mother in egging me on, but the instant the words are out, her smile slips, and her eyes widen a little like she realized she just called me handsome.

I don't expect it to make me smile, but it does. Even if she's being objective or just teasing, it still causes a warmth to fill up my chest.

"Is that so?"

She clears her throat, avoiding my eyes, and nods as she cuts into her chicken with her fork.

Her shyness is so sweet to me. She's a gentler spirit than Gabby was. My wife was feisty and would tease me into oblivion if I had ever considered going as a Disney character for Halloween. I loved that about her, actually.

But I weirdly like this, too...this shy, quiet attempt at ribbing me that fell flat and came out as a blatant compliment. I get the impression that Mara has never said a bad word about anyone, even jokingly.

"But Daddy, maybe if *you* dress up like a puppy, too, then Santa—"

"Nope. Sorry, kid. Not happening."

Linda and Doug laugh, no doubt imagining me with paint on my face and a big fuzzy brown costume.

Rosie sighs loudly, exactly like a teenager. "But Daddy!"

Movement to my right has my eyes darting from Rosie to Mara, whose shoulders are shaking. My stomach drops, thinking she's crying, but when she looks up at me, she's grinning.

Grinning.

And...*laughing.*

Her face is a deep shade of red as the elation shines on her face. I knew she had a stunning smile. It takes my breath away to see her smile that big...to see her blue eyes sparkle with happiness and humor.

Wow.

I'd do anything to keep that kind of happiness on her face.

"Please," she says through her beautiful laughter, *"please be a puppy, too."*

Okay, maybe not anything.

"'Cause it would be hilarious, apparently?"

Mara covers her beaming smile with her hands, but it doesn't matter when her eyes are smiling, too.

I pretend to smirk at her, narrowing my eyes, which just makes her giggle behind her hands.

Cute.

"Let's *all* go as puppies," my mom suggests, laughter in her voice. "Whatever helps convince Santa that Rosie should get a puppy this Christmas."

"Yeah!" Rosie shouts excitedly.

This time, I'm the one who sighs like a teenager, and I realize that whether I like it or not, come Christmastime, there will be some little yappy mongrel running rampant through this house.

And if I'm lucky, maybe Mara will be there, too.

"Oh, Mara, I forgot to ask you something," my mom says as Mara is getting her shoes on to head back to her house.

After dinner, she helped put Rosie to bed, and I couldn't

help but stand in the hallway and listen as they talked and sang quietly in Rosie's room.

"Mhm?" she says, standing up straight to face my mom, who's standing in the kitchen doorway.

Doug is making them tea, and I have every assumption they're going to have a seat and finish the puzzle on the table while they talk.

"We're all going to the last farmer's market of the season this Saturday," Mom explains. "It's the last one before Halloween, so we usually buy some pumpkins and take them home to carve into jack-o'-lanterns. Do you want to come?"

I know if Rosie were standing right here, she would be begging Mara to come with us. At first, I wasn't that excited about Mara becoming her favorite person instead of me, but I'm realizing how happy Rosie is. I can't, in good conscience, feel bad about that.

"Oh—if it's a family tradition kind of thing, I—"

"You're coming," I interrupt, her blue eyes moving from my mother to me. "If you don't have anything else going on," I add, hoping to soften my demand.

A soft little smile dances over her features. "I don't. I'd love to go with you guys."

"Great!" Mom exclaims, clapping her hands once.

"Tea's ready, Angelface," Doug says from the kitchen.

"Have a good night, Mara. And thank you again for the bread." She disappears into the kitchen, leaving me and Mara standing near the door together.

She reaches for her gray plate, which she set down on the console table so she could get her shoes on, and a very shy energy takes over her body. She hugs her plate to her chest and looks up at me, her cheeks already slightly pink.

"Um, would you mind walking me over? I wanted to talk to you about something." Her voice is small and timid, and it warms up my insides.

"Sure." I step into my boots and follow her outside, hoping whatever she wants to talk about isn't something serious. But it must be personal or important if she didn't want to talk about it in front of my mom. That makes me feel stupidly good. Just the thought that maybe she wants to confide in me puts a slight bounce in my step that I'm not used to.

The cool evening air pushes at us as we cross my yard and then hers. I'm still in denial that October is already half over. I feel like if I blink, it'll be Thanksgiving. The holidays are never great for me. They never are for people who have lost a loved one. This time of year is an unwelcome reminder of who is missing.

Mara pauses in front of her concrete steps and faces me, her hands pulled up into the sleeves of her sweatshirt to keep them warm so that I can't see her hands clutching the plate.

"Is everything alright?" I ask, sensing her nerves.

"Yes. Sorry, everything's fine. I'm fine," she rushes out as she realizes I may have interpreted this little talk as something to be worried about. She takes a deep breath, avoiding my eyes and awkwardly shuffling her feet. "Uh, I just wanted to tell you, I—" She looks up at me, her face full of...excitement? "I tried today."

"You tried?" I question, not quite following.

She nods, her smile growing. "I got out my guitar and tuned it. I played a few chords and...well, it didn't feel *right*, exactly, but... I tried."

My heart beats oddly in my chest. She took me seriously. When I told her to keep trying...she listened. My chest seizes up with emotion. She tried. I made her promise, and she kept it.

She shifts the plate to the crook of her right arm, and then I watch her peek through the opening of her left hand sleeve, bringing out her fingertips, which she looks at lovingly. Even in the dim light, I can see that they're swollen and red.

"These hurt?" Before I can stop myself, I'm bringing my fingers to hers, lightly touching where her guitar strings grated on her skin. The abrasions feel hot and irritated.

"Yeah, but..." She smiles again, almost as big as at the table earlier, "it's a good hurt."

A strange sense of pride wells up inside my chest at that response. More than ever, I want to bring her in close to me, even if just for a second. But then I realize I'm still touching her hand. I should let it go, but...I don't want to. Her skin on mine feels too inexplicably right. Touching her at all just makes it that much more real—that she still wants to try.

I swallow hard. "I'm proud of you." The words are true, though they slip out without my permission.

Mara looks up quickly, like she isn't sure she heard me correctly. And then her blue eyes soften, her brows scrunch together, and I see her lashes blink back the accumulating tears.

Without warning, she throws her free arm around my neck. The gentle pressure of her body pressed into mine both excites me and soothes me. But before I can properly return her hug, she steps back, wiping at her eyes.

"Sorry," she murmurs, and clears her throat. "I just really needed to hear that."

I nod, not liking how let down I feel without her close to

me. I feel out of my element, I realize. It's been a long time since my heart has felt this alert because of a woman.

But this isn't just any woman, I'm sure of it. Behind her depression is someone who is trying to put one foot in front of the other. And I can't even express how much relief that gives me.

"You should try again tomorrow," I tell her quietly when her eyes meet mine again. She smiles softly at me in the gentle way I was longing for when I met the school nurse this morning.

"I will. I promise."

I'm already beginning to believe that when Mara makes a promise, she keeps it. I give her a small smile in return and fight back my urge to move forward and tug her close.

"Are you doing okay after last night?"

She hugs the plate to her chest and looks away like she's embarrassed.

"I'm okay. Just sorry you had to see me like that." Her voice is small, and her shoulders hunch in slightly as she says this, and I hate it. She clearly isn't used to letting her guard down in front of anyone.

"I'm not sorry," I say sternly, drawing her eyes back to mine. "I'm glad I was there to see it."

"Really?"

I nod slowly as the cool breeze lifts a few of her long tresses, her blue eyes looking up at me so intently that I forget about keeping my own guard up.

"It was good for me to know that there's more going on inside you than you let anyone see."

"Why?"

Because I'm terrified you're still suicidal.

"I worry about you sometimes," is what I say instead. The surprise on her face has my own heating up. "I'm not the only one, you know." I nod towards my house, indicating my mother, and hopefully extinguishing the idea that I think about her more than I should.

"Hmm," she says with a funny little quirk to her brow, smiling at the ground. "Is it weird that it feels nice to be worried about?"

"No," I answer with a smile of my own.

She tilts her smile up at me, and I realize how quickly it's becoming something I want to see more of.

"Well....thanks, I guess," she says softly. "You have no idea how good you all are for me."

I nod, avoiding her eyes this time. "You're good for us, too."

She nods as well, and silence falls between us. She steps back and looks up at me with warmth in her eyes. "Well, good night."

"Good night," I say, and watch her turn away. "And hey —" She turns back to face me, and I grin at her. "I told you so."

Her grin matches mine then, and it's all I can think about for the rest of the night.

CHAPTER EIGHTEEN

Mara

I opened the curtains today. For the first time, the sun seemed inviting instead of blinding. The shape of sunlight hitting the hardwood floors beckoned me to sit there with it, my guitar in my lap.

My fingertips are sore, making each chord burn, but like I told Sean the other day, it's a good hurt, a hurt that makes my soul feel just the beginning tremors of life. With each coordinated strum, I mentally whisper to myself.

Forgive yourself. Forgive yourself for putting this aside so willingly.

And keep trying.

Sean is the only person to ever be proud of this. Mason and my mother really didn't get why I love music and how big a part of me it is. For Sean to be proud of me for trying like this...it meant more than I could express to him. His faith in me was exactly why I wanted to tell him about picking up my guitar again. I knew he would be happy for me. And I wanted him to know that I heard what he said.

He's been so different towards me lately. He's been

supportive and welcoming. It makes me think that...maybe we're kind of...*friends*. I like the idea of having more than Linda to talk to. It's nice to have warm influences in my life after going so long without anyone at all.

I hope I can be a friend to Sean, too.

My right hand breaks away from the steady strumming I was lost in, and then my pick wanders into a long lost melody that makes my heart ache. It's the melody of one of the first songs I ever put out into the world. It's a song that still sells on iTunes and is still getting views on YouTube.

So much has changed since then. I was uninhibited then. Ready to take on the music world. So passionate in my songs that I didn't give myself even a second to think about failure.

Though, to be fair, I've never done it for money or fame. Maybe that's why my mother doesn't get it. The award shows and album release parties...the media and the constant attention... None of that matters to me. I sing and I play because if I don't, my life feels like nothing.

And lately, I've felt exactly like that. Which is why I need to heed Sean's advice and keep trying.

My phone vibrates from the coffee table, and I pause my picking. My mother called last night, and I ignored it. I texted her afterward that I was busy, which wasn't a lie. I was with the Dunbars, which has become a nightly thing now. She's calling again now, no doubt to make sure I'm not still a useless lump on the couch.

Part of me wants to keep ignoring her. I'm still angry and hurt, but I also know that if I keep declining her phone calls, she'll eventually fly back here to make sure I haven't done anything stupid.

I put my guitar aside, leaned against the couch, and pick

up my phone. I take a deep breath, trying to tamp down the dread I feel, and then accept the call.

"Hello?"

"Oh, good. You answered," she huffs. "If you didn't pick up, I was about to start looking at plane tickets."

Called that one, didn't I? Despite all her harassment about being in the house all the time, she seems awfully annoyed that I'm finally starting to live my life again after Mason tore it apart.

"You're the one who wanted me to make friends and get out of the house more," I grumble quietly.

She blurts out a false laugh. "That doesn't mean you can ignore your mother. Or should I just stop calling? You've got your life together enough now that I don't have to check up on you? Is that it?"

My face heats up at that, and my teeth grind together.

It's not about you, I want to say, but I don't.

"You know I'll always need you, Mom," is what comes out, though even to me, it sounds weary.

"That's right. Without me, who knows where you'd be. Probably camped out in a tent in front of your cheating ex-husband's house." She laughs once, a derisive "ha!" that has my blood boiling.

Apparently, she's really salty about me missing her phone call. She's especially cold today. She's making me suffer for ignoring her.

"You'd like my friends," I redirect clumsily. "Linda is really sweet and—"

"I'm sure I would, Mara," she agrees dismissively. "Does Linda know any single men? Anyone she could set you up with?"

I do my best not to sigh in frustration. "Mom, I don't—"

"Just listen, okay? Mason dragged you through the mud. You need to get back at him. Find someone better looking who makes more money."

This time, I do sigh. "I'm not interested in getting back at Mason."

It's the truth. Even though he's hurt me, I'm not a vengeful person. Making him hurt would just make me feel bad. Would he deserve me giving him back a little bit of what he gave me? Probably. But at the end of the day, I'd rather just leave him in the past where he wants to be. I'd rather think about the things in my life that are going better—the things that are making me happy again.

"This is your problem, Mara. You're too nice. You don't know how to stand up for yourself. I don't know where the hell you learned that, but it definitely wasn't from me."

My eyes stray to my guitar, regretting that I picked up her call.

"My problem is that my heart is broken," I argue, raising my voice only slightly to indicate that I'm getting upset with her.

"Your heart is—" she laughs again, scoffing. "You know what fixes a broken heart? Spite. And vengeance. And pride."

I shake my head. If that's true, then she wouldn't still be bitter about her own divorce. She wouldn't insist on me turning just as bitter and hateful as she is. More than anything, I don't want to live my life that way. It's...wasteful. And pointless. Because I'm positive my father, wherever he is, doesn't give either of us a passing thought, ill or otherwise. But she's just as hellbent as she was decades ago about showing him that she's doing so much better than he is. It's like a competition that he doesn't even know exists. And I refuse to put myself through that. I've been through enough. And I don't want to end up like my mother, still hurting about a man who wronged me decades later.

"I feel sad for you, Mom," I say softly. "You did all those things after you and dad split up, and you *still* are. You're not free from the hurt; you're just distracted by it."

Silence fills the line.

I've never said something like that to her before. I've never called her out. And I'd bet money that she's thinking how much more she likes talking to me when I have nothing to say. She likes it better when she can tell me what to do and I just say, "yes, Mom."

"I love you, Mom," I add gently, knowing this isn't easy for her to hear. "But I'm finding my own way here. I have a few people in my life who are good for me, and despite what you think about it, I *am* playing guitar again. I'm sorry if I'm not going about my divorce like you want me to, but some part of me will always love Mason despite what he did. I will always have good memories of him, even if he doesn't want to make any more with me. And trying to mess with him would only hurt him and hinder myself from moving on."

That's the most I've said to her in six months. From her silence, I know I've stunned her. But saying it feels good. Better than shouting at her would.

"Well," she says finally, her voice vibrating with suppressed anger, "clearly you have it all figured out. Suddenly you have all the answers. Well, *excuse me* for trying to help you when you obviously don't need it."

"Mom, I'm not—"

"*Excuse me*," she says, talking over me, "for caring. The

next time your life is falling apart, I'll just do you a favor and butt out."

I hear a click and pull my phone away from my ear, confirming that she's hung up on me. I sigh and toss it on the couch next to me.

"That went well," I mutter to myself.

I put my face in my hands for a moment, just breathing.

It's a hard thing to face that your own mother is toxic. I don't know why she's like that. Even before her divorce, she was never the warm, nurturing, maternal person I wished she would be. How she never picked that up from her own mother is beyond me. I know that I can personally attribute my own peace-loving ways to my grandmother. I've always been a lover, not a fighter, just like her. My mother is apparently a fighter.

I get up, leaving my guitar where it is, and go outside to sit on the top step.

October is moving along, bringing barren trees and cooler temperatures that only make me want warm things. Tea. Blanket scarves. Homemade soup and bread. A friend.

What I know I *don't* want is influences that berate me for being me. Even if that includes my own mother. I told her I would always need her, and that's true. I love her. But she needs to figure out how to have a conversation with me that doesn't include bullying me into whatever she thinks would make me look like I'm doing better than my ex-husband.

But I will say that it's desperately strange to live alone. To *be* alone. I was with Mason for almost ten years. I thought I would be with him for the rest of my life. And now...I just have me. No one to talk to as I get ready for bed. No one else to cook for. No one to care about, and no one to care about me. It feels lonely, especially with more of my things put away. I have a whole house to myself, my whole *life* to myself.

For the first time in my adult life, I'm on my own. And even if it's lonely, I also feel how good it is for me. I'm slowly finding my feet, figuring out what matters to me and what doesn't. Learning to forgive myself for my own mistakes. Choosing the things that are good and well-intentioned and genuine.

I look down at my fingertips again, smiling softly at them.

Slowly, I'm getting myself back. Not for my mom, or Mason, or anyone else. For me.

I drop my hand and tilt my face upwards toward the sun, warming my skin as I close my eyes and take a deep breath of the cool autumn air.

Everything is going to be okay. I'm certain of it.

Sean's truck bounces me slightly in my seat as he drives, Rosie in her car seat behind me. She's singing softly to herself, so quietly I can't quite hear her over the radio. It felt strange to climb up into his truck, especially without Linda. But she and Doug are in the car ahead of us, leading the way to Riverside Park where the farmer's market takes place every Saturday. So here I am, sitting next to Sean, trying not to feel like I'm infringing on something sacred and familial.

I've only been to the farmer's market once, years ago. Just me and my mom, walking by everyone's handiwork while she found something to complain about. Her time has always been the most valuable thing to her, so browsing through "mediocre" produce and crafts made her feel like she'd been robbed somehow. Her attitude had spoiled it for me, of course, and we never went back.

Doug's car pulls off to the side of the road to park since the small parking lot is full. Sean follows suit, and when the engine shuts off, I'm hit with a strange flurry of nerves.

There's a lot of people here.

I don't know why that matters. But the congestion of this event has me rethinking this idea.

Sean's door opens, but he pauses with one leg out. "You okay?"

"Huh? Oh, yes. I'm fine." I open the truck door and quickly get out to avoid making eye contact.

After shutting his door, he walks around the back to get Rosie out. I can feel his eyes on me for a beat before he unbuckles her. She hops down to the grass and then clings to my hand, her nervous expression pointed at the cars passing by on the road.

"It's okay, Rosiecakes," Sean says, and takes her other hand. "Let's go check it out."

"The Hendersons better be here," I hear Doug saying to Linda as we join them. "We have to recreate the way we met, right?" He grins and kisses Linda's blushing cheek. When she turns to greet us, her happy expression freezes on her face when she spots us.

"What?" Sean asks curiously.

Her friendly face softens, and she smiles at all three of us, and I realize immediately what she sees. Sean and I holding Rosie's hands. Like we're a family. My heart pangs in my chest, and I glance at him awkwardly. He frowns at his mother slightly, and I know that he realizes what this looks like, too.

"Nothing," Linda says, waving her hand at us in

dismissal, but as she turns away, she tries to discreetly wipe her eyes.

Linda said once in passing that Sean hasn't dated since his wife died, and how that's such a shame because he's a good man. I can't argue with the good man part, but it's clear to me how badly she wants him to be happy.

"Ooh, Daddy, can we swing first?" Rosie pipes up, pulling us forward.

Doug and Linda trail behind us as we approach where all the tents and tables are set up, bordering the wide tar sidewalk that leads to the playground. Beyond that is the Mississippi River, where a couple people have waded out to a few boulders and are fishing off them, probably for the last time this season.

People are filtering through, some stopping to shop or browse, others on their way to the playground. No doubt it's so busy because it's the last farmer's market of the season, but also because the weather is turning cooler, and soon, the playgrounds will be abandoned for building snowmen or snow forts instead.

"We'll meet you by the pumpkins," Linda says, and she and Doug break off to the left where a tent is set up with produce harvested by the Henderson family.

The crowds make me uneasy, but I focus on Rosie's little hand in mine, and we weave our way forward. My eyes snag on different items as we pass. Jams, honey, and baked goods. Painted signs that read "Hello Fall" and "Autumn Blessings." Crocheted hats and scarves. And at the end of the thoroughfare is Patrick's Pumpkins, whose offerings are displayed on a large picnic table and sprawled through the grass next to it leading to the playground.

Rosie lets go of my hand and sprints for the swings, Sean hot on her heels. I fold my arms over the plaid blanket scarf bundled around my neck and shoulders as I watch him push his daughter on the swing set.

"Hi, Mara!" she calls excitedly as I move a little closer, and I lift one hand to wave at her. Her happiness puts a smile on my face.

That smile only grows when Rosie decides she's done with the swings because she insists that Sean go through the entire playground with her. Watching him climb and slide and monkey bar has my heart feeling warm and content. He's such a good dad. He's the only parent in the middle of it with all the kids, and for a second, I wonder if he wants more kids. Did he and his wife plan on having a big family? So much was stolen from him, and like Linda, I want to see him happy. He deserves it.

A tiny whisper speaks up from somewhere deep inside, then. A quiet little yearning that causes goosebumps to rise all over my body.

I wish *I* could make him happy.

But that thought instantly triggers me. Because how many times did I think it when I was with Mason? Countless. And in the end, trying to make him happy was a complete waste of time.

My gaze drops down to my feet, and I hug myself a little tighter, feeling cold inside and out. I can't let myself fall into that again. Sean's happiness isn't my responsibility. The only person's happiness I'm responsible for is my own.

When I look up again, he's moving toward me with Rosie in his arms.

"Phew," he says as he gets closer, "I think I need a nap."

Rosie giggles. "Silly Daddy."

"What? I'm an old man."

179

She giggles again, and I do, too. Sean flashes a smile at me that makes my stomach flip and then puts Rosie down.

"Alright, let's go get some pumpkins." He takes her hand, and we head back the way we came.

I take in the multicolored gourds and different varieties and sizes of pumpkins as we come upon them. Rosie oohs and ahhs over the white pumpkins, and as soon as Doug and Linda join us, Doug jokes about taking home the biggest one of the bunch.

I smile at them all as they bicker and argue about which ones are the best for carving, and I feel...content. This is clearly a family outing, but every time I see these wonderful people, I feel more at home with them. I don't feel like I stick out with them or feel like I don't belong. It's balm for my lonely soul. Especially now that Sean's withering looks and frowns are gone. He doesn't even look surprised to see that I'm in his house anymore when he gets home from work. He seems to have accepted me into the pack, and I feel deeply privileged.

Family wasn't like this for me. The closest thing I had to it was Mason and his family, even though my mom never liked them and refused to share holidays with them. Family for me has always been sort of broken and jagged around the edges. The few times in my life that I actually felt like I was a part of something was when my grandma was alive. But it's been decades since then, and until I met Mason, I was mostly on my own. No wonder I dove headfirst into that relationship. I was desperate to feel like I belonged somewhere, like I was wanted.

Tears fill my eyes as I realize that the reason, I didn't want to get divorced was because I had nothing else. It wasn't because I loved him. It was because he had become the thing I felt secure in. Mason became something I didn't think I could exist without. I disappeared into him, and when he left, I had nothing.

I take a deep breath and let it out slowly.

That isn't true anymore. I'm more myself than I've been in a year. I'm not standing still anymore. I'm doing better. Without him.

"Mara?" Linda asks, jarring me from where I was staring at a pumpkin.

"Uh, hi," I blurt out, and quickly wipe at my eyes with my sleeve.

"Sweetheart, what's wrong?" She comes close and puts her arm around my shoulders.

"Nothing. I'm sorry. I'm fine. Just got lost in my head for a second." I sniff, blushing that she caught me sifting through the pieces of me I'm still trying to fit back together.

"Come here," she murmurs, and hugs me tightly.

I sigh and hug her back, eased by her gentle mothering. Over her shoulder, I see Sean frowning at me in a concerned sort of way. I give him a tight smile and then step back from Linda.

"Thank you. I'm okay," I assure her, and she loops her arm through mine to bring me closer to her family.

I focus back on the pumpkins, this time joining in on the bickering, and ten minutes later, we've each selected what we have decided are the best pumpkins for carving. Doug has a monster that weighs at least twenty pounds, Linda has a manageably-sized one that Doug doesn't approve of, Sean has an oblong one that he says will be perfect to carve a ghost into, Rosie has a small white one that she wants to paint instead of carve, and I have a smallish, perfectly round pumpkin with a curly stem.

Thankfully, Patrick's Pumpkins has a few grocery carts

to help folks bring their pumpkins to their cars, so Sean offers to run our picks to the truck. While he's gone, the rest of us go through the tables and tents, Linda buying a couple things while Doug wanders over to a tent with handmade jewelry. Rosie and I are looking through some scarves and mittens when Sean passes behind us with the empty cart, but then I notice he doesn't come back.

I crane my neck, looking back down the way toward the pumpkins and spot him standing a little ways' from it, sans cart, talking to a very familiar looking blonde woman.

The breath catches in my throat, and I instantly break into a panicked sweat.

Sarah.

She looks beautiful, as she always does. Every time I saw her at the hospital or a holiday party, she was always picture perfect. Her blonde hair is cut and styled to frame her smiling face, expert eye makeup paired with ruby lips, wearing a maroon-colored sweater dress that hugs her curves. No wonder Mason couldn't stay away from her. Especially with how bubbly and personable she is.

I actually thought we were friends once. Not close friends. But I considered her a good person who I could call on for a favor if I needed something. I thought she was friendly to everyone, not just Mason. What a fool I was. And I let him fall in love with her.

No.

He chose to fall in love with her. He chose to leave me. Nothing I could've said or did would have changed his mind.

Oh no...is he—is he with her?

The panic crescendos as I quickly glance around at all the faces nearby, but I don't see Mason anywhere. All I see is

Sarah leaning toward Sean, touching his arm as she laughs.

The thought of seeing Mason dissolves instantly as she touches Sean. Anger slithers through me, burning my throat and making me feel reckless.

"My friend Cheryl is going to *love* this," Linda says, suddenly next to me.

"Let me see, Grandma," Rosie says. My eyes stay on her father.

The chatter of the market grows quiet in my ears as Sean attempts to walk away, but Sarah stops him by the hand. Heat rises on my face as I watch the woman who stole my husband flirt with the man who—the man who what? Sean isn't...mine. He's...

I bite down on my lip as my fists clench.

He's *something* to me.

And there's no way I'm letting this woman sink her claws into him the way she did with Mason.

I start forward, Linda calling after me, and move through the smattering of people between me and Sean. I'm almost there when I catch his gaze, looking in my direction like he was trying to tell Sarah he should find his family, but when he spots me, his previously perturbed expression changes. He smiles at me.

My heart beats strong.

But it isn't until I'm standing in front of him and Sarah that I realize what I've forced myself into doing. Confronting Sarah is the last thing I ever thought I'd do.

Sarah's eyes land on me and instantly widen. But then she smiles, like we're old friends.

"Mara," she says warmly, though with a bit of a surprise.

"Hi, Sarah."

Sean stiffens, looking between us. "You two know each other?"

Sarah's smile deepens on one side, her eyes narrowing slightly. "We do know each other. Would you like to tell him, or should I?" Her smile turns smug as she looks at me, like she's daring me to say it.

My pulse spikes as I stand here, feeling weak and yet strengthened by my need to protect Sean. But then I see a familiar shape materializing from behind her. My eyes move over her shoulder to see Mason approaching, holding a handful of bags. Their purchases, apparently.

What strength I had leaves me then, and Sarah knows it.

Every bit of him is achingly familiar, yet I can see a difference in his face. Where before he was angered and irritated whenever I saw him, now he looks exhausted and worn down. Though his navy sweater looks the same, he wears it differently now.

"Mara?" Sean asks, seeing the way my expression fell.

I could run. I could turn and run and run and never stop. I could hide in my house for the rest of my life.

Or I could stand my ground. Face this. Face him.

I feel Sean's warm hand touch my lower back, and I brace myself as Mason looks up and sees me.

The last time I saw those green eyes was when I signed the divorce papers. He was impatient then and irritated. Now he looks stunned and displeased. The coldness of his gaze cuts me deep.

I swallow hard as he comes to a stop beside Sarah. She

leans into his side, smirking at me. And Sean, utterly confused, speaks first.

"Uh, hey. I'm Sean."

My past and my present colliding right in front of me.

CHAPTER NINETEEN

Sean

I don't know what the hell is going on right now. No one has answered my question about how Mara and Sarah know each other, and now here's this guy, whose presence has Mara looking like she's about to pass out.

I move my hand from her back to her waist, just in case she does faint. Just touching her at all gives me comfort. Before she came over here, Sarah was flirting to the max even though I was not responding. And from the way she's pulled herself against the guy next to her, I'm assuming he's her boyfriend. What a class act.

"Uh, hey," I say awkwardly, even though he isn't looking at me. "I'm Sean." Hopefully if I start off the introductions, I can figure out how everyone knows each other. But he ignores me.

"Hey, Mara," he says, not sounding happy at all to see her. "Funny running into you here."

Mara gives him a tight smile that looks much more like a grimace.

"I know," Sarah says with a loud laugh that tenses my

shoulders. "So funny."

He glances at Sarah, and then his eyes finally land on me, following my arm to where my hand is grasping Mara. Then he looks at her, a shadow of some negative emotion darkening his features.

Mara clears her throat, and I feel the shake of her knees all the way up her spine.

"I didn't catch your name," I blurt out irritably, done with being in the dark.

"This is Mason, my soon to be fiancé," Sarah answers for him with that teeth-bared smile, placing her hand on his chest. "Right, honey?"

Mason? Why does that name sound familiar?

Mara quivers under my hand, and when I look at her, she's wearing a number of expressions. Pain. Anger. Embarrassment. Grief.

I smooth my hand up and down her side, and she finally responds to me.

"Mason and I were—" Her small voice abruptly cuts off, and Mason rolls his eyes at her.

"We used to be married, and now we're not," he finishes for her.

Wait. *This* is her tool bag ex-husband? The one who cheated on her? Tension rolls through me as I look between the three of them.

"Wait, wait. Let me get this straight. This is your ex-husband?" I clarify.

Mara nods awkwardly, looking like she wishes she could disappear into the ground she's standing on.

"So, *this* is who he left you for?" I add, pointing at Sarah.

She nods again, her face more solemn and humiliated by the second.

Sarah just smiles that huge smile, like she's proud that she won Mason from his wife.

And all I can think is...wow.

"So, you chose *her* over Mara?"

Mason shifts uncomfortably on his feet and glances at his ex-wife. "I did."

I cover my mouth with my free hand, but it slips out anyway. "On...*purpose*?" And then a laugh rumbles up out of me before I can stop it.

All three sets of eyes are staring at me as I belly laugh like a little kid.

Sarah's smile slowly slides off her face. Mason's face turns red with anger. But I can't stop laughing. It's the best joke I've ever heard.

I can feel Mara staring at me like I've lost my mind, but I keep chuckling.

"So...so you left this sweet, amazing, kindhearted woman because you fell in love with this disingenuous, vain, serial flirt?" I slap my leg. "Great choice. Just, amazing job working that out."

I glance at Mara to find a small bit of amusement and appreciation in her eyes. I pull my arm around her shoulders, still chuckling.

"Well, this has been great. But we gotta run," I say, and steer Mara around with me. "Nice meeting you, Mason."

And then I turn us toward where my family is, leaving

that pair of fuming idiots behind.

"What a fool," I say to Mara as we make our way through a handful of people.

"Yeah," she agrees thoughtfully.

I look down at her, realizing my arm is still around her shoulders. "If you want me to let go, I will," I offer. "Not sure if you wanted to make him think we were—"

"No, I—I wasn't trying to make him jealous," she explains quickly. "I mean, my mom said I should but I—"

"It's alright, Mara. He got what he deserves anyway." I glance over my shoulder to see Mason and Sarah walking away from us, the tension visible between them.

I slide my arm off her, feeling a pang of regret as I do, but when I catch sight of my mother and notice the way her mouth slowly stretches into a knowing smile, it's obvious she saw my arm around Mara.

I caught the way she looked at us earlier when we all got out of the truck. She didn't have to say a damn thing for me to know how it felt for Mara to walk hand in hand with Rosie and me.

But all that is out of my mind now that I've just met the man who broke Mara's heart. And even though there's a part of me that really wants to go back there and put my fist through his teeth, I can't get over how satisfying it is to learn how massively he messed up.

Good for him, really. He deserves what he got. He deserves to be engaged to someone who, if her track record is any indication, doesn't give a damn about faithfulness or monogamy. Serves him right for running out on Mara.

"Who was that?" my mom asks us as we reach her. Rosie is holding her hand and smiling up at us, just like my mom is smiling at us.

"No one," I answer, biting my lip to keep from laughing again. "Where's Doug? Let's find him and head out. We've got some pumpkins to carve, right, Rosiecakes?"

She nods up at me, her light blue eyes wide and excited. I smile down at her, feeling oddly light, and bend down to pick up my little girl. I bring her up and plop her on my shoulders, her legs hanging over my chest as my mom spots Doug moving toward us.

"We'll see you at home," I say, and without a thought, the hand that isn't clutching Rosie's shin reaches for Mara's. My fingers intertwine with hers as we set off towards the truck, and suddenly, everything in the world feels right.

She fits with us. Like she's always been in our lives. Like this is where she belongs. With me and with Rosie. And not with that fool of an ex-husband.

And I want to believe that she thinks so, too. I imagine she would've let go of my hand by now if she felt differently. If she was just holding my hand in order to spare my feelings, her fingers wouldn't be tangled in mine so comfortably, like we've done this a thousand times.

Mason didn't know what he had, that much I'm sure of. No smart man would choose someone like Sarah over someone like Mara. He made the biggest mistake of his life when he divorced Mara, whether he realizes it or not.

And for the first time, I'm grateful for his mistake. If he wasn't such an idiot, I never would've met Mara. For the first time, I feel what Mara could be to me if I let her, if she wants to.

But as we get in the truck and I get Rosie buckled in, I remind myself that Mara is newly divorced. The way she clammed up when she saw Mason is proof that she's still reeling from what happened between those three. She needs time, I'm sure of it.

So, when I get into the driver's seat and pull out onto the road, I fight back the urge to reach over and hold her hand again. She's looking out the passenger's side window, her fingers playing with the hem of her scarf.

"You alright?" I ask quietly over the hum of the engine.

Mara looks over at me, her expression unreadable.

"I...I'm not sure, honestly."

I put my eyes back on the road. "Well, I know whose face I'll be picturing while we carve pumpkins," I say, throwing her a smile that she returns with her own little signature smile.

Even though we covered the kitchen table with newspaper, the kitchen is a mess. Every year, my mom comes up with a plan of attack that will keep us from finding pumpkin seeds behind the fridge or in our shoes a month later, but it never works. The mess is part of the fun, according to Doug.

My ghost is coming along pretty well, I think, even though I got a late start because I'm the designated scooper-outer of each pumpkin. Doug's is huge, with a perfectly carved jack-o'-lantern face cut into one side. Mom's is barely even touched, because she keeps stopping to clean up whatever pieces fall on the floor. Rosie's little white pumpkin is almost totally covered in every color there is, some of those colors also painted on her hands and face. Mara decided to paint her pumpkin, too, though the heart she's painted on it in red and pink isn't as vibrant against the orange backdrop.

She's been quiet, like she's inched back into the shell

that me and my family have coaxed her out of the last month. She could probably use some time to herself to work through what happened at the park earlier, but at the same time, I'm glad that we can all distract her from it. I don't want her to disappear back into herself where she's too far for me to reach.

"Angelface, will you just leave it? We can clean up when we're done," Doug insists, pulling my mom from her bent over position where she's gathering pumpkin pieces from under the table.

"He's right, Mom. You're missing the fun."

"Don't be a fun sucker," Doug adds with a laugh and gives her a peck on the mouth. "Come on, I'll help you."

I shake my head and go back to my own pumpkin, working on carving the eyes all the way through so the light from the flameless candles we bought can shine through them.

And when Mom and Doug finally get her pumpkin finished, Rosie and Mara have gone to wash up their hands in the bathroom. We've placed all our pumpkins out on the front porch, even Mara's, and I'm crumpling up the newspapers on the table when my mom stops me, leaning over the table.

"So, who were you talking to at the park? Mara went rushing off when she saw you talking to that woman."

For good reason, I think. Though there's a tiny part of me that hopes maybe Mara was jealous. But I really have no business hoping that.

"She's the school nurse," I explain blandly.

"Oh," Mom says, and watches me carefully as I throw away the newspapers. "She was pretty."

I raise an eyebrow at her. "Hmm. Didn't notice." I hold her suspicious gaze for a moment as she tries to work out what happened earlier. Whether I was interested in Sarah. If Mara was jealous. If I'm full of crap.

Before she can ask any more questions, Mara and Rosie return with clean hands and faces.

"Well, thank you for letting me join you guys today," Mara says to all of us, like she's about to leave and have dinner alone at her house. The idea of her not being at the table with us feels like a blunt knife being slowly pressed into my stomach.

"Of course," my mom says with a smile. "You're more than welcome to stay for dinner."

"Thank you, but I'm feeling a little under the weather. I think I need to just go home and rest," Mara says, and even I know it's a lie.

"Oh no! You're sick?" Rosie asks, and quickly hugs Mara's legs. "It's no fun to be sick," she says to her thigh. Mara smiles down at my daughter and strokes her hair.

"I'll be okay, sweet girl."

"Can I walk you back?" I offer.

She eyes me for a moment, knowing that I don't buy her claim of being under the weather. She nods, and I can feel her nerves from here.

She says goodbye to my family and Doug and then follows me to the front door where we get our shoes on. She wraps her big scarf around her neck and shoulders, avoiding my eyes, and then we step out onto the porch.

"You don't have to walk me back, you know," she says as we descend the steps.

"I want to."

She's silent the rest of the way, and I let her be. When we reach her steps, she turns to face me. The lingering sun through the naked trees behind us puts a soft glow on her face that I can't help admiring.

"I just wanted to make sure you're okay," I tell her.

Mara takes a deep breath, looking down at her shoes, and then lets it out slowly.

"I don't know, Sean," she answers, her voice so soft I can barely hear it. "I wasn't expecting to see them, obviously, so I was caught off guard...and of course it hurt to see Mason." Her brow gathers into a funny squiggle as she looks up at me with a puzzled smile. "But then you—you *laughed* at him."

My heart pounds as her face changes to something appreciative and warm.

"Of course, I laughed at him," I reply simply. "The guy made a horrible choice, Mara. You and I both know that."

She nods, her smile lessening but still present as she looks down again. "I guess I just expected you to hit him or give him a piece of your mind."

"Oh, believe me, I wanted to. I still do. Hell," I say, and gesture to the phone in her pocket, "call him up and get him over here if you want me to rough him up for what he did to you. I'd be more than happy to."

Her face tips up towards me, her blue eyes sparkling. "I'll keep that in mind."

I smile softly at her. "So, what are you going to do tonight?"

She glances behind her to her house and then back to me. "I think I need a date with my guitar."

My smile turns into a full-on grin. "That's my girl." My grin drops, and my eyes widen instantly.

Damn. It.

Why the hell did I say that?

Even in the glow of the sun, I can see her blush in surprise.

"I—I didn't mean *my* girl." I clear my throat awkwardly, feeling the pain of what I said bounce around my body like buzzing bees. "I just meant—you know, *attagirl*." I swing one fist through the air in front of me in some lame attempt at enthusiasm. "Uh, well..." I step back, realizing that I'm blushing, too, and Mara is probably doing her best not to laugh at my discomfort. "Have a good night."

"You, too," she says as I back away from her. She smiles at me sweetly and then turns to go up her steps. I turn around as well and book it back to my house, feeling like a teenager who doesn't know how to talk to the girl he likes.

It dawns on me how long it's been since I've been in a situation like this. Clearly, I'm out of practice. If Rhys had witnessed that, he would be on my case about it for the rest of my life.

I shake my head and go inside where I do my best to distract myself from thinking about it again.

But dinner and Rosie's bedtime routine do nothing to distract me. All I can think about is that little blush on Mara's face with maybe just a flicker of pleasure in her eyes. Maybe I imagined that part. But it makes me feel better to think that Mara wasn't disgusted by my little flub.

"Alright, lights out, Rosiecakes," I say, and get up from her bed to turn off her lamp. I look back at her before I turn the switch, making sure she's settled in and comfy, and it's then that I see a sad look on her little face. "What's the matter?"

Rosie sighs. "Mara will be better tomorrow, right?"

My stomach does a little flip. "Of course, sweetie."

"There's a boy in my class whose daddy got sick, and he didn't get better."

"Don't worry, okay? Mara will be fine."

She nods, but I can still tell something is bothering her, so I leave the light on and go back to lie down on her bed next to her. I watch her think for a long moment, her blue eyes pointed up at the ceiling. My own eyes follow the little slope of her nose, the exact slope her mother had, and I feel a little pang of grief.

"I'm the only kid in my class that doesn't have a mommy," Rosie says finally, her voice just above a whisper.

I inwardly curse.

Is this it? We have to have this conversation? The one where I tell her there's no replacing her mother? Are we finally going to have the talk my mother has been telling me will come someday? The one about needing a mother...?

"You do have a mommy," I remind her gently.

She sighs again and turns onto her side to face me. I lift my hand and brush her blonde hair back from her face.

"But she's gone," Rosie reminds me back.

"That doesn't mean she didn't love you." My chest aches as I say it. Because after it happened, I doubted Gabby's love. For Rosie. For me. But it isn't about whether Gabby loved us because she was beyond being able to express it. Whether she loved us or not, she still chose death. I tried to love her better, but sometimes, it isn't enough.

Rosie's eyes meet mine and stay there. "Do you still love Mommy?"

The question hurts like a blow to the head. Gabby is the only woman I've ever loved. I dated a few women before

196

her, but each one was short lived. Gabby's lively spirit is what captured me the first time I met her, and by the second date, I knew I was a goner. But even so, since her death, I feel so many other things for her than love. I'm angry at her for doing what she did. I'm angry at myself for not doing anything to stop her. I feel grief and longing for what I had and what I lost.

But those are things Rosie will never need to know about. I'm not sure I'll ever tell her how Gabby died. At least not until she's an adult and has the emotional capabilities to process it. I just don't want my daughter to think that Gabby didn't love her because she didn't stay alive for us.

"Of course. I'll always love your mommy."

Her blonde eyebrows pull together. "So, you'll never love anyone else? Ever again?"

I sigh. "I don't know, Rosiecakes. I'm okay being alone. My heart is full enough with you and your grandma."

I've really never seriously thought about moving on with someone else. Even though Gabby has been gone for five years, I still am just as filled up with her as I was when she was alive. Filled up with her choice and my own guilt.

Rosie thinks about that for long enough that I assume she isn't going to say anything else, but then she opens her mouth and says the last thing I expected.

"You were holding Mara's hand at the market," she whispers, big eyes blinking at me in a sad, yet hopeful way.

"I—I was," I stammer hoarsely. Of course, she noticed that.

"Do you like Mara?" she asks before I can think of an explanation for why I was holding Mara's hand when I really had no business doing that.

"I do like Mara, but we're friends, Rosie."

I don't have to guess what Rosie is thinking. She wants Mara to be her mom. Something about that idea confuses the hell out of me. Because part of me understands what Rosie sees in her—this warm, understanding soul who fits in with our family so well. But I also see the same darkness in Mara that stole my wife away from me. Even though I know Mara is trying and is taking steps to get back on her feet after her divorce, I'm still scared that something could change, and she would leave us just like Gabby did.

"It's okay if you hold her hand, Daddy," she says, bringing my focus back to her. She pats my stubbly cheek lightly. "She likes holding your hand, too."

"Oh? And how do you know that?"

"Because she was smiling the whole way back to our truck."

She was? Why does that information light up my insides? It shouldn't. It shouldn't make a difference to me whether it felt as natural to her as it did to me. But it does.

Damn.

CHAPTER TWENTY

Mara

The days are shorter now. The evening sets in earlier and earlier, bringing the dark cover of night even before each dinner with the Dunbars. The trees are bare sticks, each leaf having drifted away from its woody perch. The house across the street went all out with Halloween decorations, but my stoop is empty. Dressing up for Halloween has never been my favorite thing about the holiday. I've always liked opening the door to each witch, pirate, monster, and princess.

So, when my neighbors come around, I'm more than pleased to see them. The minute I open my door, Rosie barks in between the words "trick or treat" and I take in the three of them. I laugh, because somehow Linda convinced her son to dress up like a dog, and he does not look pleased about it.

Rosie's cheerful face is painted brown with a white spot around one eye and a red tongue painted down her chin. She's wearing a headband with two black dog ears attached, and so is Linda. But Sean's ears are pinned to his baseball cap, and he's foregone the face paint.

"What are you supposed to be?" he asks me gruffly,

gesturing with Rosie's pumpkin candy bucket.

I glance down at my jeans and t-shirt, which is very obviously not a Halloween costume, and then dart inside to grab my guitar. I sling it over my shoulder and reappear at the door.

"I'm a rockstar," I claim.

Sean chuckles under his breath. "Nice save," he mutters. I'm sure he's wishing he could've gotten away with a "costume" like mine, but I personally love that he's caved for his daughter.

"Yay! Play us a song!" Rosie says, clapping her hands.

I laugh softly at her. Her enthusiasm pleases me, even though I know I could just strum a few chords, and she would be excited.

"Maybe later, Rosie Posie. You have more trick or treating to do," Linda reminds her and tugs affectionately on one of her granddaughter's floppy dog ears.

Rosie doesn't seem convinced but immediately perks up when I dump three handfuls of candy into the bucket her dad is still holding for her.

"Say thank you," Sean demands gently.

"Thank you, Mara!"

"You're welcome, sweetie."

"When the trick or treaters are all through, make sure you come over for some apple cider, okay dear?" Linda says, her brown face paint wrinkling as she smiles in the exterior light.

"I'll be there."

I watch my friends head back down the sidewalk, remembering how hard it was for me to accept Lindas invitations when I first moved here. Now I'm over almost every night, sitting with them at their kitchen table like I'm part of their family. I basically *am* part of their family...more so than I'm a part of my own now that me and my mom aren't talking. Without the Dunbars, I'd be totally alone.

I thoroughly enjoy handing out candy for the next two hours. Seeing all those happy kids warms me up and has me thinking once again about having some of my own one day. It stings a little still that it won't be with Mason, but there's nothing I can do about that now. At this point, I don't even *want* to do anything about it. Mason is moving on with Sarah.

It's been almost a year since Mason asked me for a divorce. And even though I fought like hell to change his mind at first, now I'm feeling the deep breath that is my new life. It feels good for my focus to be shifting away from him and on myself and what makes me happy.

Over the last week, I've been playing for hours every day. Sometimes just random things. Sometimes old songs of my own or someone else's. My calluses are back. And yesterday I felt the tiniest little push inside to sing. Like *really* sing. Not just sing a lullaby or nursery rhyme to Rosie.

I'm coming back to myself, and I have more hope than I did before that things are getting better. That *I'm* getting better. My heart is being filled little by little with the things I love, and the things that broke my heart are slowly being drained out. This is my beginning, and I'm feeling more and more ready to leave the hurt in the past where it belongs.

The only thing I can change is my future. And so far, I'm happy with what the future looks like. Me, singing and playing again. And me, making dinner and eating with the Dunbars.

This is what's on my mind as I walk over to my neighbors' with a plate of homemade caramel apples in my hands hours later. Even though it's Halloween and not

Thanksgiving, I feel extremely thankful for them.

The chilly evening air sends a shiver down my spine as I step up to their porch. It won't be long now before the snow starts falling I smile to myself as I knock and open the door, thinking that I'll need to shovel a path from my front door to theirs soon.

Inside, I find Rosie still in her dog costume, on her knees with all of her candy spread out in front of her on the blue living room rug. She doesn't look up or greet me as I close the door behind me; she's too concentrated on sorting her candy.

The TV is on, playing *It's The Great Pumpkin, Charlie Brown* with the volume only a little louder than the talking going on across the room between Doug, who is dressed up like a dog as well, Linda, also still in costume, and Sean, who has removed his dog ear hat.

Standing next to him is a man I've never met who's apparently stolen Linda's dog ear headband and is wearing it instead. He laughs at something Doug says, his acquired dog ears flying as he throws his head back.

Sean's brown eyes find mine, and he returns my smile. Just that alone has my heart beating a little faster. That quiet little nudge I feel whenever I see him is almost second nature now. I haven't bothered to dissect it, mostly because I know that nudge is a gut feeling. And it's a good gut feeling.

"Happy Halloween, Mara," Doug calls across the living room.

"What did you bring?" Linda asks, coming closer. "Wow, those look delicious! Rosie, look—Mara brought caramel apples."

But Rosie continues her sorting, a very serious expression hiding beneath her face paint.

I just laugh and give the plate to Linda.

"Let's go put these in the kitchen and get you some cider."

It isn't until I turn to follow Linda that I realize the stranger next to Sean is staring at me with his mouth open. He snaps it shut as soon as I move forward.

"Hey, Mara," Sean says warmly, gesturing to me in welcome with his mug of cider.

"Hey."

"Wait," the stranger says, sticking out his muscular arm to keep me from following Linda through the kitchen doorway. His dark blue eyes widen as he looks at me. "*This* is Mara?"

"Uh...yeah," Sean answers skeptically.

He looks back and forth between me and Sean for a moment.

"You didn't tell me she was so beautiful," he scolds, and promptly smacks Sean in the stomach with the back of his hand. Sean heaves a vehement *oof* and clutches his stomach with a glare.

Doug chuckles heartily at Sean.

I blush at his words, mostly because I get the sense that this guy isn't trying to hit on me. He's meaning to pay me a compliment and not flatter me.

"I'm Rhys," he finally introduces, offering me his hand to shake as he takes a step closer. When I put my hand in his rough palm, he gives it a friendly squeeze. As he moves back slightly to stand next to Sean again, I notice that he has a white scar bisecting his left eyebrow.

"My *best friend*," Sean adds, raising his eyebrows at Rhys, who doesn't notice.

"It's nice to meet you, Rhys."

"You, too. I've heard so much about you. Sean won't shut up." Rhys gets a back hand to the stomach this time.

"*Oof.* Hey!"

"*Dude,*" Sean hisses, and then looks back to me. "I don't talk about you that much."

I chuckle, blushing again, and a little thrill goes through me when I realize Sean is blushing, too.

"Uh huh. Riiiight," Rhys agrees sarcastically, rolling his eyes as he absently rubs at the spot where Sean hit him.

Linda reappears, a white mug of steaming cider in her hand, outstretched for me to take.

"Oh, thank you," I say, and bring it close to my lips. The delicious autumn scent of cinnamon, clove, orange, and apple swirls in front of my nose, and I smile.

"So, if I asked Mrs. D if you talk about Mara all the time," Rhys continues, smirking, "she would—"

"Do *not* ask—"

"Of course, he does," Linda happily interrupts her embarrassed and irritated son. Doug laughs again.

"Mom, really? You talk about her more than I do," Sean argues. The blush staining his cheeks is one of the sweetest things I've ever seen.

"Why wouldn't I talk about her?" she replies with a casual shrug. "I'm her biggest fan." She winks at me, and I giggle softly and take a sip of cider.

"No, I think that's Sean," Rhys claims, and quickly steps out of the way as Sean tries to smack him again. He laughs, his head tipping back again, those dog ears flopping.

"That's it," Sean snaps. "You've been demoted. You're no longer my best friend." He stalks off past me into the kitchen.

"Ah, come on!" Rhys calls after him, and then winks at me with a huge grin. "Don't be so dramatic!" He steps a little closer to me. "I was just kidding," he says, lowering his voice conspiratorially. "He doesn't really talk about you all the time; I just love getting under his skin."

I chuckle at that.

"It really is fun," Doug agrees. "Glad you're around to give him a hard time, Rhys. He needs to loosen up a little sometimes."

"I think he might disagree with you on that one," he replies with a snicker.

"I can hear you!" Sean shouts from the kitchen, and we all laugh. I lean forward to look around Linda, trying to see if he's coming back to join us, but I can't see him from here.

"Anyone want a caramel apple?" I ask the group with a smile.

"Absolutely," Rhys answers. "Let's do this." He heads into the kitchen, and I follow behind his tall frame.

Sean is sulking by the sink, his mug of cider refilled and held in one hand, resting on his arm folded across his chest. He glares at Rhys and leans his hips back into the counter behind him.

"You're not really demoting me, are you? We've been best friends since we were kids."

Sean says nothing and sips his cider. I try as hard as I can not to smile, but I can't help it. I have to agree with everyone else; it really is fun to get under Sean's skin a little.

"Guess I could be your best friend," I say to Rhys, and he beams like I just told him he won the lottery. "Seems you have a vacancy."

"That's right," he agrees, and moves towards me. He throws his arm around my shoulders. He smells like Irish Spring and sawdust. "Have you met my best friend, Sean? Get ready, 'cause I'll be talking about her all the time."

I glance over at Sean and find his face is so red that he's about to erupt steam from his ears. My heart stutters. He's really mad. Like not just irritated or annoyed...he's actually angry. He's glaring between me and Rhys, looking like he's trying to use his eyes to burn off Rhys's hand where it's resting on my shoulder.

But then, something changes in his expression. In a split second, the anger is gone and replaced by pain. It's a pain I don't understand, but also a pain I recognize. It's the pain of grief.

I gasp to see it, feeling like I've been stabbed, and instantly step out of Rhys's grasp.

"Sean," I croak out, but it's too late. He sets his mug down on the counter and charges out of the room. A second later, I hear the front door open and then close.

Rhys curses under his breath, and I look at him. Deep remorse and worry cloud his expression as his eyes stay on the doorway to the living room.

"I'll go after him," I say, already needing to explain myself.

"No," Rhys argues quietly. "He needs a minute. Then I'll go out and talk to him."

I nod even though I can barely keep myself standing in this room when I know Sean is hurting.

"I shouldn't have said that. About being your best friend. That was—"

"Hey, you didn't do anything wrong," he says, clutching my shoulder. "His reaction has nothing to do with what you said or even what I said, okay?" He releases me. "He was well aware that we were teasing."

"Then what happened?"

Rhys sighs and hesitates for a moment. "I think he realized—"

"What's the matter with Sean?" Linda asks worriedly, appearing in the doorway.

"He's all right, Mrs. D. I'll go talk to him." Rhys gives me one more consoling look, and then he leaves the house.

Linda and I share a concerned look, and then she nods me out to the living room where she and I sit with Doug on the couch. We pretend to watch the movie, but I know we're both thinking about her son.

I sip my cider distractedly, my mind continuously on the muffled sound of Rhys's voice on the other side of the front door.

Rosie has laid down on her stomach on the floor in front of me, her chin rested on her hands as she examines her spoils.

Rhys stays out on the porch with Sean for at least twenty minutes. It takes all my focus to stay seated and not rush out there, too. And when Rhys comes back in without his best friend, my chest aches.

"Is he okay?" I demand, getting to my feet.

Rhys shrugs off his jacket and hangs it up on one of the hooks next to the door. "He's okay. He said he'll come inside in a minute."

I nod and sit down again next to Linda. I study Rhys's face, trying to get an idea of what they talked about, but I don't know how to read him. He gives me a reassuring smile and then disappears into the kitchen.

Linda squeezes my hand and then goes to wash off her face paint, leaving me and an oblivious Doug sitting on the couch.

My eyes go to the front door. I wait. And wait. Five minutes pass, and I can't take it anymore. I hop up, move carefully around Rosie and her littles piles of sorted candy, and sink my feet into my shoes.

I step out into the cold and see Sean standing to the left, his arms folded across his chest and his chin tucked down against the collar of his plaid jacket. My heart wants to break knowing I had a hand in making him feel like this.

"I didn't mean what I said," I tell him, my nerves dancing in my stomach.

He stays perfectly still, but I know he heard me. I step closer until I'm a few feet in front of him.

The laughter of a few older trick or treaters drifts across the dark street towards us, reminding me that he and I aren't the only ones in the world.

"I know," he says at last.

I nod, not sure what else to say. I watch him, his tumultuous body language holding my attention hostage as his mind whirs.

"Gabby used to joke around with him like that," he tells me, his voice rough.

My stomach drops.

"They used to rib me like that all the time. And

tonight...it just reminded me of that." He scrubs one hand down his face. "I miss her, you know?"

My heart cracks as he avoids my eyes. "I'm so sorry, Sean."

He nods, still looking down at the decking below our feet.

I wish I could steal his pain. I wish I could heal his hurt and ease his grief. But I know just as much as he does that it doesn't really work that way. Not if we don't let it.

I swallow hard, and before I can stop myself, I move forward and hug him tight. He hugs me back, breathing in and out against me. The nudge this time feels much more like a kick to my stomach, and I squeeze him tighter.

"I want you to know that..." I trail off, my emotions ramping up. I clear my throat. "I consider you to be my closest friend."

He pulls back, but his arms stay around my waist. "Really?"

I nod slowly, my heart aching. "You've seen me at my worst, Sean." I sniff, tears springing to my eyes. "You're the *only* one who's seen me at my worst," I correct myself. "I don't take that lightly."

He stares at me, his expression filled with surprise and vulnerability. My heart beats harder in my chest. When a tear slips down my cheek, he lifts his hand and wipes it away with his thumb.

"I don't either," he whispers, making goosebumps break out over the surface of my skin.

Relief sinks in, and I breathe easier. The depth of unease I felt at hurting his feelings caught me off guard. It makes me realize that Sean is a bigger piece of my newfound happiness than I thought.

My shoulders tense at that. I don't want another man to step up onto the pedestal that Mason vacated. I can't let my peace be dependent on a man's role in my life. If there's one thing I've learned lately, it's that.

Even if Sean is important to me, I need to make sure I don't lose myself again. Because the soulful way he's looking at me...it would be far too easy to disappear into him just like I did with Mason.

"Good." I take a step back, mostly because I think I should and not because I want to. I miss the warmth of his arms around me almost instantly.

"Mara?" he asks softly, his hands slipping into the pockets of his jeans.

"Yeah?"

He hesitates for a long moment, making me nervous and reminding me of the early days when he and I didn't quite know how to talk to each other.

"What were you really doing on the bridge that day?"

My body stills.

Sean's question hangs in the air between us as I tremulously comprehend what he's really asking me. I blush slightly in embarrassment and look away. But despite my discomfort, he doesn't take back his question or apologize for asking. This is something he really wants to know. And maybe he deserves to know if it's still something he thinks about.

I fiddle with the sleeves of my sweatshirt as I go back in my mind to that moment.

"I was out walking," I explain quietly to the space between me and him. "Mason had just called me for some menial thing and...I don't know, everything just sort of hit me at once." I swallow down the lump in my throat. "I was upset and..." My heart beats loudly in my ears as I gain the courage to say it. "...and for just a second, I thought about jumping."

I blink back my tears and look up at Sean. His dark eyes peer into mine fearlessly, but the furrow of his eyebrows gives away how terrified he really feels.

"But I swear," I choke out, "I wasn't going to. The second I thought it, I knew I could never do it. I...I didn't *want* to do it. I still don't."

The dim porch light highlights the moisture accumulating on his lashes. A moment's worth of silence passes, the air thick with all the words he isn't saying.

"I'm so—" His gruff voice breaks. "I'm *so* glad you didn't."

I give him a watery smile. "Me, too."

He weakly gestures for me to come close again, and I do without hesitating, forgetting already that I don't want to let myself disappear into him. I bury my face in his shoulder and cling to him like I'm allowed to. Like he's mine. Like I'm his.

And when his hand strokes the back of my head and my long hair intertwines in his fingers, I close my eyes at how intimate it feels. The warmth of his body and his sawdusty scent wrap me up and take me to a place where my entire history with Mason never existed.

My spirit breathes in a peaceful, healing breath.

"Promise me," he says in a low voice near my ear, "that if you ever feel like that again, you'll call me, okay?" His soft voice makes my heart melt. "I don't care if I'm working or if it's in the middle of the night; I'll come find you."

I nod into his shoulder. "I promise."

He strokes my back. "Promise me again." His voice is weak and filled with emotion, bringing more tears to my eyes.

I pull back enough to look him in the face, seeing his concern and his fear in the tears welled in front of his golden-brown eyes. It makes my heart squeeze to see with my own eyes and hear with my own ears just how much he cares about me.

"I promise."

He sniffs slightly, and before he releases me, he does the last thing I expect. He leans down and casually brushes his lips against my temple, like it's something he does all the time.

That nudge kicks hard from deep inside me, forcing me to analyze it for the first time. Only one word forms in my mind.

You.

"Let's go in," he says, and I mindlessly obey, my brain a tangle of things I can't separate.

CHAPTER TWENTY-ONE

Sean

All I can think about when we go inside is that I almost kissed her. I barely got myself to swerve in time so my mouth landed on her temple and not her lips. But I couldn't help wanting to kiss her...not after she said she never wanted to jump, and she still doesn't.

Something dislodged in my heart when she promised me that she would reach out to me if she ever felt that upset again. She's more than trying. She's doing. She's actively choosing to participate in her new life without Mason. And with me.

Not *just* me, obviously. My family, too. And if anything, that just makes me want her all the more.

She's down on the floor with my tired daughter, asking about her favorite candy and which house gave it out. I see Mara's gentle smile and intentionality with Rosie, and a slow joy fills me up.

I couldn't describe this relief even if I tried.

She doesn't want her life to end.

Not anymore. Not ever. She's here, and she plans to stay. She's safe. I'm not going to lose her like I lost Gabby.

Oh, Gabby...

I almost lost my mind with grief earlier in the kitchen. Seeing my best friend rib me in a way he hasn't since Gabby died hurt like hell. It was like old times for a second, except sweet Mara was standing there instead. It was like losing Gabby all over again.

"This is getting itchy," Rosie whines as she scratches at her face paint, catching my attention. I know that tone. She's exhausted.

"Let's go wash it off," I say and carry her through the living room and kitchen to the bathroom across the hall from Rosie's room.

I set her down on the counter next to the sink and grab a washcloth from the drawer below her feet.

She yawns wide as I scrub at the face paint my mother so carefully applied earlier, the wet washcloth turning more and more brown as Rosie's pink skin is revealed.

"You have fun tonight, kiddo?"

She nods a little, her eyes closing as I finish my job.

"You look pretty tired, Rosie. Let's get you to bed."

I toss the washcloth in the hamper and pick her up. Her head rests on my shoulder as I take her across the hall to her darkened room.

I hold her for a moment, closing my eyes, trying to soak in the age she is. She won't need me like this forever, and I know she'll be a teenager before I know it.

When Gabby died, I was terrified of raising her on my own. I was scared I'd do everything wrong and that I'd never be the parent I could've been with Gabby by my side. But I know Rosie gets the best parts of me. She deserves it.

I take in a deep breath and then let it out slowly.

"Love you, Rosie."

She says nothing in response, and when I lay her down and cover her up, she barely stirs. I kiss her forehead and then close the door behind me.

I lean against her door and look up at the ceiling, feeling grief and anger because of Gabby's final act. Thank God I'll always have a piece of her in Rosie. I know I can do right by both of them as long as I keep doing my best to love that little girl.

"Well, I think I'm going to head out," Rhys says, his voice carrying from the kitchen. "Thanks for having me, Mrs. D."

I head down the hall to the kitchen as my mother answers.

"Of course. Don't be a stranger, okay? Especially because it seems like you and Mara hit it off."

I pause in the hallway, my mind zipping back to him with his arm around Mara. To say my blood was boiling is an understatement. I've never felt that kind of burning jealousy in my life. And when he called her beautiful? Well, he"s lucky I only smacked him in the stomach.

For just a few minutes, I entertained the thought of Rhys being interested in Mara, and I nearly snapped. My best friend is a good man. But Mara doesn't belong with him.

She belongs with me.

I swallow hard at that thought.

"Yeah, she's great," Rhys agrees warmly. "But we both know our boy is falling for her."

My mom chuckles. "Yes, we do. But does *he* know he's falling for her?"

"He is a little dense," Rhys teases, and I roll my eyes when they both laugh.

"Dense, huh?" I ask as I enter the kitchen. Neither one startles or seems to care that I heard them talking.

Rhys grins at me. "Just calling it like I see it, man." He removes my mom's dog ear headband and gives it back to her with a wink. She puts it on her head even though she already washed off her face paint.

I glance through the doorway into the living room where Mara and Doug are talking quietly on the couch. When I look back at Rhys, he's eyeing me seriously.

"What?"

His expression softens. "Don't be afraid to go after her if you want her."

My heart stutters in my chest.

The question isn't *if* I want her. My fear of losing her like I lost Gabby has been eradicated by what she said tonight. Now that I know I can trust Mara to keep living, I can't keep myself from entertaining what Rhys is saying.

"Gabby would've liked her," he adds with a sad smile, his voice quiet and honest.

"Yes, she would've," Mom agrees, sounding like she suddenly has a head cold.

I clear my throat, uncomfortable with this topic, but I know they're right. Mara is one in a million. And even though moving on from Gabby feels like shards of glass puncturing my lungs, I know I can't live in the past forever. No matter how much I deserve to for not saving her.

"Just think about it," Rhys presses, and then slaps a hand on my shoulder in farewell. I watch him retreat into the living room where he waves to Mara and Doug, and then he disappears through the front door.

When I look back at my mother, she's wiping her eyes with a paper towel. She tosses it in the garbage next to her and then folds her arms.

"You haven't been happy in such a long time, Sean," she says quietly. "I know I'm not imagining how much happier you've been lately."

Unease prickles my stomach. "I know."

"I think she feels the same way," Mom whispers.

I don't know that for sure. I've learned that Mara is the kind of person who would do anything for anyone. Her kindness to me and my daughter could be strictly platonic.

Then again, I know I'm not imagining that she feels what I feel whenever I touch her. Holding her feels like heaven to me, and the way she sinks into me like she finds just as much contentment in my touch as I do must mean she has a sweet spot for me.

But I also know that Mason hurt her deeply. Being cheated on has probably affected how she views love and relationships. It hasn't even been that long since she got divorced.

I bite my lip and shake my head slightly. "I don't think she's ready, Mom," I whisper back. "She just got divorced and—"

"And she's getting over him. I'm sure of it," she insists, whisper-shouting at me like she used to when I would act up in public as a boy.

I sigh heavily and grip the back of my neck. "It's too soon. She needs more time."

"*She* does? Or *you* do?" she hisses.

I narrow my eyes slightly. I don't appreciate her lecturing me on this, and I've about had enough.

"What about *you*, Mom?" I drop the whisper now.

"What?" she asks, confused.

"I know Doug wants to marry you."

She flushes red. "We're not talking about me right now; we're talking about you."

I roll my eyes at her defensive tone. "Don't act like I'm the only one who's holding back from taking the next step."

Her lips press into a straight, angry line. "It's not the same."

I scoff loudly. "Right. Keep thinking that." I stride to the fridge, throw it open, and reach for a can of beer.

Before she can offer a retort, I escape to the living room and sit next to Mara on the couch.

"Angelface, you ready for the movie?" Doug calls towards the kitchen doorway.

"Movie?" Mara asks.

"We watch *Beetlejuice* every year when Rosie goes to bed," I explain as I crack open my beer. I take a healthy swig, not in the mood for watching a movie.

"Oh. I've never seen that," she says.

"You haven't?" Doug asks. "My kids loved it growing up." He chuckles. "Especially the part where they all sing." And then he does a horrible impression of the scene where everyone is possessed.

Mara, who's never seen this movie, and has an ear for music, goes wide-eyed and tries to stifle her laughter with her hands. Her sweet smile has the tension leaving my shoulders.

But then my mother paces into the room and stands between the coffee table and the TV. Her face is set and pensive, and when Doug sees her expression, his singing thankfully commences.

"What's wrong, Angelface?"

Mom stares me down for a moment, and I feel completely clueless as to what's about to come out of her mouth.

She places her hands on her hips and moves her very serious eyes to Doug. "I love you," she says matter-of-factly.

Confused, Doug says, "I love you, too."

She nods, all of us watching her. After a moment where she seems to collect her thoughts, she takes a deep breath.

"You've been nothing but sweet to me from the moment I met you," she says to Doug calmly.

He glances at me, still confused about what's going on.

"I wasn't sure if I was ready to move on after Grant died." Tears appear in her eyes as she talks about my dad. "But you were patient until I was ready. And you're still being patient with me now." She sniffs and takes another deep breath. "I've been holding off on taking the next step with you because I wasn't sure if my family was ready. But I realized tonight that I need to lead by example. I need to show them that it's okay to move on."

What she's doing dawns on me then.

"Mom, you don't have to—"

She holds up her hand to me, and I fall silent.

"I love you, Doug. I didn't think I could love someone like this again, but I can't help it. Loving you is easy. And I want to spend the rest of my life loving you."

Mara gasps next to me, catching on.

Doug's face is wet as he smiles lovingly at my mother from where he still sits on the couch on the other side of Mara.

"Douglas Arnold Gabrielson, will you marry me?" Mom asks, smiling through her tears, too.

He laughs and gets up. He hugs her close and kisses the top of her head, right next to the dog ear headband she's still wearing.

"Do you realize you just proposed in a dog costume?" he chokes out through his laughter.

My mom laughs too and then pulls back. "So?"

Doug beams down at her for a second, but then he looks over at me. For his blessing, I realize. I've always had a lot of respect for Doug, but he just gained some more. I look between them and then give him a nod. He more than has my blessing.

He grins at me and then looks back to Mom. "Yes."

And then they kiss, and I try not to throw up and cry at the same time. Mara is beaming that beautiful smile and yet there's a wistfulness to it as well that makes me wonder how Mason proposed. I shake my head, deciding I don't want to know.

"Where's the ring?" Doug teases, holding out his hand.

My mom rolls her eyes at him and turns toward me and Mara. She gives me a knowing look, like she's trying to say, "it's your turn now."

"Congratulations, you guys," Mara exclaims, and gets up to hug them both. I follow suit as well.

When I pull back from Doug, I offer him my hand. He shakes it firmly.

"Promise me you'll take good care of her," I say before I release his hand.

"It would be my honor."

After that, we spike the cider with some celebratory rum and settle in to watch *Beetlejuice*.

The mid-morning November air is brisk, even with the sun shining down on me as I buzz through the last branch with my chainsaw. The forecast for the week includes a frost warning, which is making our job more complicated. The last thing I want is to slip and hurt myself.

But if I had to guess, business should slow down a bit now that winter is approaching. Rhys has a couple of roof rakes, so in the winter, we also service people's homes to prevent ice dams on roofs. He's also been talking about getting a plow for the front of his truck so that we can get in on the plowing business as well.

I let off on the chainsaw as the limb drops. I look down to where Rhys drags it towards his truck.

My life has been incredibly consistent since Gabby died. It took me some time to soldier through what happened, but I did see a grief counselor for the first year after I found her dead in the tub. I know that without that help, I don't think I could've ever given Rosie a bath myself or even *look* at a bathtub. After that, I went back to work climbing trees while my mom stepped in to watch Rosie. We each settled into a comfortable routine that I didn't see changing any time soon.

But that was before the house next door went up for sale and Mara bought it. That was before she befriended my daughter and my mother. That was before her gentle smile became my favorite thing.

Before, I used to zone out up here in the treetops and not think about the hole Gabby left behind. But now, I find myself thinking about Mara instead. Now I feel myself in a permanent state of anticipation until I can see her again.

It feels strange to be so filled up with someone. It feels...good, but...I also feel guilty. I married Gabby. She was my best friend. I still love her. Having feelings for Mara seems unfaithful.

But it isn't. I'm not in a relationship with Gabby anymore because she chose something else. She released me from our wedding vows when she sank down into that water.

"You good, man?" Rhys calls up to me.

I wave down at him and then start my descent.

His chat with me the other night on the porch hasn't left my mind. He didn't apologize for ruffling my feathers, but he did remind me that I'm allowed to be happy again. It wasn't easy for me to hear. Losing Gabby has weighed on my shoulders every second since she's been gone. I could've saved her, and the guilt I feel over failing has never left me.

Rhys doesn't get it. I don't deserve to be happy. I don't deserve to find a nice girl and settle down with her. Not when I could've prevented Gabby's death.

But I know better than to voice that to anyone. Most all Rhys, who knew Gabby before I did. He wouldn't hesitate to call me an idiot.

Hell, maybe I *am* an idiot. Because I'm falling for the woman next door whether I deserve her or not.

Rhys meets me at the bottom and helps me take apart the rest of the dead tree. By the time we're done and the wood is taken care of, it's past noon, and sawdust is stuck to the sweaty skin on my face and neck. I'm thankful for the cool temperatures today.

We pack up our job site, and as I'm removing my harness, I hear my phone beep from inside my pocket. Rhys honks at me as he drives away, and I throw the last of my things into the backseat. I check my phone once I get into the driver's seat and am surprised and stupidly elated to see that Mara has sent me two text messages.

The first says, *Look what I did today.*

And the second contains a YouTube link.

I tap on it, and my mouth curves into an unrestrained smile as the video comes up. It's Mara, sitting on the floor with her guitar in her lap. Her long dark red hair hangs over her shoulders, a few tendrils touching the blue guitar body. She smiles a little nervously, and I crank the volume on my phone as she begins to expertly pluck the guitar strings and sing. I don't know the song. It could be a cover or an original of her own, but either way, I'm gob smacked.

I've heard her sing to Rosie. I know she's more than capable of carrying a tune. But this is something entirely different. Her voice has a beautiful sort of rasp to it, just enough to rub on each note and bring it to life. I watch her body relax as she plays her guitar in a way I've never seen her relax before. This is a Mara I've never seen. Gone is the timidity and meekness. Confidence and contentment wash over her as she gets lost in the words and the melody. The music embodies her, and if I wasn't already sure I was falling for this woman, I would be now.

When the video ends, I watch it again. And then I text her back the first thing I think of.

Sean: *Beautiful.*

CHAPTER TWENTY-TWO

Mara

It happened this morning. I was making coffee and washing a couple dishes, doing nothing at all out of the ordinary. It took me several minutes to notice the sound in the air. But when I heard it, I had a strange moment of recognition.

It was *me*. *I* was singing. Like I used to, back when it flowed out of me effortlessly and thoughtlessly. I was singing again in a way I was terrified I would never be able to again.

Sean told me it would come back, and he was right. His faith in me wasn't misplaced.

I immediately broke down in tears of joy and abandoned the coffee and dishes. I went straight to the spare room and grabbed my guitar. I played and sang all morning, reveling in finally feeling home within myself again after so long.

Everything looks different now. Like the sun hitting each surface has warmth to it now and not just light. Like the walls around me and roof above me are more than just a skeletal structure designed to keep the elements out. Now these floors and those stairs feel softer, more alive than before.

My soul can breathe again, and it brings me such a deep sense of relief. I've been feeling so out of sorts without that all-consuming need to sing that now I finally feel *right*.

There's nothing I can't do now.

The most important thing that I cast aside is back again, and whether or not Mason is with me is irrelevant. Because he isn't the first person I want to tell. Sean is. The man who has never doubted that I would get through the worst and get back the best part of me.

So, I forward him a song, and butterflies flutter in my stomach at his response.

Beautiful.

I've thought about his little kiss far too much in the last few days. Every time, I tell myself it was just a friendly thing, that he didn't mean anything by it, but deep down I still wonder.

I *shouldn't* wonder.

I shouldn't let myself think about him like that. I've only just regained my sense of self, and I'm scared to lose it again. I don't want to shove myself at Sean the way I did with Mason.

I just need to focus on me, and not how every love song I sing makes me think of my handsome neighbor.

I need to focus on the newly rediscovered push to sing from that precious place inside of me and not how Sean's arms feel a lot like home.

But if anything has come into focus lately, it's him. Before, I noticed he had a bright smile reserved mostly for his daughter, but now I know the shape of his mouth almost as well as I know my own—how the right corner of his mouth indents a little deeper than the left, and how his stubbly cheeks wrinkle and roll when he grins. Where I once only saw him as a man like any other man I'd ever seen, now I see beauty and warmth and character. And I like what I see when I look at him. More than the physical attributes I liked about Mason. Sean is no longer a stranger to me, and if anything, that feels like something deeply precious held in my hands.

He *is* precious to me, I realize.

I shake my head. No. No good can come from acknowledging how warm he makes my life.

Don't imagine him in the room when I sing and notice how much better it sounds.

Don't let him dwell in the same sacred space that my urge to sing does.

Don't wish he could be something to you that he isn't.

I take a deep breath and let it out slowly.

Just sing and let that be enough.

It's been almost three weeks since my fight with my mom. I'm not surprised she hasn't called. She holds grudges and is always the last to apologize or make amends. I have never known the exact details about why my parents divorced, but I have a feeling that even if my dad had wanted to fix things, my mom would've rather worn her pain like armor than reconcile with him.

Making up with my mom won't be an overnight thing. I've never said anything like that to her before, and her three-week silence is proof that her stubbornness is alive and well. Not for the first time, I wonder why she's like that. My grandma was full of warmth and light. Why did that only translate to me and not to my mom?

When Linda asked me if my mom and I are close, it made me realize that we aren't. I've never been close to her, and it's even more glaringly obvious now that Linda is part of my life. Because Linda shares her life with people, even people like me whom she hasn't known since Adam. My mom redirects conversations and twists things around to always come back to herself, but not in a way that reveals anything personal about her.

I don't know if she still wants me to come to Arizona for Thanksgiving. She hasn't canceled my ticket, which is a good sign, so maybe I should go. Even if my heart wants to be here. Even if I can't imagine not seeing the Dunbars for more than a couple days. But my mom is the only family I have left, and even if our mother-daughter relationship will never feel as warm and homey as my relationship with my grandma or with Linda, she's still my mother. And I should still try to be her daughter.

I set my guitar to the side and grab my phone from where I set it down next to me on the floor, and I start typing out a text.

Mara: *Hey, Mom. I just want to say that I'm thinking about you.*

I frown and delete it. I watch a few brown leaves drift past the window, trying to think of what to say.

Mara: *Hey, Mom. Hope Arizona is treating you well. I miss you.*

I delete that, too.

It makes me sad that I don't really miss her. I *should*

miss her, right? She's my mom. But if anything, the lack of conversation with her lately has felt like a breath of fresh air. I don't hear her commenting on my life and bearing down on me with her unsolicited advice every couple of days. It's been nice.

I sigh and toss my phone back on the floor. My eyes follow the corners of the room as I realize how much more devastated I would be if something happened to Linda than I would be if something happened to my mom. Yes, I'd be sad, and it would hurt, but...it wouldn't feel like it felt when my grandma died. I wouldn't feel like I was genuinely *losing* something.

I pick up my phone again.

Mara: *Mom, I wish you would talk to me. I mean really talk to me. Not about Mason or what sort of progress you think I should be making. I wish you and I were close. I wish I was as important to you as saving face is. I wish you were more like Grandma. But that doesn't mean I don't love you. You're my mom, and I will always love you.*

I hit send before I can think twice and let out the breath I was holding in. I don't think she's going to like that text, but it's all true. I reach for my guitar again, but my phone vibrates. I'm surprised to see my mom has already answered back.

Mom: *Wishing is for fools, Mara.*

My brows pinch together at her words. She's saying that she'll never be what I wish she was. She'll never put down her guard or try to approach our relationship differently. I guess I just need to accept that, but it hurts too much.

Mara: *I'm here if you change your mind.*

I wish Sean was home from work. I'm remembering what it's like to have friends to rely on, and it feels good. Every one of my friends distanced themselves from me during the divorce. And some of that was my fault because I definitely put them on the back burner while I tried to convince Mason to stay. I haven't missed them much, but it's times like this where I'm deeply grateful for Sean and Linda. Their friendship is something I know I can depend on.

I wonder how that will change once Linda and Doug get married. I'm sure Linda and I will still keep in touch, but it will be weird when she moves in with Doug and it's just Sean and Rosie in the house. I haven't had much of a chance to ask Sean how he feels about that, but he seems happy for them and not worried about his mom living somewhere else.

I've replayed Linda's proposal in my head at least a dozen times, and every time, I can't help but chuckle. I can't believe she proposed wearing a dog costume. It's the most endearing and funny thing I've ever seen. I'm so happy for them, especially having overheard their argument. I'm so glad that Linda is taking the next step with Doug.

But something didn't sit right with me about her little speech. The part where she said she was going to lead by example. I know she meant Sean, but there's a bigger part of me than I'm comfortable with that squirms at the idea of him moving on, too, and getting married to someone. It doesn't matter. He isn't mine. He's being friendly to me. We both agreed that we're close friends. And friends support each other. So, if I need to support him in dating again, then that's what I'll do. Even if it kills me inside just to imagine him with someone else.

I sigh and reach for my guitar again. It doesn't matter how I feel. It's not like I'd do anything about that nudge I always feel around him anyway. I'm finally finding my feet again, feeling like my old self. I don't need to invite someone else to step into Mason's footprints and knock me off balance again.

And yet, my stomach wiggles uncomfortably as I think about my mom and how she handled divorcing my dad. She's been hell bent on never needing anyone, including me. I don't want to follow down that path...the path that robs me of the joy of loving other people. I don't want to spend the rest of my life alone just because I'm scared of getting hurt again. My mom's way is totally black and white, and I know I'd much rather look at it as the gray area in the middle.

I want to learn to love myself while also loving someone else. I want to love someone without losing me in it. That isn't something my mom is capable of doing. It's harder to do than just leaning into the absolutes. Pride and anger and spite are all too easy to make a home in. But love, trust, and faith are much more worth pursuing to me.

My fingers begin to play of their own accord, my mind continuing to whir and ponder as the beautiful sound of guitar strings fills the room.

My mother and I may never understand each other or see eye to eye, but I know that when it comes down to it, I will still love her despite our differences. And unfortunately, I don't know if she will.

The temperatures continue to plummet as another week passes. We're approaching mid-November, and the passing of time since the divorce staggers me if I think about it too much. But at least I can realize that things are okay now, better even.

Next month, I have a gig set up. It isn't a big thing, and I don't plan on getting back on my old social media handles to broadcast it. But it's one toe in the pond of getting back out there again. Hopefully, the people who followed my music before will still be interested in giving me a shot. If they're anything like Linda, I'll be fine. Thankfully, the manager of the coffee shop remembered me and immediately agreed to let me play a small set. It'll be after Thanksgiving, so I have a couple weeks to decide which songs I want to do.

I told the Dunbars about it last night, and they promised they'd be there. I knew they would, but it still meant a lot to hear them say it. To see the pride and excitement in Sean's eyes had my heart stuttering. And little Rosie gave me a hug and said she couldn't wait.

I'm surer than ever that only good things are waiting for me in the future. The worst has passed, and now, all there's left for me to do is reach out and grab a hold of those good things as they come.

Tonight is pizza night, and Sean mentioned to me when he walked me back to my door last night that Rhys would be joining us. I'm looking forward to seeing him again, but I know Sean told me about it ahead of time because he was preparing me. I'm not sure exactly for what, but I have to imagine he doesn't want me to be caught off guard again if something happens. This time I have no intention of teasing Sean, even if I have every right to do so. I don't want to give him another reason to hurt all over again because of losing his wife.

Because dinner is covered and I don't really need to bring anything as a side, I spend most of the morning making an apple pie. The sweet scent of apples and cinnamon perfume my kitchen as I take the crumble-topped deliciousness out of the oven and set it on the stove to cool.

It's been rainy and cold these days, and I've been craving apple pie now that Thanksgiving is coming up. I still haven't decided whether I'm going to Arizona, but I'm leaning towards not. It sure would be warmer there, but even the promise of not enduring the freezing drizzle we had this morning isn't enough to sway me.

I turn off the oven, remove my oven mitts, and head out into the living room, intending to tidy up a bit when I spot the mail carrier truck through the front window, stopped at my mailbox. I watch it slowly pull away to the next box and I waver on whether I should go out to get my mail now or later when it might be less miserable outside.

At length, I decide to suck it up and do it now so I won't forget. I slip my feet into my shoes by the door and throw my fall jacket around me. I really should dig through what's left in the spare room to find my winter jacket, but I haven't been bothered enough to. I'm usually only outside for a few minutes at a time anyway.

I step out and make sure the interior door is shut to keep the cold out and then clutch my jacket around me tighter as I make my way down the steps.

The wind is damp and cuts through me like I'm wearing nothing. I shiver and immediately quicken my pace once I hit my sidewalk. But I only take about two steps before I realize my error in walking so fast on my sidewalk after the freezing temperatures we've been having at night. This morning's drizzle has hardened into glass, and I feel too late my foot moving under me without my doing.

The world tilts up, the cloudy gray sky coming into view for only a second before I instinctively reach out behind me to try and break my fall. With a surprised gasp, I fall backward, and then everything is dark and silent.

CHAPTER TWENTY-THREE

Sean

My stomach has been squirming all afternoon. It shouldn't be, and I'm annoyed that it is.

I'm not sure why I invited Rhys over tonight, but I did. I feel like I'm just asking to have a replay of Halloween night. But part of me wants him to be around Mara. Not because I want them to hit it off, of course, but...because I think deep down, I want to make sure his approval of me moving on is something he really means. Part of me hopes he might be able to tell if Mara feels anything for me that goes beyond friendship. Rhys isn't a fantastic people reader, but I weirdly feel like I need back up in deciding what I should do with these new feelings living inside my chest.

I sigh. Maybe I would be better off asking Doug what he thinks. He's been around Mara enough to have a good idea of who she is. Maybe he would be able to give me an unbiased opinion about what it looks like when Mara smiles at me.

I know I'm being stupid. I *know* that. It's just been a long time since I've had to try and figure out whether a girl liked me.

And this time, it's a hell of a lot more complicated. Because I have a kid. Because she just got divorced. Because I'm scared.

"What's with all the sighing?" my mom questions, narrowing her eyes at me from the table where she's working on a puzzle.

I didn't realize I had sighed more than once, but apparently, I had. I glance at her over my shoulder and go back to unloading the dishwasher.

There's no way in hell I'm going to ask my mom for advice or input of any kind. There's no way she would be unbiased or even calm about it. Besides, I already know what she would say.

"Nothing," I mutter.

Mom doesn't make a retort to that, surprisingly. I pile a couple plates in the cabinet in front of me and then reach back down for the last one. It's a gray plate, the one Mara always brings food over on.

It's funny how just one inanimate object like this can set off a nervous warmth in my chest. It's just a damn plate. But it makes me think of her.

"If you sigh one more time, I'm going to assume you're a lovesick fool."

I whirl around and glare at my mother, who's giving me that look. That *mom* look. Like she knows all my secrets. I fight hard to keep my cheeks from blushing.

I open my mouth to argue that I'm *not* a lovesick fool, but she cocks her head slightly and raises her eyebrows, like she's just *daring* me to deny it. 'Cause it's apparently that obvious.

Despite what she just said, I sigh again, and she cracks up laughing.

"Oh, Sean," she cackles.

My glare intensifies, and I set Mara's plate on the counter. Instead of addressing her, I turn back to the dishwasher and put away the silverware.

"You're never going to admit it, are you?" she tosses out, causing my back to stiffen.

"Admit what?" I answer with a huff.

She chuckles. "You're not fooling anyone, Sean."

I roll my eyes at that and place the last fork in the drawer. "When are you moving out again?"

Mom just laughs as she fits a piece into place. "You get your stubbornness from your father."

I bark out a laugh. "Right. 'Cause you're not stubborn at all."

She and Doug haven't set a date yet, but they're thinking about having a spring wedding. Rosie is already excited to be the flower girl. I've never seen my mom happier, and despite how the household will change when she moves into Doug's house in St. Cloud, I know everything will be okay. Rosie and I aren't losing her. And besides, we'll always have Mara next door.

The front door opens, and my breath hitches, thinking it's Mara. But then I hear Rhys's voice greet Rosie who's coloring at the coffee table in the living room.

"I just want you to stop acting like you don't like Mara when you obviously do," my mom continues, pulling my attention back to her. "You can't pretend away feelings."

I close the dishwasher a little harder than necessary, and when I turn around, Rhys is striding into the room with a big smile on his face.

"Hey, Mrs. D."

My mom's face lights up, and I'm grateful for the distraction that is Rhys's hug.

"Here he is," she says as she squeezes him.

A melancholy shadow crosses over me as I watch them hugging. Rhys and I have been friends since high school, back when his home life was falling apart, and he needed a safe place to land. Even though Rhys rarely talked about what was happening at home with anyone except me, my parents seemed to figure it out anyway. I tease my mom and Rhys's relationship, but I know she was there for him when he needed a mother figure the most. That kind of bond doesn't go away, even a decade later.

"Where's your mister?" Rhys asks as he pulls back and stands back up to his full height.

"Should be here any minute." My mom turns back to me. "And when he does get here, that'll be three of us trying to get your head out of your butt."

Rhys rubs his hands together, and his smile turns mischievous. "Ooh, are we already starting in on him?" He cracks his knuckles.

"And Cheryl. She and I talked all about it this afternoon when I went over for coffee." Great, she and her best friend have been talking about me. No wonder Mom's all riled up about this. Cheryl always rallies around whatever Mom's passionate about.

I narrow my eyes at them. "You all need to butt out."

"Maybe we'll butt out once you get up the courage to ask her out," Rhys replies, wiggling his eyebrows at me. I hate that he knows exactly what Mom is saying without any sort of context.

"No."

"Don't be a chicken, dude."

I grit my teeth at him, and he just smiles back at me pleasantly.

"I'm not a chicken, I just..." I trail off, my chest clenching tightly as I imagine myself standing in front of my beautiful, sweet neighbor who blushes at my question and says an uncomfortable "no, thanks" in reply. My stomach jumps with nausea at the thought.

"Sean, no one is saying you have to propose like I did," Mom interrupts. "Just ask her out on a date and then take it slow."

I groan at the both of them, hating this conversation and how it makes me feel like a teenager. Despite how easy they both make it sound, it just isn't. Even if I feel like a teenager, I'm definitely not. I have a daughter, and grief, and other responsibilities. Everything is normal and predictable now. Asking Mara to be something more than friends will change everything. Actions have consequences, and I'm afraid of those consequences.

"What if she says no, alright?" I blurt out irritably. "Then it'll be weird."

Rhys scoffs loudly. "She won't say no, dude. It'll be fine."

So simple. *It'll be fine.* Yeah, easy for him to say. He isn't in my shoes. And besides, he hasn't even had a girlfriend in a couple years. Who is he to be giving me dating advice?

"I'm done talking about this." I point a finger at each of them. "And you better not say a damn thing about it in front of Mara, got it?"

Rhys heaves a sigh and leans his head back in defeat.

"Fine." He holds up two fingers in the Boy Scouts salute. I'm pretty sure he was never a Boy Scout, but I'll take it.

My mom says nothing, and I get a sinking feeling that she has every intention of making some comment tonight.

With the determined way she's looking at me, I'd be smart to tell Mara myself before she does. I wouldn't put it past her to take things into her own hands. Thankfully, Doug shows up a minute later and distracts Mom long enough for me to sneak back to the living room with Rosie.

She's been doing so much better in school since she switched teachers. Rosie comes home from school in a good mood and goes to school each morning looking forward to her day. I'm so relieved, and frankly, I feel a little bad for not switching her sooner. I guess I was just hoping she would warm up to Mrs. Jacobson somehow.

I watch her coloring for a moment, admiring the blond hair that reminds me so much of her mother. A mother she doesn't know or remember. And when Mom moves out and marries Doug, she'll just have me.

What am I even thinking—going after Mara? My daughter should be my focus. She should be all I need to be a happy man.

Guilt slaps me in the face, then. I know she likes Mara, but I shouldn't let myself be so consumed by this. Rosie is my whole world. She has been since the moment Gabby died. My turmoil over how I feel about Mara isn't as important as this little girl.

I lean forward and kiss her temple.

"When is Mara coming?" she asks me without acknowledging my affection.

I glance at the clock on the wall, realizing it's well after five o'clock. My brow furrows. She's usually here before I even get home from work. It isn't like her to come over late, but maybe she got caught up in playing her guitar.

"I don't know, Rosiecakes," I answer thoughtfully, and get up to look out the window facing Mara's house. The front windows are dark, but the window of the spare room has a faint light glowing through it, like the kitchen light is flooding into the room.

That's weird. I take my phone out of my pocket and send her a quick text.

Sean: *Ready for pizza?*

After I hit send, I go back to sit by Rosie. But when I don't get a response after a couple minutes, I return to the window. No other lights have turned on.

Is she not home?

Maybe she went for a walk.

"Hey, did you order the pizza yet?" Doug calls to me from the kitchen.

"Not yet," I call back. I didn't realize I was waiting for Mara to show up before I called, but I guess it's later than I usually call it in.

"Well, hurry up!" comes Rhys's laughing voice. "We're starving in here!"

I roll my eyes and call the pizza place to put in our usual order, plus extra cheesy bread since Rhys is here. When I hang up, I go back to the message I sent Mara to make sure it went through.

A nervous pull spreads through my upper body as I press the call button and bring the phone to my ear. It rings and rings and eventually goes to voicemail. Not sure what to do, I listen to her instructions to leave a message and then decide to hang up at the last second.

I give it a couple more minutes, and then I start to feel a little panicked. This isn't like her. Not anymore, at least. There hasn't been a day in the last two weeks that she hasn't been over for dinner. She's been happier. Just last night she told me about booking her first gig in more than a year.

So why isn't she answering her phone?

Something isn't right.

Without saying a word to anyone, I throw on my boots and quickly make my way outside.

The sky is already dark with only a slight reddish tinge to the west, and both the darkness and the cold make me shiver.

Don't panic. Don't panic. She's fine.

But the words don't ease the anxiety coursing through me as I jog over to her front steps. I open the screen door and knock on the interior door. I distractedly shift my weight from one foot to the other as I wait. And wait. I raise my fist and knock again, louder this time. Still nothing.

Why wouldn't she be home? I turn to look over my shoulder, glancing up and down the street, but I don't see her familiar shape on the sidewalks. Where is she?

I reach for the handle, and it turns easily, so I take a deep breath and push the door open.

The living room is dark and still, the only light coming from the kitchen doorway. Blood pounds in my ears as I take a small step forward.

"Mara?" I call out and get no reply.

The panic increases as I reach for the light switch with a

shaking hand. I squint for a second and sweep my gaze over the empty living room. Everything is as it should be. A partially done puzzle lays on the coffee table, along with her coffee mug placed near the corner. A cream throw blanket is casually tossed over one side of the couch. But no Mara.

My eyes move toward the kitchen doorway, and the hairs on the back of my neck stand up. Time slows down as I walk toward it. Part of me hopes that when I step into the kitchen, it transforms into Gabby's and my apartment, because then it would make this whole situation a dream. I feel a disturbing sense of Deja vu that I pray is just me being paranoid.

But the kitchen is there when I enter, and I frown at the apple pie sitting on the stove. I reach out and touch the glass pie plate, finding it room temperature and not hot in the slightest, meaning she probably baked it this morning.

"Mara?" I call out again, louder and more desperate.

But the quiet of the house remains, sinking like weights on my body.

Fear adds to the anxiety as I frantically check every room in the house. It's obvious she isn't home, but because of Gabby, I have to make sure she isn't hurt somewhere and unable to reply to me.

The spare room is empty; her guitar sits in a stand in the corner. The bedroom upstairs is still, her bed made. The bathroom has me hesitating with a pounding heart, but she isn't in there either.

Where is she?

I pace through the living room, trying not to hyperventilate as I call her again.

A ring tone breaks the silence in the house, and my

stomach drops when I follow the sound to the kitchen where her phone is vibrating on the opposite counter of the pie she clearly made to bring over for dessert tonight.

I hang up and reach for her phone, thinking maybe Mason called her again and it set her off like last time. But my text and two calls are the only correspondence she's had today.

I take her phone with me as I head back into the living room. It's then that I notice her shoes are gone and so is her jacket, but I spot her purse and car keys hanging on a hook next to the door.

Uncontrollable terror thunders through me, swarming my brain with the facts and what they mean.

She left her house on foot, likely hours ago, without her phone or wallet.

I do hyperventilate then, because I can't stop the worst-case scenario from coming to mind.

She went back to the bridge.

Where else would she have gone? I can't think of a single damn place she could be besides there. My fingers are trembling so badly that I can barely dial Rhys's number. As it rings, I open the front door and start making my way to my truck.

"Uh, hello?" Rhys answers uncertainly, and I wonder if any of them even noticed I left.

"Mara's gone."

"What?"

"She's *gone*. I went over to get her for dinner, and she wasn't there." The damp wind pelts me in the face as I nearly break into a run. "She left her phone, wallet, and keys behind," I continue, my voice shaking.

Rhys says nothing, probably because I've caught him off guard.

"I'm going out to look for her," I say roughly, wrenching open the driver's side door.

"What? Sean, she could be anywhere."

I climb into the seat and slam the door shut, blocking out the weather—the weather she's out walking in, or at least she was.

"There's only one place I can think of, Rhys," I tell him gravely. "I never told anyone, but a couple months ago, I found her standing on the highway 10 bridge."

Rhys makes a choking sound.

"I have to find her." I dig my keys out of my pocket and crank the truck to life.

"I'm coming with you," Rhys says, and I can hear him saying something away from the phone, probably explaining to Mom and Doug what's going on. Then the line goes dead before I can argue, and I look to the right to see him running out the front door and across the lawn.

He gets in and looks over at me with wide eyes. "You really think she went to the bridge?"

I put the truck in drive. "I sure as hell hope I'm wrong."

Rhys is quiet as I drive. I notice him looking up and down every street we pass, like maybe she's still out walking somewhere. I doubt that. But maybe, just *maybe*, she ducked into a coffee shop or something to dry off or warm up. Maybe she's not on the bridge. But I have to know.

The bridge comes into view, and I suck in a terrified breath as I steer my truck to the shoulder, beneath a street light near where I saw her standing that one afternoon. The bridge is vacated. Not even another car driving across. I throw the truck in park and dart out. I can feel my heartbeat jumping throughout my entire body as Rhys gets out, too, and we rush to the side of the bridge.

I feel like the fate of my life is on the other side. Like I could very well die inside if she did in fact jump.

I can't lose her. I can't lose her like I lost Gabby.

My lungs seize painfully in my chest, and I look down at the water.

I don't know what I expect to see, looking over the edge. Maybe her jacket floating in the water, or her body washed up on the riverbed, but there's nothing. Just lapping water and inky darkness.

Rhys touches my shoulder as I grip the concrete and try to breathe.

"She's not here," he says, his breath coming in and out quickly.

She probably wouldn't be if she jumped. She'd probably be miles down the Mississippi by now. My stomach rolls, and I wretch over the side of the bridge.

Rhys pats my back weakly, like he might be sick, too. When I step back and look at my best friend, I see the terror in his eyes, and I know he sees it in mine, too. He swallows hard, the cold wind pushing at his hair.

"Let's call the police. Maybe they know something."

My entire body shakes, but I nod.

CHAPTER TWENTY-FOUR

Mara

The dark nothingness is like the most restful sleep I've ever experienced. It's peaceful enough that I don't want to move, hoping to drift back into it and not be brought forward into consciousness. But there's a dull ache throbbing at the back of my head that forces me to bring my hazy attention to the other side of my closed eyelids where there's a gently glowing light. I stay still as my other senses kick in. The faint, stringent scent of rubbing alcohol. The little high-pitched beep sounding steadily. The pulse of pain and soreness settled around my left elbow. Something warm and firm clutching my right hand. My entire body feels weighed down and heavy, perforated only by the aches in my head, elbow, and left hip as well.

I don't have the presence of mind to put all these pieces together. These are just facts I'm vaguely aware of, like my neurons are only firing on the periphery of my subconscious. Though I'm aware of my injuries, it doesn't occur to me then to question what's happened to me or even where I am.

But then, something moves over my right hand, startling me slightly. I turn my head toward it, and that's all it takes for me to wince as the ache in the back of my head revs into a radiating pain that grips my entire skull. I let out a little groan, and that warm thing squeezes my hand.

I languidly open my eyes, squinting against the light and the pain, and find Mason sitting in a chair next to me, holding my hand.

What? Mason?

A twinge of nausea erupts in my stomach as I slowly glance around, the hospital room coming into better focus. There's a whiteboard ahead on the wall with some scrawled handwriting on it. A window with the shades drawn and no light from outside reaching in. The environment is in stark contrast to anything homey or comforting, and I instantly long for something familiar.

When I bring my eyes back to Mason, the room swings wildly. I slam my eyes closed, but it does nothing to stop the whirling dizziness.

"It's alright," he says gently, squeezing my hand again.

My brain clunks from thought to thought, trying to make sense of what happened and why Mason, of all people, is here. I peek my eyes open again and continue to squint at him, like maybe he isn't really here and I'm just imagining it. Despite my dizziness and pain, I can see that he looks tired, but his green eyes look back into mine steadily, like he's actually concerned about me.

Oh, no.

Are we still married? Panic crawls up my spine and sinks sharp talons into my shoulders. Did I dream up the Dunbars in some weird comatose illusion? I quickly glance at my left hand, regretting it instantly because the dizziness only increases and so does the nausea. But I'm deeply relieved to see my hand devoid of a wedding ring.

Then it hits me how weird it is to be relieved that I'm not still married to Mason. *No*, I decide, *that isn't weird*. That's reality and that's where I want to be. Not in the past but in the present, where he's at the bottom of my list of people I want to see.

"What...what are you doing here?" I croak out slowly.

"I work here," he explains patiently. "And I'm still listed as one of your emergency contacts." He sits back a little but doesn't let go of my hand. "They couldn't get a hold of your mother."

I try to lift my hands, realizing there's something wrapped around my head, but I immediately grimace at the pain shooting through my left elbow. I breathe in sharply, which causes the nausea and dizziness to swell. I close my eyes tightly again.

"What happened?"

I hear Mason sigh in distress. "Someone driving by on your street saw you lying on the sidewalk outside your house."

Oh, that's right. I was walking out to get the mail, and I slipped and fell.

"She called the ambulance when she couldn't revive you. The EMTs don't know exactly how long you were lying there, but it was probably close to an hour."

I take a deep breath in through my nose and out through my mouth, willing the spinning of the room and the rolling of my stomach to cease.

"You've got a concussion and mild hypothermia," he informs me, his voice getting quieter as he continues. "The hypothermia has been remedied, but obviously, you had a pretty hard fall. You'll probably be staying the night."

I realize then that I'm covered with a couple of warm blankets, and that's why my body feels so heavy.

Wait, staying the night?

My eyes pop open, and I stare at my ex-husband. "What time is it?"

He glances at the watch on his left wrist. "Almost eight."

I gasp. "At *night*?"

"Yes."

I've been here for that long? My brain struggles to think back to what I was doing before I slipped, and with difficulty, I remember making that apple pie to bring over to—I gasp again.

The Dunbars.

"Sean," I blurt out in alarm.

Mason glares at me almost suspiciously. "Who's Sean?"

"Sean Dunbar. And Linda Dunbar. They're—they're my neighbors—my friends," I explain through the panic. "They must be worried sick; I was supposed to be over for dinner."

Instinctively, I look to the right, expecting for my phone to be sitting on the little table next to me, but there's only a big glass of water. The quick movement has my stomach clenching.

"Oh, no, they don't know what happened," I groan, tears pricking at my eyes.

I imagine my sweet neighbors pacing through their house, trying to call me and being scared because they don't know where I am. I remember saying to Sean how it was nice to be worried about, but I didn't mean like this. The last thing I ever wanted to do was cause them any kind of pain, and here, I disappeared out of nowhere.

"Relax," Mason orders, his hand clutching mine in an ungentle way.

"Please," I whisper, looking back at him as the room continues to spin. "There has to be a way to—"

"I said *relax*," he repeats, even more sternly. "He's in the waiting room."

My heart leaps. "He is?"

"He showed up about an hour and a half ago," Mason informs me gruffly. "He's been harassing the front desk for information about you, but he isn't family or an emergency contact, so we can't release any details. Twice now I've threatened to—"

"I need to see him," I plead, tears welling in front of my already swimming vision. "Please, Mason."

He stays perfectly still and studies me with those green eyes that were once as familiar to me as my own. His hesitation throws me off, but my need to see Sean only intensifies.

"Why?" Mason asks, the word coming out slow and low. There's a harshness to it that I don't understand, even more than I don't understand his question.

"What?"

"Why *him*?"

I stare back at my ex-husband in pure confusion. "What do you mean?"

"Why is *he* the first person you want to see right now? Why isn't it—" His rough voice cuts off abruptly, and I feel his hand tighten slightly around mine. His eyes lower as I watch him, the room still spinning like a carousel around me. "When

I got the call that you were here, Mara, I—" He stops again, and looks up at me with a strange expression on his face. Maybe if I wasn't concussed, I would be able to identify it. Mason shakes his head slightly. "Things haven't turned out the way I thought they would," he admits quietly. "I thought I knew what I wanted, but... Well, this just seems like fate bringing us back together."

My head, which is already roaring with pain and dizziness, begins to pound. "Mason—"

"I miss you," he interrupts sternly, his eyebrows dipping from my apologetic tone of voice. "Sarah's not...she's not who I thought she was. And I miss you."

I close my eyes and take a few breaths to keep my nausea at bay, and as I do, I feel irritated for more than one reason. One, because he's springing this on me *now*, in a compromised state in which I don't have the ability to properly think this through. And two, because he's exactly the fool that Sean said he was. I knew the mistake he was making in divorcing me so he could be with her, but he didn't listen. And now it's all too little, too late.

"I know I messed everything up; believe me, I know. But sometimes, you have to lose everything to understand what you really want. And what I really want is you."

I open my eyes, my temples feeling like they're being squeezed by a vice and keep my gaze on the swaying ceiling. He's saying everything I wanted him to say back when I was doing whatever I could possibly think of to get him to choose me, to choose us. But his timing is unfortunately way off because even though a part of me will always love him and the memories I have with him, there's no denying that I don't want any of it back.

Mason squeezes my hand. "Please, Mara. I—"

"You didn't lose me," I ground out to the ceiling. Tears resurface in my eyes, this time filled with anger and hurt. "You left me, Mason. It isn't my fault that you made a bad choice." I slowly follow the moving ceiling down to his astonished face. "This isn't love, Mason. What you're doing right now isn't what you think it is. This isn't fate, or romance, this is just… desperation." Shock crosses his rugged features, but I keep going. "You don't get to push me out of the life we built and then demand it all back like this. That's not how it works." I swallow hard and then pull my hand out of his. "Thank you for making sure I didn't wake up alone, but you can go now. There's someone waiting in the lobby, and from what you've said, he's very eager to see me."

Mason's face slowly fills up with a hideous red tinge. "Mara, you can't be serious. Come on. You *know* me—"

"No," I whisper, a tear slipping down my cheek. "You're not the man I fell in love with, and you're not the man I'm in love with now." I lift my hand to wipe at my eyes. "I'm sorry that you figured it out too late, but I've moved on. You should, too."

My ex-husband gapes at me for an uncomfortable moment, and then his anger takes over. He slams his chair back as he gets to his feet, glaring down at me like *I'm* the one to blame for all this. Like it was *my* idea to ruin our lives. His volatile reaction rolls my stomach, amping up my concussion symptoms even more.

"Fine. Be that way," he growls. "You don't want me here? *Fine.* I'm going home." And then he leaves the room in a fury.

I'm not sorry for what I said. On the contrary, I'm proud of myself. I know that if Mason had wanted me back even two months ago, I would've considered taking him back. But I've come a long way from begging for the scraps of his love. I deserve something better…something steady and pure.

I sniff back my tears, feeling so helpless that Sean is here, probably a worried mess, but not beside me. So close and yet so far away from me. I lay there blinking up at the ceiling as it swings around.

A soft knock on the doorframe pounds my aching head, but I jerk it towards the door anyway, hoping it's Sean. I squint, groaning. The discomfort bouncing around my body makes it difficult for me to focus on the man standing in the doorway in a white coat.

"Hello there," comes a man's voice, very clearly not Sean's. "I'm Dr. Peterson. Mason let me know you're awake." He comes into the room, rubbing his hands together with hand sanitizer between them. "How are you feeling?"

"Horrible," I squeak out. "I want to see Sean."

The doctor gently touches the side of my head, inspecting my head bandage. "We'll see. Let's get you checked out, okay?"

He shines a painful light in my eyes, asks me a few questions, including where my pain rates from one to ten. I answer his questions impatiently, each one draining me more and more. He tells me that when I slipped and fell, I landed just slightly more on my left side, with my left elbow and my head taking the brunt of the impact.

"I'll order you something for the pain and vertigo, and I'll be back to check on you later. Hang in there." Before I can ask about Sean again, he's gone.

Alone again and hating it, all I can do is close my eyes and long for my favorite family. I don't want my mother. I definitely don't want Mason. I just want to see Linda smile at me, and hold Rosie's little hand, and look into Sean's brown eyes. They're the only comfort I need. The only people I want to talk to right now.

Before this, I was well aware what they meant to me, but lying here without them makes everything so much clearer. There is a definitive before and after in my life, and I want the after so much more than I want the before. Mason is nothing to me now. And I wouldn't go back for all the money in the world. I'd give up my voice before I gave up Sean, Linda, and Rosie. Even if they aren't here beside me, just thinking of them comforts me enough to relax. And then the blankets over me pull me down deeper into exhaustion. The steady beeps become quieter, more far away. My eyes close, the nausea and vertigo fading slightly as I unwillingly sink back into the quiet darkness.

When the ambient noise of the room lifts me from my sleep again, the pain in my head is better. The dizziness is less, and the achiness in my elbow and hip feel less angry. My head feels less clunky, which must mean my bandage has been removed.

But there's no hand holding mine.

I open my eyes slowly, disappointed that I drifted back to sleep and that no one let Sean come in while I was out. I reach my right hand around for the bedrail and find the call button for the nurse.

A moment later, a nurse enters my room with a smile. I recognize her from one of the work parties I used to attend with Mason, though I can't recall her name.

"Hey, Mara. What do you need?"

"Sean," I reply softly. I look over at the clock and see that it's past nine-thirty now. "If he's still here."

"Mason tried to kick him out," the nurse tells me with an eye roll. "I know you guys were married," she adds, lowering her voice, "but I've always thought he was a jerk. Anyway, Sean's still here, and Dr. Peterson said he could come up if you're feeling better."

"I'm feeling better," I assure her instantly.

She chuckles. "You're a lucky woman," she says, her voice warming. "He's been a wreck. He obviously loves you very much."

I blush at that, but before I can explain that he's just my friend, she takes a step back.

"I'll go get him for you." She spins on her heel and disappears through the doorway, leaving my heart a little gushy.

I *am* lucky. Lucky to be alive, and lucky to have moved into that particular house. My heart aches to think of what things would be like if I had moved somewhere else...if I had never met them.

I glance at the clock again. Sean's been here for hours. For *me*. Though the nausea and dizziness are much better, I feel my nerves kick in as I realize he's walking through the hall right now, on his way to my side. I need to tell him I'm okay and that I'm sorry for causing so much trouble.

I should've just waited to get the mail. *Why* did I go out then? There probably wasn't even anything important waiting for me in that mailbox. If I had just gotten the mail tomorrow, I wouldn't be here, and Sean wouldn't have spent his entire evening here worrying about me.

But besides how guilty I feel, it isn't lost on me that I really am lucky. Lucky that I'm not more seriously injured, sure, but even more so because without a doubt, Sean cares about me.

I take a deep breath, grateful for my life, and grateful that I'm someone important to Sean Dunbar.

My heart beats fast. What a privilege. I close my eyes

and try to calm myself, but it's no use. Any minute now, he'll be walking through that door, and I'll somehow have to not show how much I wish I belonged to him.

He isn't mine, I remind myself.

But when I open my eyes and look over at the doorway, I see him standing there with wide, scared eyes, and I know. I know there's no hiding how desperately I wish he was mine.

He starts toward me, his face filled with emotion, and without a word, he bends down and brings me to his chest. Encouraged, I don't hesitate to cling to him as tightly as my sore elbow will allow. His hands are shaking, and his breath matches my own ragged intakes. The warmth of him close to me is all I want. This is where everything feels okay. This is where I want to be.

"I'm okay," I assure him, burying my face in his shoulder, already feeling the apologetic tears forming in my eyes. "I'm okay."

He pulls back, his eyes a little wild as his shaking hands gently frame my jaw and cheeks. He looks me over like he's never seen me clearly before. I'm not sure what exactly he sees, but I can tell he's trying to commit every detail of my face to memory.

"The nurse said you fell." His voice comes out choppy and scared, and it twists my heart.

Embarrassment and shame clench my stomach. I grasp his wrists and get myself to look him in the eyes as I speak. "I'm so sorry. It's such a stupid thing, and I've caused so much worry." My bottom lip trembles, and when I close my eyes, several tears drop onto my cheeks.

I don't see him shake his head slightly; I just feel him move close. I welcome the warmth of his arms around me again, comforted by his closeness.

"I'm just glad you're okay," he says into my hair. His words are shattered and terrified. "You scared the hell out of me. I thought...I thought you went back to the bridge."

I pull back, staring at him in horror. "What? Sean...I promised you. I promised *twice*."

"I know," he assures me. "I know you did, but I—I couldn't find you and...I just panicked."

More tears fill my eyes as I realize what he's been dealing with while he was sitting alone in the waiting room.

Maybe once, for just a second, I thought about making everything go away. But every moment since then has strengthened me and assured me that I want to get up every morning so I can see his face and the faces of his family.

"I could never...I love my life now. I...I could never leave you and your mom and Rosie." I sniff as his eyes become glassy and wet. When a tear rolls down his tortured face, I can't stop myself from touching it. "I love you all so much. You make life worth living."

His face crumples slightly as my words sink in. He closes his eyes for a moment, another tear slipping out that I have to keep myself from kissing away. Instead, I lift my hand and gently smooth it over his chest. The motion feels intimate, even if it's only meant to bring him some comfort.

After a moment, he opens his eyes and brings his hands back to either side of my face, his weathered fingers still shaking slightly as he holds my head in his hands. His sawdusty scent drowns out the sterile hospital stench, and I welcome it.

"We love you, too, Mara." One thumb smooths over my cheek as something unspoken passes between us. Some exchange of trust and understanding that I will never leave my

257

life by my own hand, and he will choose to trust in the promise I made him.

Then he blows out a breath that he must've been holding in and moves closer, bringing his lips to my forehead and then resting his own against the tingling place he just kissed.

I close my eyes tightly, savoring this sweet, intimate moment. And despite how I don't want to fall so quickly, I can only think one word.

Yours.

Even if he doesn't belong to me, I know without a doubt that I belong to him. Nothing could ever change that. And in the terror I feel in realizing it, I feel a deeper stillness that feels a lot like peace. A kind of peace I never felt with Mason or even my mother.

I don't want to lose myself. I don't want to undo all the progress I've made in loving myself and choosing what's best for me. But this man...he feels an awful lot like what's best for me. And to know how stressed he's been...it just makes me feel horrible.

"I'm so sorry for all this," I whisper, my heart beating fast. "I didn't mean to worry anybody."

One hand lifts from my face to gently run his fingers through my hair, but his forehead stays against mine.

"Don't, sweetheart. You're okay, and that's all that matters," he whispers back.

I savor that, too. That little endearment. It feels like he's bestowing something upon me, and I tuck it in close where it will stay protected and safe. I don't care what he means by it. I just know that everything will be okay. Without my permission, my hand rubs across his chest again.

"I'm so glad you're here," I murmur, my eyes closed, enjoying the warmth of his face so close to mine. My cheeks blush a little at my admission.

"Where else would I be, Mara? Mason would've had to drag me out of here before I would've left on my own."

At the mention of my ex-husband's name, I sigh and pull back a little. "I'm sorry about that. He was here when I woke up and—"

"Wait, what?" Sean's hands drop from where they were touching me. "He was here?"

I give him a small nod, being mindful of my injury. "I forgot to take him off my emergency contacts," I explain absently. "It was so weird," I tell him genuinely. "For a second, I thought I was still married to him and—and it felt...*wrong*."

Sean's face relaxes slightly, relief creeping in as I continue.

"For a second, I thought you and your mom and Rosie had all just been some really vivid dream. It was...terrifying." I look down at my left hand again, still relieved to see it without a ring. "Mason was the last person I expected or wanted to see." And I definitely didn't expect him to want me back.

Sean moves his hand over mine, his warm, rough skin a reminder of how much better it feels to hold his hand than Mason's.

"He really is my past now," I say, my heart beating fast as my fingers slowly thread through his. I close my eyes and let out a deep breath of relief. "It feels good to be free of him." I open my eyes and look up at Sean, into those deep brown eyes peering so steadily back into mine. "*This* is the life I want. A life with you and your family in it."

One side of his mouth lifts up, and he rubs his thumb

over the back of my hand, making my stomach squirm.

"That's what I want, too," Sean's low voice rumbles. "I thought I might have lost you tonight, and I *never* want to feel like that again…" The exhaustion and stress in his expression deepens as he takes in my face again like he's memorizing every inch of it.

"You won't," I vow. "I'll do everything I can to make sure you won't."

He lifts his free hand and pushes my long hair over my right shoulder. It's a sweet gesture that warms me up inside.

More than anything, I know this man is something important and vital to me.

"Are they keeping you overnight?" His hand trails down my arm all the way to my wrist, warmth awakening at his touch.

"Yeah, just to be on the safe side."

He nods. "Do you need anything? Water or pain meds?"

I shake my head and look back down at our intertwined hands.

The only thing I really need is him and his sweet family. Right now and forever.

CHAPTER TWENTY-FIVE

Sean

I hold back the groan that wants to escape me as I resituate myself in the hospital chair. My neck hurts, and my butt is asleep from how I was slouched, dozing. I lean forward in the low light of Mara's hospital room and rest my forearms down on the bed next to her thigh so I can lay my cheek on them.

I told her I would only stay until she fell asleep. That was hours ago now. I couldn't leave. I don't know if I'll be able to leave her side ever again.

She may not have gone to the bridge. She may not have left my life like I thought she did. But for those miserable hours I spent in the waiting room dying for any scrap of news, she *was* gone. I didn't know if she had been mugged, or shot, or stabbed. All the police told me was that she was found unconscious outside of her home and was taken to the hospital.

So even though Mara is going to be fine, I'm not fine. I'm beyond shaken up. I'm still getting myself to understand that what I feared isn't what happened.

I can't leave her. I can't go home and expect to sleep any better than I would here. I'm not okay. And I need to be near her.

Me. Not goddamn Mason. Not her ex-husband who pretended not to remember me from the farmer's market and wouldn't let me see her. To hear her say that Mason is her past helped, but I'm still angry as hell that *he* was there when she woke up and not me. By staying here all night, I'm making certain the first face she sees in the morning is mine.

The only thing rolling through my mind is what the nurse said when she was bringing me back to Mara's room.

She's been asking for you.

Me. Not her mom, or even my mom. *Me.*

I don't want there to ever be a circumstance going forward in which she asks for me and I'm not there.

I know what this means. I know how much I'm risking in letting myself feel so much for Mara. But it's too late now. I'm already in too deep.

Mara shifts in front of me, her left hand brushing against my elbow. I stay still, but it's no use.

"Sean?" comes her tired voice, raspier than usual.

I lift my head and yawn.

"It's late," she says in surprise.

"I know."

"I thought you were going home when I—"

"I know," I repeat, and sit all the way up, my back stiff. "That's the first and last time I lie to you; I promise."

The dim lighting in the room leaves shadows across her

face, but I can still see the mixture of emotions at finding me asleep at her bedside. Mostly trying to decide whether she should send me home and risk me falling asleep behind the wheel.

"I'm staying."

"You don't have to," she says softly.

I swallow hard. "I want to."

She's quiet for a moment, and I'm dying to know what she's thinking. Does she not want me here? Does she think I'm being clingy or possessive?

"Why?" she whispers.

Why?

She really doesn't know, then. She doesn't understand that my presence here is because I'm crazy about her. Maybe that's okay. At least for right now. It isn't the time for me to lay it out there for her. She's still recovering, and it will likely be a few days before she's feeling back to normal.

Besides, I'm not sure she's ready to hear me pour my heart out. Just because she's over Mason doesn't mean she's ready to jump into something with me.

So, I clear my throat and decide to go with the simplest explanation.

"Because I care about you. Very much."

"I...I care about you, too."

My heart pounds at her gentle tone.

"And if it were you in this bed, I wouldn't want to leave either," she adds, and then I feel her hand reach for mine. I let her slender fingers smooth over the back of my hand, and I find so much gratification in feeling the rough calluses on her fingertips.

"Good," I say quietly, buoyed slightly by her admission.

"I can't imagine that chair is comfortable," she murmurs, almost to herself. "If you insist on staying, then I insist on sharing this bed with you. It's the least I can do for putting you through all this."

Before I can say a word, she lowers the head of the bed down a little more and turns onto her right side. The gaps in her hospital gown give me a little shadowy glimpse of the curve of her bare spine.

Goosebumps erupt all over me. I haven't laid in bed next to a woman in more than five years.

"You'd do the same for me," her quiet voice throws out after a moment in which I can't get myself to move.

She's right. If roles were reversed, I wouldn't hesitate to do whatever I could for her to sleep comfortably.

I steel myself and acknowledge that the fatigue pulling at my body as I rise from the chair is a reminder that I really do need to rest. And sleeping any other way will give me nothing but a backache.

I lift back the blankets and pause, a wave of nerves hitting me straight in the gut. Mara wiggles over just a little more, as if encouraging me, and I step out of my boots. I climb in, feeling deeply vulnerable.

The hospital bed is obviously meant for one person, but there's just enough room for the both of us...if we're touching. I pull the blankets up over Mara's shoulder, my heart trembling, and then settle in behind her. My knees to the backs of her calves, my chest to her back, and my arm...

My heart stutters then.

"Can I...?" I trail off, and then she wordlessly takes my hand and pulls my arm around her.

Tears instantly prick at my eyes. Holding Mara is... *everything.*

"Goodnight," Mara murmurs, her hand staying on mine where she's tucked it against the front of her body.

"Night."

Despite how exhausted I am, the devastation I feel keeps me awake. The part of me that loves Gabby is guilty as hell for holding Mara close like this. Holding someone who isn't my wife just makes it that much more real that she's gone. And she's gone because I didn't save her. I don't deserve Mara and her sweet spirit. But I know it would take a firing squad to remove me from this woman right now.

I forgot how good it feels to be this close to someone. The gentle, radiant warmth is like balm, relaxing the tension in my shoulders. Mara fits perfectly against my body, like she was made for me. And the soft scent of her long hair smells like home to me.

I close my eyes, hurting just as much as I'm healing, and settle into sleep.

The morning comes quicker than I like and arrives with the sound of a nurse's voice.

I pry my eyes open, barely conscious, and it takes me a moment to realize that we're still at the hospital, and not at home in my bed.

"Sleep okay?" the nurse asks us, the same one who showed me to Mara's room last night.

"Mhm," Mara answers with a yawn.

With a lot of reluctance, I release Mara and get out of her

bed. She turns onto her back as I get my boots back on.

The nurse says something about checking vitals, so I back up out of the way. As I do, Mara catches my eye. She smiles this tiny little smile, a smile that's just for me. It's shy and sweet, and everything that makes me sure I'm in love with her. I don't hesitate to return that tiny smile.

"I'm gonna grab some coffee," I tell her, and then go off in search of the hospital cafeteria.

My mind is full of her as I wander the hallways, barely glancing at signs. I can smell her on my clothes. I can still feel her body wrapped up in mine. I want more of her. My conscience feels incredibly guilty, but the rest of me is already addicted to falling asleep with Mara in my arms. That's where she belongs.

I duck into line at a little cafe and purchase a coffee. I sip it on the walk back to Mara's room and check my phone when it buzzes in my pocket.

"Hey, Mom," I answer.

"How is she?" she asks without pretense. After Mara fell asleep the first time last night, I texted my mom to fill her in. I know she told Rosie that something came up and Mara couldn't make it to pizza night, but I'm not sure what she told her in regard to myself. Maybe that I had to help Rhys with something.

"She's good, I think." I approach Mara's door and peek in, finding the nurse entering something into the computer next to her bed.

Mara has moved the bed back up so she can be in a reclined sitting position. Despite the tiredness, she seems much more mentally alert than last night.

"Well, you tell her that whatever she needs, we've got

her covered," my mom says in my ear as I walk in.

"I will, Mom."

Mara visibly perks up. "Is that your mom? Can I talk to her?"

I smile at her. "Of course." I come forward and sit on the edge of the bed. I put my mom on speakerphone, but Mara takes my phone anyway.

"Hey, Linda," she greets, and I can already see her blue eyes filling with tears.

"Oh! Hello! How are you feeling, dear?" At the sound of my mom's voice, I see a change come over Mara. Her expression softens and relaxes. I know my mom is awesome, but it's clear that she's become something important to Mara. It makes me feel good.

"I'm okay. I feel better this morning."

"Oh, I'm so glad. Did you sleep okay in that hospital bed?"

Mara slides me a timid look, her cheeks blooming pink. "I actually slept the best I have in a really long time."

Her blush spreads to my cheeks as well, and I can't stop the smile that hoists up the corners of my mouth. I watch her speak with my mom like a mute, letting the sounds of Mom's and Mara's voices wash over me. I've missed this. There's been a missing piece to our family puzzle since Gabby died, and now I feel like our family could be complete with Mara in it. Her soft heart is matched by her indestructible fierceness. I admire that so much, and it comforts me even more.

Without thinking, I take her hand in mine and settle in as she finishes up her conversation with my mom. I probably have stars in my eyes, but I don't care. I didn't ask for the lesson but losing Gabby did teach me that time isn't always guaranteed. So, when Mara is ready, I will be, too.

It takes nearly two hours for Mara to be discharged. I pay close attention to the instructions from her doctor and intend on carrying them out myself when we get back to her house. I almost offer to take her to my house, but there's no doubt in my mind that Rosie won't let her rest. She'll want to play or color or read a book. That doesn't mean I'm going to let Mara be alone in her house. The last thing she needs is to lose her balance and fall down the steps. Mara is precious to me and to my family, and I want to take care of her accordingly.

But I should've known she would object. The first thing out of her mouth after I get her inside is that I can go.

"You should go home and see Rosie," she says, cradling her sore elbow with her right hand as she stands in the middle of her living room.

I raise one eyebrow at her and then take off my boots.

"I'm serious, Sean. You were gone all night and all morning. I'll be fine."

I take off my jacket too and hang it up next to hers. "Are you hungry? I can make you something." When I turn back to face her, Mara's eyebrows have lowered. She isn't exactly scowling, but she definitely isn't smiling. "What?"

"You're needed at home, Sean. I've already put you through enough."

My eyebrows lower, too. "Put me through enough?" I scoff at her. "Do I look like I'm ready to throw in the towel here? Absolutely not. And I never will. So, tell me what I can cook for you."

She looks at me curiously, like I'm a book written in a different language. "You don't have to."

I glare at her, starting to feel insulted. "I *know* that. I want to take care of you, all right? So, if you could get with the program, that would be great. Now, lunch?"

A few different expressions flicker over her face. Surprise with a tiny little blush, then a shadow of sass wiggling one eyebrow, and then acceptance. She follows me into the kitchen where her apple pie still sits on the stove, and I get to work.

It's clear to me that she isn't used to people caring about her. She mentioned this morning that the hospital never got a return call from her mom. And who knows how Mason treated her. If he cheated on her with Sarah and then divorced her, I can't imagine their marriage was equally loving. Thinking about it just makes me want to scoop her up in my arms and hold her until she understands that I'm not doing this just out of obligation. I'm doing it out of love.

"You should at least go home and change," she pipes up as I flip her grilled cheese. A little sizzle hisses on the hot pan and causes the smell of toasted bread and browned butter to momentarily drown out the scent of simmering tomato soup, which I made from a can of crushed tomatoes and some seasonings.

I look over my shoulder at where she's standing near the doorway to the spare room, arms folded.

"Do I smell that bad?"

She gives a little gasp, like she had no intention of being rude. "No, no, I—"

I cut her off with a chuckle and turn to grab a plate from the cabinet above the dishwasher. "Don't worry about me, Mara. But if you'd like to change after you eat, I'll help you get upstairs."

"You don't need to go up with me," she disagrees.

"I don't want you to fall," I say sternly, and use the spatula to place her sandwich on the plate. I step over to her, holding it out. I nod to the living room. "Take this, and I'll bring the soup."

Mara holds my gaze for a moment with a coolness I've never seen before. I may be pissing her off by being overbearing, but I'd rather her be a little upset with me than risk her hurting herself further.

At last, she takes the plate, and as she does, I realize it's the first time I've given her something that I've made on a plate. I guess I'm joining the club with her and Mom.

"Thank you," she says softly, glancing at the grilled cheese and then back up to me. This time there's more warmth there and a little gratitude, too.

I give her a lopsided smile and go back to the stove to stir the soup one more time before I get down a bowl.

Gabby could never resist that lopsided smile. She found it endearing or charming or something. Even if she was boiling mad at me, she would always quiet if I gave her that smile. My chest feels tight as I realize that's the first time I've smiled Gabby's favorite smile since she died. I still wish that smile could've saved her, but it didn't.

I shake my head slightly, willing that thought away even though it eats at me day and night no matter what I do. I dig around for a ladle and scoop out enough piping hot soup to fill a bowl. I carefully put it on an oven mitt and bring it into the living room. I find Mara sitting on her couch, slightly hunched over the plate on the coffee table in front of her, half of the grilled cheese already gone.

I try not to smile too much at that, but I'm pleased that she's eating. I lean over to set down her soup and something stops me from straightening up. I have the thoughtless notion to turn my head and plant a kiss on her forehead like I did last night. Her eyes flit to mine, slightly curious, as she notices the hitch in my motions. I quickly stand tall, ignoring the squirm in my gut.

"Good?" I ask her.

She nods, chewing. When she swallows, the sandwich in her hand lowers. "I'm sorry if your back hurts."

My back? I clear my throat. Oh. She thinks I stopped mid-stoop because my back hurts.

"You really didn't need to stay last—"

My heavy sigh cuts her off. I can't blame the woman, I guess. She doesn't know I care about her more than I've cared about anyone in a long time. So maybe it doesn't make sense to her why I would go so far out of my way to take care of her and make sure she was okay.

Soon, I promise myself. Soon, I'll tell her. But not now. Not when she's in pain and still mildly concussed. My stupid feelings can wait.

"Quit it with that, alright?" I nod towards her food. "Just eat."

Without giving her a chance to reply, I head back into the kitchen and get some soup for myself. But when I bring it back with me to sit next to Mara, she's looking down at her untouched bowl of soup, sandwich gone.

"What's the matter? You don't like tomato soup?" I question.

A tiny little smile hovers on her lips as she turns her

head to look at me. "It's not that," she assures me. "Mason just never cooked for me." She looks back at her soup and smiles a little more. "It's nice."

A warmth fills me up that has nothing to do with the soup. I'm glad she appreciates my effort, even if she fought me on it the whole way.

"Gabby was a horrible cook," I chuckle. "We used to say that she could burn a pot of water."

Mara laughs softly at that, and I watch as she takes a tomatoey spoonful into her mouth. Then I do the same.

"Was Mason a bad cook, too?"

"No," she tells me with a bit of a shrug. "Cooking just didn't interest him."

I cock my eyebrow at her. "A basic life skill didn't interest him?"

"I guess. He didn't have to cook because I did it, and before we were married, he ate on campus. Before that, his mom cooked everything."

I hate that explanation. What a spoiled baby. My parents made sure I knew how to cook and do laundry before I even graduated high school. Though the laundry thing started just because Mom refused to put her hands on my sweaty basketball uniform.

"That's stupid," I comment, aiming it at my soup. "At least Gabby had a good reason to not be allowed near a stove. Believe me, she tried to cook for us many times. I endured a whole list of charred food that no sane man would."

The memory of her first casserole burnt to a crisp still sends a shiver down my spine.

Mara smiles sweetly at me. "Just a man who's in love

would." Her smile fades quickly, but before I can wonder why, she goes on, looking away. "What was she like?"

It's an innocent question that I don't mind answering, but my mind flashes through what Gabby was like before she died, instead of what she was like before Rosie was born. It must show on my face because Mara quickly backtracks.

"I'm sorry. I shouldn't have asked." She takes a distracted and guilty swallow of soup as her cheeks redden.

It's the sweetest thing, that blush. That extra-large-sized conscience she has. I never would have expected to be so attracted to it, especially because Gabby didn't bat an eyelash when it came to something she wanted to know or something she wanted to say. It's so strange that I can still love that about Gabby while also love Mara's lack of it.

"It's alright," I assure her gently. "The holidays are the hardest. Rosie doesn't know any different, but for me, it's just an extra dose of reality that she's gone." My blood goes a little cold at the last two words out of my mouth, even though I'm eating hot soup.

"I'm sure," she murmurs. "I'm glad you talk about her, even if Rosie doesn't remember her."

I heave out a sigh. "I don't know." I shake my head slightly, remembering the other night. "Sometimes I think it sort of confuses her and just reminds her that she doesn't have a mom like her classmates do."

"One day she'll be glad you did, though."

I glance at her, beautiful red hair flowing over her shoulders, and take the encouragement she's giving me with appreciation.

"I'm a little biased because I grew up without a good example of a father, but I think you're a great dad. She's amazing."

I return the little smile she gives me. "Yeah, she is."

"I hope one day I can have a little girl like her."

"Yeah? You want kids?"

"Mhm, I always have."

My eyebrows flicker. Always? "Then why didn't you and Mason—?" I stop that sentence abruptly. It's not my business, really. But she answers anyway, like it isn't a personal question at all.

"He said he wanted the same things I did, but when it came down to it, he made excuses. Obviously at this point I'm glad we didn't... It would've been heartbreaking to have a child who isn't wanted by their father, like I was."

My heart thumps painfully in my chest. *Like I was.* Ouch. She doesn't deserve to think that about herself— that she wasn't wanted. I can't imagine anyone, including her idiot ex-husband, not wanting her.

"I'm sorry, Mara. He has no idea what he's missing." Even though I mean them, the words fall flat. Nothing I say will change what her father did or even change how she feels about him.

But Mara nods, not seeming particularly ruffled by speaking about her dad. "At least Rosie was loved. She might not remember her mama, but at least she doesn't realize what she's missing. Like I did when he left."

I watch her for a moment as she takes more soup into her mouth. She speaks so passively about him. But she said once that she hasn't spoken to him since she was nine. That's a long time to come to terms with his absence in her life.

But what I can't get past is how the two most important

men in her life have left her. The two men who should've been by her side forever had elected to leave. What the hell is wrong with them?

I reach for her hand without a thought and let my fingers move over hers as she looks up at me. My chest tightens.

"We haven't known each other forever, but I can honestly say that you're not someone who would be easy for me to leave." I pause, wondering if I should just blurt it all out there. Nerves hit me like a train, so at the last second, I bail on that idea. "Leaving isn't something I do unless my daughter's well-being is at risk. Okay?"

She eyes me warily, like she isn't sure why I'm telling her this. But then that wariness eases back, and a genuine smile emerges, tiny and sweet in that way I'm addicted to.

It's then I realize I'm still touching her hand, so like an awkward teenager, I abruptly remove it and turn back to my mostly uneaten soup.

"Sean," she murmurs, to get my attention again, and I give it to her. She has a soft look on her face. "I've never been the one to leave." She glances around my face, taking in my eyes and hair and then my mouth before pointing those blue jewels at my eyes again. "I stay to a fault."

I study her expression, noticing the warmth as well as the bitterness.

"You didn't want to leave him? After what he did?" With *Sarah* of all people?

Mara gives me a sad smile and shakes her head. "I tried to make him love me again. I...tried to give him reasons to choose me." She looks away, toward the scattered puzzle pieces on the coffee table in front of her bowl. "I regret that now, but...I can't go back."

If there's anyone who understands wanting to go back to change something, it's me.

"It doesn't matter now. Besides, at least something good came out of it," she adds as she looks back up at me with light in her expression. "You. And Rosie and your mom."

I smile at her. "Yeah, we're pretty awesome."

She laughs softly, and I do, too. Then Mara gazes at me with warmth. "You really are."

CHAPTER TWENTY-SIX

Mara

With my good arm, I run the brush through the long strands of my wet hair. It was difficult taking a shower. Not only does my head still really hurt from the impact, but bending my left arm around to wash my hair didn't feel great. Not that I'll mention that to Sean if he asks, which he probably will.

In the mirror, I glance down at the gap between the floor and the closed bathroom door. There's a shadow there, and I have no doubt in my mind that Sean has been standing there for the entire twenty minutes it took me to shower and dry off.

He's being protective, which I'm not used to. I don't know what to do with the way he watches me like a hawk with every move I make, like he's trying to figure out when I'm hurting. It should feel nice to be looked after, and it does, I guess, but it mostly just feels...strange. Foreign.

I put the brush away and then turn around to face the door. The shadow is still there, so I prepare myself to come face to face with him when I open the door. With a slightly self-conscious glance at the gray joggers and black sweatshirt I'm wearing, I turn the handle and find Sean's anxious expression as soon as I step out.

His brown eyes look me up and down quickly, assessing whether I've hurt myself even more somehow in the shower. Before I went in, he announced that he would be close by so he could hear me if I slipped and fell.

I sigh at him. "Okay, here's what's going to happen now," I tell him as sternly as I can, which isn't coming off that stern at all, "I'm going to curl up on the couch and not move while you go home and brush your teeth and change your clothes and see your daughter."

Sean blinks at me as he brings his hands to his hips.

"I'll be *fine*, Sean. Please."

"No one's ever tried to get rid of me before," he mutters, a flash of amusement glinting in his eyes.

I stifle a chuckle. "Just go. Bring your family back with you for dinner, if you like."

He glances at his watch and sighs. "But that's hours from now."

I roll my eyes and then regret it when pain slices through my head. "I'll be fine," I repeat. "If I need anything, I'll text you."

Sean frowns, his hands still on his hips. It reminds me of Linda, and I smile at him. "*Anything*, okay? Even if it's nothing. Text me," he stipulates seriously.

"Yes, sir."

He narrows his eyes at me, but I still see the smile he's trying to hold back.

"Thank you," I add, before he can change his mind.

He helps me get settled on the couch, propping my poor head with a pillow and tucking a blanket around me like I'm a little girl. Then he hands me the remote and moves my phone, which he brought with him to the hospital last night, closer to the edge of the coffee table.

"Let me get you some water—or do you want tea? I'll get both." Then he disappears into the kitchen as I try to remember the last time someone took care of me like this.

Mason never did. I can't even remember a time when my mom did. The last person to look after me when I was ill was my grandma, decades ago. And she had done it the way Sean is now, without a hint of irritation or selfishness. I sigh softly. I miss her. She had a knack for always knowing when I needed a hug or when I needed space to think. She was kind and funny, and always made time for me. And I wonder if she's the last person in my life who loved me. Like *really* loved me. It's clear to me after the divorce that Mason got along well enough with me to marry me, but you don't do what he did to someone you love.

Sean returns with a glass of water and a hot mug of tea. He places them both on the coffee table in front of me and then straightens up. He looks down at me, and I already know he's going to offer to stay longer, so I smile at him.

"Thank you. I'll see you later."

His mouth twists to the side, eyes slightly narrowed at me, but then he nods.

I watch him head to the front door, where he pauses with his hand on the doorknob, looking over his shoulder at me.

"Go," I urge him, laughing. "I'm not dying. I'm fine."

He sighs but does as I say and disappears out the front

door.

I smile to myself and close my eyes, but then I hear the door open again.

"You're due for Tylenol in an hour," Sean says, already striding through the living room towards the kitchen. "I'll get it."

I bite my lip, feeling a strange mix of amusement and gratitude. Sean reappears and places the medication bottle next to the glass of water. I smile up at him while he stands in front of me for another moment, his brown eyes on the ceiling thoughtfully, like he's making sure he isn't forgetting anything else I might need.

He nods to himself and looks down at me. "Okay. Text me. Even if you just need another blanket or something."

"I will."

He sighs and then goes back out the front door.

I wait, fully expecting him to make another appearance for some silly reason, but he doesn't. So, I settle in as comfortably as I can, intending to let myself drift off, but my mind stays focused on one thing: the way it felt to fall asleep with Sean last night. I know I shouldn't think about it. I have no business thinking about it. But...I do. I've never slept in the same bed with anyone besides Mason. And I wasn't lying when I told Linda that I slept better than I have in a long time. Maybe it was the concussion that caused me to rest so completely, but deep down, I know it was because of Sean.

My eyes slowly open, and I stare up at the ceiling as my mind continues to sort through the last twenty four hours. Falling. Sean almost getting kicked out of the hospital. His stricken face when he saw me. The way he kissed my forehead. The way he asked if he could put his arm around me. Waking up next to someone for the first time in a year. Him making me lunch.

So many of his actions have been completely filled with care and concern that I don't know what to think. He didn't need to go that above and beyond for me, but he did. And all I can ask myself is *why*. I know he isn't purposely trying to get that sweet spot I have for him to grow, but that's what's happening.

My stomach churns at how pathetic I feel. A man is being decent and kind to me, and that's apparently all it takes for me to want something I shouldn't be wanting. Mason left me so hungry for love that the second anyone else shows me just a little bit of it, I'm a goner.

No. I can't let myself get swept away in Sean's well-meaning intentions. That's all he feels for me. Good intentions. He's taking care of me in the same way Linda would. I'm not the object of his affection or desire. I'm a family friend. That's all. I can't let myself forget that. I can't let myself get hurt because *I* took his actions to mean more than they are.

This is my fault. And maybe Mason's. He's the only experience I've ever had with relationships or romantic feelings for the opposite sex. And now that he's out of the picture, I just feel...clueless. Because clearly Sean isn't a damn thing like my ex-husband. And as much as I'm grateful for that, I can't take that out of context, no matter how hungry I am for affection. It isn't Sean's fault that I'm a dry sponge ready to soak up any kind of moisture I can get.

We're friends. Friends take care of each other. And...sleep in the same bed sometimes...

I let out a heavy sigh.

What was I thinking, inviting him into bed with me last night? I could blame it on the concussion, but... I shouldn't have done that. Even if it was amazing. He only took me up on it because that chair was so uncomfortable.

I palm my achy forehead as embarrassment floods me. Could I have been any more obvious? *Sleep in my tiny hospital bed with me.* I'm so pathetic. And I need to reel it in. He's my friend. That's where it begins and ends. I don't want to ruin things, not when I could really use a friend like him.

I do my best to put it out of my mind, then. I try to think about other things until I sink into a doze. The next thing I know, there's loud knocking coming from my front door.

I rub my eyes. Did I sleep that long that it's already dinner time?

"Come on in," I call out to who I assume is the Dunbars. But when the door opens, the smile I had ready for my favorite family slides off my face.

My mother steps inside, rubbing her gloved hands together and shivering. "Damn, I didn't need the reminder of how cold it is here in the winter," she exclaims crossly. She stomps her shoes on the rug and closes the door.

I sit up, and immediately, my head throbs. "Mom," I say in surprise. "What are you doing here?" My mind quickly whirs through the information I have of the hospital not being able to reach her and wonder...did she come all this way to make sure I was okay? Did she drop everything and get on the first flight available?

She turns toward me, still rubbing her hands together, and I don't miss the almost timid look on her face.

"I came as soon as I could," she admits.

"You...?" I trail off in shock.

She finally drops her hands and places them on her hips as she looks me over with a frown. "You're okay, aren't you? The hospital said they released you this morning."

To say I'm surprised is an understatement. She came all this way. For me. Emotion trembles through my chest.

"Yeah, I'm okay," I answer, fighting the tears stinging my eyes. "I—I didn't think—" I stop, not wanting to admit it...but I didn't think she cared. I assumed her radio silence was her way of saying she didn't, even if I was in the hospital.

My mom removes her gloves and unzips her jacket, avoiding my eyes. Her back is to me as she makes a production of hanging up her jacket. When she turns back to face me, she looks nothing like the woman I know.

The nicely styled brown hair and blue eyes framed in mascara look the same, but her face is blotchy and scrunched up, with all traces of her usual composure gone. When her eyes meet mine, I don't recognize the remorse in her gaze because I have literally never seen it before.

"I'm sorry," she whispers.

I blink. What? She's *sorry*?

What is happening? Am I still sleeping? Am I somehow still unconscious in my hospital bed? Because I have *never* heard my mother genuinely apologize. Ever.

"I know I'm not the mother you need. I never have been." She sniffs and wrings her hands. "I know how I am, Mara. Everything you said was dead on, and I deserved to hear it."

"Mom," I gasp out, utterly gob smacked.

She smiles bitterly. "You get that from your grandmother, you know. She always knew what I needed to hear."

I watch her hesitate to come closer, so I pull my legs in closer to my body to make room for her on the couch. She steps forward slowly, with dread and almost humiliation, and stiffly sits next to me.

"When I got the message from the hospital, I..." She pauses, her face reddening. "I realized—I realized that I could've lost you and never gotten the chance to make things right. So, I had to come right away."

I stare at this woman who's behaving so unlike herself that I almost don't know how to talk to her. "I...I appreciate that, Mom," I stammer out.

She nods, and in the slightly awkward silence that follows, she takes in my living room. I wait, expecting something critical to come out of her mouth about the state of my house, but she says nothing, and eventually, her attention returns to me.

"So, what happened? The hospital said you slipped and fell, but that's the extent of what I know besides you being discharged this morning."

I explain how I was getting the mail, slipped, and woke up in the hospital. I hesitate then, because she won't be happy to hear that Mason was there when I woke up and tried to get me to take him back. I decide to skip that part and then hesitate again to mention Sean, because I know she's going to jump on that and assume he and I are something that we're not...something I foolishly wish we could be.

"They kept me overnight as a precaution, and my neighbor Sean drove me home this morning," is what I go with, keeping our little night in the hospital bed a secret. It really isn't any of her business anyway, but I also want to keep last night tucked in close to my heart where she can't pick it apart or warp it with her own opinions.

My mother eyes me, and I can feel her suspicions even if she doesn't voice them. She's more perceptive in person than she is over the phone and I'm not particularly grateful for that at the moment.

"I thought your neighbor's name was Linda," she says slowly.

I nod slightly. "Linda is his mother."

Mom's brows scrunch up. "I didn't realize Linda was old enough to have a teenage son who can drive."

My cheeks heat up. I know the second I explain their ages she's going to pounce on the idea of me using Sean to make Mason jealous. But I also feel a little stab of sadness that she knows so little about my life...about the people who've come to mean so much to me.

"Linda is your age," I tell her quietly. "Her son, Sean, is a single dad to the most amazing little girl."

Her previously scrunched eyebrows rise and rise with each word out of my mouth, and I brace myself for what she's about to say.

"Hmm."

Hmm? That's it?

"Um, if you want to meet them, they'll be here for dinner." The offer is genuine, but I half hope she turns it down.

"I would; thank you."

Silence falls again because she doesn't know how to do this. She doesn't know how to talk with me honestly, in a way that isn't pushy or self-serving in some way.

"Thank you for being here," I throw out. "I didn't expect you to—" I break off abruptly, because I'm not sure how to say I expected her not to be bothered without it sounding harsh and cold.

She nods. "Even though you're fine, I'm glad I came. It's time we sorted things out."

I assume she means our little fight, but when she continues, I'm shocked even more by what she says.

"Being a mother has never come easily to me," she admits awkwardly to her hands, clasped tightly in her lap. "I'm not like my mother. I'm much more like my father...detached, cool."

I never knew my grandfather. He died before I was born and neither my mother nor my grandma spoke about him much.

She swallows and meets my gaze. "But I hope you know that even though my attempts to be a good mother have fallen short, I've only ever wanted the best for you. And I hate that you married someone who hurt you like that. I hate that I couldn't protect you from it."

Her words feel like a gentle, warm breeze. She cares. She actually cares.

"All I want is for you to be happy. To leave that horrible man behind and build your future without him."

I nod, smiling a little. "I am. My life is better now than it's been in more than a year."

Her blue eyes, darker in color than mine, soften. "You are?"

"Yes. I'm playing and singing again, and I spend a lot of time with Linda, Sean, and Rosie. They make my life so full, Mom."

Her expression softens now, too. "Good, Mara." She reaches out and pats my knee, which I know is as physically affectionate as she gets. "Hang on to that as long as you can because happiness can be fleeting."

I study her, wondering if she's even been happy. I can't remember a time when she wasn't some combination of grumpy and judgmental.

"Are you happy, Mama?"

The term of endearment forces her eyes to mine.

"Were you happy with Dad? Are you happier without him?"

She grimaces at the mention of her ex-husband and sighs as she looks away. "I never loved him, Mara. Not really."

What?

"Then why did you marry him?" My head spins with questions. Why did they have me? Was I an accident?

She gives a little shrug. "He was a good choice. He was from a good family and was in law school. He was nice enough and fine to look at."

This is the most I've heard her talk about him, and I see how much it pains her even after all these years.

"The truth is that I loved someone else, someone who chose what his family wanted over me," she murmurs, speaking from a vulnerable place that makes me want to cry. "So, when he broke my heart, I proved to him that I was good enough to be loved by someone just like him—from a family just like his."

I know my mom grew up with less than other kids her age. She and her sister wore secondhand clothing and worn down shoes for many years, simply because my grandfather was an electrician and my grandmother made extra money by cleaning people's houses. They were humble people. That's one of the big reasons she worked so hard as a realtor and was gone so much. She wanted to prove to everybody that she was successful.

"It didn't take long for your father to realize I didn't marry him for love. It ate at him. I thought giving him a child would help...that a baby would love him like I didn't. But you were born, and nothing changed. I think he thought I was trying to trap him into staying."

All of these words have me listening raptly, each one hitting me like a seismic wave.

"He found someone new almost immediately after the divorce was final, and seeing how much happier he was because of someone else just...hurt. He moved on so quickly, and I had no one. Just you, a reminder of all my failures, and my mother, who loved you better than I did." She sniffs, the splotches on her face sharpening. "And then she died and...and I just didn't know how to be who you needed me to be."

I touch her hand as she gives in to her tears, her shoulders shaking slightly. Even in this moment of truth, I can feel how uncomfortable she is. These are things she probably never thought she would tell me. This is a side of her she never lets anyone see.

"Mama, you did the best you could," I tell her, leaning closer. "I know you did. It's okay."

She nods and takes a few breaths to get herself under control. "I'm sorry for pushing you so much, I just told you to do the only thing I knew. So, when you pushed back, I just...fell apart, because you have so much goodness in you. A goodness that reminds me so much of my mother."

I squeeze her hand as my eyes sting. She looks up at me with her mascara beginning to seep onto her cheeks. I've always thought she was beautiful, but she's never looked more beautiful to me than she does in this moment.

"She would be so proud of the woman you've become, Mara. And I'm proud, too."

I smile, tears leaking out as I do. "Thank you, Mama," I whisper, and scoot forward to hug her. She lets me and responds by simply patting my wrist. When I pull back, she wipes beneath her eyes.

"So, tell me about these neighbors of yours," she says lightly, changing the subject. "I want to know everything about the people who make you so happy."

I swipe at my eyes with the back of my hand and smile. I tell her about Linda baking me things, and how Rosie befriended me. I gloss over Sean, mostly because I don't trust myself not to be obvious about how I feel about him. It doesn't matter though because she notices.

"Does this Sean have a significant other?"

I swallow hard and shake my head. "His wife died not long after Rosie was born, and he's been single ever since."

My mom frowns, watching me carefully. "That's a shame about his wife. How did she die?"

I open my mouth to answer her but then realize I don't actually know. He's never told me, and I've never asked. It's not my business, and it felt insensitive and too personal to ask.

"I don't know. He doesn't talk about it," is what I say, even as my mind goes back through the conversations I've had with him and with Linda. I can't recall a time that either one of them mentioned how Gabby passed.

"Hmm," she says for the second time since she's arrived. "Well, I look forward to meeting him."

I squint at her slightly and decide to just get it out there so she can't say anything to make Sean uncomfortable later.

"There's nothing going on between me and Sean. We're just friends."

I've never been a good liar. The fact that Sean and I are just friends isn't a lie, but the first sentence isn't exactly true. At least not for me. Not for my pathetic, lonely soul who invited him into my hospital bed last night.

She carefully studies my face, making my stomach squirm, and then she says the last thing I expect. "Okay."

Okay?

No, *well you need to snap him up so you can move on?*

No, *thank goodness you finally listened to me and found someone to make Mason jealous with?*

Who is this woman?

This is so strange. A...*good* strange. But I hate to let myself hope that maybe my mom is trying to *really* change. I would be too disappointed if I was wrong.

CHAPTER TWENTY-SEVEN

Sean

My little girl is a mess. My mom told me she was worried last night when I didn't come home and Mara never showed up for pizza night. I instructed her to tell Rosie in the morning that Mara had a fall and I was taking care of her. But what I didn't know until I finally tore myself away from Mara on the couch was that Mom had mentioned the H word: hospital. So, when I walked through the door, tired and still concerned about our neighbor, Rosie broke down in my arms. It was heartbreaking to hold her little body and try to assure her that everything was fine and she could go see Mara later.

The promise of seeing Mara soon helped her to calm down, but I can feel how on edge she is. After I hop in the shower and change, I try everything I can think of to keep her mind off Mara. Puzzles, card games, movies, baking cookies, but none of that changes the pinch in her blond eyebrows.

I know Mom is just as eager to see Mara as my daughter is, even though she knows more information. She tries to keep busy, too, mostly in the kitchen where she's throwing together a casserole to take over to Mara's for dinner in a couple hours.

And when Rhys shows up unannounced, I'm not surprised. He knows what it's like to lose someone. He knows how panicked I was last night when I couldn't find her. I'm sure all of this is taking him back to losing Gabby, just like it has for me.

"Hey," he greets quietly, his face somber, though he tries to smile through it.

I nod at him from where I'm sitting on the floor next to Rosie. We're coloring pictures for Mara at the coffee table.

"Is that Rhys?" my mom calls from the kitchen.

"Hey Mrs. D," he calls back, and then puts his eyes on me. I feel him trying to figure out Mara's condition by studying the expressions on my face.

Mom appears in the doorway of the kitchen. "We're going over to see Mara later; are you coming?"

"Of course," he replies at once and comes forward to sit on the floor across from me and Rosie. He reaches for a blank piece of paper and a green crayon, eyeing both of us.

Electronic chimes ring out from somewhere in the kitchen, and my mom disappears to answer her phone. Probably Doug checking in. He went to the Twin Cities this morning to help his daughter move into her new apartment. I hear her talking quietly in the other room as the three of us silently color.

I think I can speak for all of us when I say the waiting is unbearable. It's taken everything in me not to text Mara or just go back over there. I know she's okay, but... It doesn't stop the thoughts ping-ponging around in my mind.

What if no one had spotted her outside and called 911?

What if I never got to tell her how much she means to me? To us?

What if my time with her had been even shorter than my time with Gabby?

Life is so short. I hate that it's so damn short, and there's so much out of my control. Regardless of where Mara is at in moving on from Mason, I need her to know where I stand. I need her to know even if she isn't ready. Even if she doesn't feel the same way. I'm willing to risk it all just so she knows how much I care about her, including my pride.

I glance up at Rhys, noticing how tight his jaw is clenched as he colors with us. He's been telling me that it's okay for me to be happy again and to reach out to Mara, but he knows more than anyone how hard it is for me to leave Gabby in the ground. It's second nature for me to dig her up in my mind over and over again to say the things I didn't say when she was alive. If I move on with Mara, I'll have to leave her buried. I'll have to come to terms with the fact that I didn't save her.

And how the hell do I do that?

I swallow down the lump in my throat.

Like he can tell what I'm thinking, Rhys's eyes flick to mine and then the porch, indicating he wants to talk outside where Rosie won't hear us.

Instead, Mom comes back into the room, apparently done with her phone call. "Rosie girl, I'd love some help with the casserole. Mara will like that we made it together."

My daughter's shoulders stiffen slightly at my mother's words, but she gets up and sulks into the kitchen without a word.

When I turn my head back to Rhys, he holds my gaze.

"How is she doing today?"

"Fine. Better."

My short answer does nothing to lessen the concern on his face. He looks behind me into the kitchen, where I can hear Mom giving Rosie directions.

"And you?" he asks when he looks back at me.

My stomach clenches. I open my mouth to answer but nothing comes out, so I close it again and toss my black crayon on the coffee table.

"Come on," he says, doing the same. "Let's talk outside."

We get to our feet and head outside to the front porch. The temperatures are warmer today, but I still put a liberal amount of salt down on Mara's sidewalk earlier. Despite the sun, I feel nothing but gloomy and sick to my stomach.

Without the presence of my family, I feel the things I've been trying to ignore, and I don't know how to get it out.

"Talk to me, man," he says, his voice reaching through the haze of grief and anxiety.

I look beyond his shoulder to Mara's house as my mind swirls to when I was standing in her living room. The moment I was so sure she had gone back to the bridge.

"I...I thought that was it, Rhys." I shake my head as bile rises up my throat. "I thought I had lost her just like I lost Gabby. Hell, it was like losing her all over again because for hours I thought I had failed Mara, too...I thought I had failed the only two women I've ever loved." I sniff as I remember racing to that bridge. The panic comes back to me like the rushing water splashing the lonely riverbank. "Maybe it's me, you know? Maybe I'm just cursed."

Rhys clears his throat and rocks back and forth from

one foot to the other, like he's gearing up to say something I don't want to hear.

"Sean, you didn't run that bath."

My ears start ringing as I stare at my best friend who speaks brokenly through the moisture welling in his eyes.

"You didn't force her under. She chose that. Trust me, I feel guilty, too. I didn't check in with her as often as I should have. I didn't speak up and insist she see her doctor. It's not just you, okay? We lost an amazing woman, but there's nothing we can do about that now. She's gone. And it will always hurt that she's gone, but she wouldn't want you or me blaming ourselves for her actions."

I curse under my breath and swipe at my eyes with the back of my hand. "Rhys...I—I don't know how to let go," I whisper.

He smiles at me just slightly. "You don't have to let go of Gabby. You just need to let go of the guilt." He clears his throat. "We both do."

We stare at each other, the truth linking us and making me that much surer that this guy is a brother to me. I nod slowly because he's right.

"She loved you," Rhys says. "You know that, right?"

My mouth goes dry, then. "Rhys..." I mutter warningly.

"She *did*. Say it."

My teeth grit together, and I feel myself shut down. "Stop." Every inch of me tenses, like if I try hard enough, I can erect a tough enough barrier to keep this from weakening me.

"You weren't the reason she wanted to die," he continues, stepping closer to me.

My lungs seize up, and everything starts to close in on

me. Every moment of her hurting flashes through my mind, every moment that I missed the signs, and then the last moment. The moment I pulled her out of that bathtub and wept.

"Sean," he says from a long way off as his hand grips my shoulder. "Look."

Through my blurry eyes, I see the illuminated screen of his phone.

"It's the last text she sent me."

I take his phone with shaking fingers and force myself to read the text message.

Gabby: *Tell Sean that I love him.*

The words move and blur as my hand visibly trembles, and then Rhys takes the phone out of my grasp.

"You were the last thing she was thinking about before she died," he whispers roughly. "And I will remind you of that for the rest of your life if I have to, because she asked me to."

She didn't want to leave *me*. She just wanted to leave her suffering. The reason for her last breath wasn't because I wasn't enough for her, it was that her pain was too much.

And the fact that Rhys saved this text for more than five years... For him to show it to me now when I need it the most...

Something crumbles in me.

"She loved you," he says again, squeezing my shoulder. "And loving Mara doesn't mean you love Gabby less."

A choking sound comes out of my throat. I feel strangled by Rhys's words but also freed by them.

It has to be enough that I would've saved Gabby if I could have. There's nothing else I can do about her death now.

The guilt doesn't change a damn thing. The guilt won't bring her back.

"Why couldn't I have saved her?" I whisper through the wetness on my face that is running down into the scruff on my chin and jaw. "If I had just come home an hour earlier—"

"But you didn't. And you can't go back. She wouldn't want you to. She would want you to find the happiness she couldn't find for herself." He roughly smacks his hands down on both of my shoulders. "It's time, Sean. It's time you put down the blame. It's time for both of us."

I clear my throat and nod weakly with my eyes at my feet. "You're right," I mutter. "It's just..."

"She isn't here to tell you not to be an idiot," he says through a watery grin. "So, don't be an idiot."

A sad chuckle pushes out of me, and I pat him firmly on the back as he releases his grip on my shoulders. "She did love calling me an idiot."

"And a lot of the time it was deserved," he adds, chuckling too as he wipes his nose with the sleeve of his sweatshirt.

When I move my eyes to his, an affirming look of understanding passes between us.

"Thanks, man."

"Of course."

My conversation with Rhys is heavy on my mind as we walk over to Mara's. Rosie is practically jogging to get there as quickly as possible while my mom attempts to hang onto her hand. Rhys walks two steps behind me, a silent supportive shadow that reminds me of where my life needs to go now.

I can't go back. I can't keep standing still. I need to forgive myself for not helping Gabby when I was able to. And I need to forgive her for being a flawed human who just wanted out. I need to be the best damn father I can to Rosie. I need to support my mom as she takes the next step in her life with Doug.

I need to tell Mara that I love her.

And like Rhys said, I can still love Gabby. And I will. I will always love her. And the best way to show it is to love Rosie with everything I've got. The best way to honor Gabby is to not run from the things that make me happy. And Mara? She makes me really damn happy.

"Whose car is that?" Rhys asks from behind me.

We walk around the red Honda Civic parked in Mara's driveway to get to the concrete front steps. Mara has company? Now?

"No clue."

Rosie finally succeeds in wrenching her hand out of Mom's and races up the steps to pound her little fist on the screen door. I beat my mom to Rosie's side and shift the casserole dish I'm carrying to my left hand.

"Remember, Rosie," I warn, "be gentle—"

The interior door opens, and a middle-aged woman stands there. My head cocks to the side in confusion, and I'm about to ask about Mara when Rosie squeezes beside this woman and into the house.

"Rosie—" I call out. The woman steps aside to let us in.

I step inside and what I see has my heart twisting in my

chest. Mara is sitting on the couch with my daughter on her lap, their arms around each other tightly. I couldn't ask for a better woman to love my daughter than Mara.

"Hi, sweet girl," Mara coos into Rosie's blond hair.

"These must be your neighbors," the stranger says, eyeing my family and Rhys.

"That's correct. I'm Sean," I introduce as Mara continues to talk softly with my little girl. "That's my daughter, Rosie, and this is my mom, Linda, and my friend, Rhys."

This woman, who I'm beginning to see has a slight resemblance to Mara, takes each of us in and then her blue eyes—darker than Mara's—return to me. "I've heard a lot about you," she says stiffly with a wariness to her expression that I'm not sure what to do with.

"This is my mother," Mara adds, "Vivian."

Her mother. I fight to keep my face neutral, but all I can think of is what she said to Mara that made her so upset—how hurt she was because of this woman. How she wanted Mara to get back at her ex-husband and make him jealous. How she was happy that Mara wasn't playing or singing.

"It's nice to meet you, Vivian," my mom says, and even I catch the slight iciness to her voice. She obviously remembers those things, too.

"I was scared," Rosie's little voice squeaks out. "Sometimes people don't come back from the hospital."

I swallow hard, forgetting Vivian, and glance at Rhys.

"I'm so sorry I scared you," Mara says soothingly. "I'm just fine, Rosie. Only a little bump on my head and my elbow, okay? I'll be back to normal again in no time."

My daughter nods solemnly but stays close to Mara.

"Uh, we brought dinner," I say, lifting the dish in my hand. My attention goes back to Vivian, who I can tell is trying to read between the lines of whatever my relationship is with her daughter.

"I helped make it!" Rosie informs Mara, who smiles at her.

My heartbeat picks up. Damn, that smile. That smile could heal wounds, I'm sure of it. It could heal *my* wounds even…if I let it. She looks up at me then, her blue eyes happy and clear, and I almost think she can see it in my eyes. The love. The vulnerability.

"Rhys, will you help me with the plates?" Mom asks and takes the casserole from me. He follows her without a word, looking between me and Vivian, and they disappear into the kitchen.

I clear my throat and offer my hand to Vivian. "It's nice to meet you, Vivian. You must've flown in today."

She shakes my hand thoughtfully as I examine her a little more. Her features don't remind me of Mara. The shape of her eyes, maybe, but Vivian's hair is brown and stick straight, and she holds herself just as straight, like her spine is an iron rod.

"I did. I got on the first flight available," she says, looking back at her daughter and mine.

I don't know very much about her relationship with Mara, but what I do know isn't great. As far as I know, this woman says hurtful things and doesn't apologize for it and harasses her daughter into moving on instead of supporting her. But Mara doesn't seem at all bothered or uncomfortable by her mom's presence here, so I decide to take that as a cue.

"Your mommy is pretty," Rosie whispers loudly, and I

crack a smile. Vivian blushes just the tiniest bit, and then she seems to relax slightly.

"She's very sweet," she says to me quietly and then raises one eyebrow at me. "Does she get that from you?"

"Yes," Mara answers for me warmly, that smile still out for everyone to see.

A fuzzy feeling warms up my chest, and I return her smile. "Mom might argue she gets it from her," I say with a chuckle, and Mara chuckles, too.

"What does she get from Mrs. D?" comes Rhys's voice as he appears with plates and forks. He sets them down on the coffee table.

"Her sweetness," I answer as he sets the plates out.

He snorts. "Sweetness? From her? No way; she gets it from me."

Mara giggles, and I roll my eyes with a smirk. Mom brings the tater tot hotdish in then, with a serving spoon stuck into it. "Mara we really need to get you a dining room table," she says as she places our dinner in the middle of the coffee table.

The women all sit on the couch, with Rosie sitting as closely as she can next to Mara, and me and Rhys take the floor. I notice Vivian frown as she takes the first bite, and I brace myself for whatever criticism is about to come out of her mouth. But instead, she looks over at Mara, and her expression turns sad.

"I haven't had tater tot hotdish in decades," she admits, almost to herself. "The last time I had it was when my mother was still alive." She sniffs, looking down at her plate. "It's just as good as hers."

Mara reaches over and squeezes her hand with an

understanding smile. They share a moment of unspoken thoughts that makes me sure Mara and her mom had some kind of catharsis.

"There's nothing better than your mom's cooking," my mom joins in, "especially when you aren't feeling so well."

Mara nods and releases Vivian's hand. I go back to my plate but notice that Rhys has his fork frozen above his plate, an unreadable expression on his face. I elbow him as discreetly as possible, and that snaps him out of it.

"My daughter is very lucky to have you all," Vivian says softly. "Thank you for looking after her while I've been away."

"It's been an absolute pleasure, Vivian. You raised her well," Mom gushes on the other side of Mara.

Vivian clears her throat and goes back to eating, clearly uncomfortable with that compliment. "So, what do you do, Sean?"

"Rhys and I own a tree trimming company."

"Hmm." She turns her sights on my mom. "And you, Linda?"

"Retired and loving it," Mom replies with a grin. "I worked as the school secretary for our local high school. That's where I met Sean's father, actually. He was a music teacher."

I just barely catch the nerves that flash through Mara's eyes, nerves I don't understand. She watches her mom like a hawk, as if worried she might say something rude. But Vivian gives Mom an almost approving smile.

"That's lovely," she says, sounding totally genuine. Mara visibly relaxes. "Has your husband passed?"

"Seven years ago," my mom replies, sounding only a little somber.

"And now she's engaged to Doug," Mara adds, looking at Vivian. "They've been together for a few years and are getting married in the spring."

"I'm going to be a flower girl!" Rosie announces joyfully, and I grin at my little girl.

Mom beams. "Yes, Rosie Posie, you're going to be the most beautiful flower girl ever."

"You know, I'm still waiting for you to ask me to be the ring bearer," Rhys teases, pretending to be put out over it.

Mom laughs and leans over the coffee table to pinch his cheek. "I had no idea, Rhys. Of course, you can be the ring bearer."

Rhys winks at her and goes back to cleaning his plate.

"Are you married, Vivian?" Mom's question has both mother and daughter tensing.

"Uh, no, I'm not."

Mom nods. "Good men can be hard to come by. My philosophy is that if you find a good one, you keep him."

I narrow my eyes at her not-so-subtle hint. She pretends not to notice.

"I've been telling Mara she needs to start dating," Vivian agrees, "but she's—"

"Okay on my own," Mara interrupts.

I try not to let that sentence get to me. She *is* okay on her own, there's no doubt about that. But that means she isn't looking to be in another relationship right now. It reminds me that there's a pretty big chance my little confession will just make me feel like a fool, but I'd rather be a fool than regret saying it.

"But it's okay to hold Daddy's hand if you want to," says Rosie sweetly.

Everyone's eyes turn to me as Mara blushes. I clear my throat and break out into a sweat as I try to come up with a way to explain away what she's said.

"I know for a fact that he really likes holding your hand," Rhys adds with a big smile. I shoot him laser beam eyes that do absolutely nothing.

"Mara, I thought you said you and Sean were just friends," Vivian says suspiciously to her ever-reddening daughter.

"Uh, we are," she answers, and if I hadn't been looking at her as she spoke, I would've missed the flicker of disappointment in her eyes. It makes my heart squeeze, because...maybe she feels the same way. Maybe she isn't the only one who wishes there was more than just friendship between us. Maybe just being friends with me isn't what she wants after all.

A little bit of hope buoys me up.

"Friends who hold hands sometimes, apparently," Rhys snickers.

I elbow him hard this time.

"Ow!"

Mara chuckles awkwardly, looking at me for help. The only thing I can think of is to change the subject, which isn't exactly subtle, but oh, well.

"So, Thanksgiving is almost here," I say too loudly. Mom and Rhys are both trying not to laugh and clearly enjoying watching me flounder.

"I love Thanksgiving," Rosie says with a smile.

304

Vivian doesn't take the bait and assesses me as she finishes her last bite.

"I've been meaning to ask what your plans are, Mara," Mom says brightly.

"Oh—uh, Mom already bought me a plane ticket to Arizona for Thanksgiving."

Wait, what? She isn't going to be here for Thanksgiving? Even though I can feel Vivian's eyes on me, I can't take mine off Mara. I can't imagine her not being with us for Thanksgiving. She's the thing we're most thankful for. It wouldn't feel right if she wasn't at our table.

Mara's eyes meet mine, and I see the apology there. She wishes she could be with us, too.

"Oh, of course," Mom replies, but I can hear how caught off guard and disappointed she is.

The rest of the conversation goes over my head. Even after the dishes are cleared, apple pie is eaten, and everyone helps with finishing Mara's puzzle, all I can think about is how badly I wish I didn't have to go a single day without seeing her. Nothing feels right without her.

But it wouldn't be fair of me to ask her not to be with her mother for Thanksgiving, especially because it seems like they're on good terms. It wouldn't be my place. Mara may feel like she belongs to me, but she doesn't. Not yet.

Eventually, Rhys heads out, and not long after, Vivian goes home as well. It isn't easy to get Rosie to leave, but Mom and I talk her into it by telling her Mara needs rest to get better. I can tell she's still worried about her as I get her tucked into her bed. But I turn the light out anyway, give her one last assurance that Mara is okay, and then close her bedroom door.

Mom is on the phone with Doug again, filling him in

on dinner and the evening at Mara's house. I head upstairs to my room and close the door behind me. I have every intention of changing into pajama pants and watching TV in bed, like I would on a normal night, but I don't. Instead, I stare at my bed. The queen-sized bed that only I have ever slept in, besides Rosie a few times. The bed I sleep in but find no rest.

I realize it, then. I only find rest with Mara in my arms.

CHAPTER TWENTY-EIGHT

Mara

I t's good to be home. It's a strange feeling, really. That this house is my home, and it feels like my home. Especially with my favorite people inside it with me. Especially with Rosie's drawings taped up on my fridge.

It's the first time I've realized how much my life has changed since I moved in. I've come a long way in starting anew, and I owe it to the Dunbars. They've eased me out of the shadow I was living in until the brightness of the sun no longer made my eyes sting. I thought my life was over after Mason divorced me, but now it feels like it's just beginning. Now it feels like my future has opened up, and Mason's actions can no longer drag me down.

I feel…loved.

Because Sean stayed with me last night. Because Rosie was scared. Because Linda made me dinner. Because Rhys came, too. And because my mom flew here as soon as she could.

My heart is full.

A knock startles me out of my warm thoughts, and I glance at the clock. It's nearly nine o'clock. Did Mom decide to stay here tonight after all? I make my way to the door and open it to the cold November air outside. On the other side of the screen door is Sean, looking pensive in the outdoor light.

I give him a little smile, realizing he's probably here to make sure I get tucked in safely and have taken my Tylenol. But before I can tease him about this, he speaks with a stern tone edged with nerves.

"Can we talk?"

My smile melts away as my stomach drops. I study the way his eyebrows hover low over his dark eyes and immediately my nerves go haywire. He wants to talk, and it seems serious. I nod and step back as he opens the screen door.

As I close the interior door behind him, my mind races, wondering what's going on. I take a deep breath and turn to find him standing directly in front of me with a very serious expression that only has me even more worried.

"Is...everything okay?" I ask hesitantly.

His Adam's apple bobs nervously, and he clears his throat. "Everything's fine." But he doesn't sound like everything is fine. He sounds incredibly anxious. I can feel the tension tightening his shoulders and spine as he stands in front of me.

"Okay...?" I prod.

My eyes glue themselves to his bottom lip as he bites it, and a blush steals across my cheeks. He clears his throat again, the rough sound seeming much louder in the silence around us. I feel a funny sort of tingling throughout my body when I raise my eyes back to his.

"Don't go to Arizona for Thanksgiving."

His words catch me completely off guard. I blink at him in surprise and don't even bother trying to mask the expression on my face. He doesn't want me to go to Arizona? My heart beats erratically for a second as I try to figure out why, but then I realize he must be here asking me on Rosie's behalf. A little bit more affection for him sneaks in then, because there's really nothing he wouldn't do to make his daughter happy.

"Rosie wants me to stay, huh?" I ask, easing a smile onto my face to try and lighten the mood, but his stony expression remains unchanged.

He stays stock still as he stares at me and everything else fades into the background. "I'm sure she does," he mutters, seemingly to himself, and then with his eyes still on mine, he steps closer until all I can see is him.

I swallow hard at his proximity to me, standing toe to toe with the gentle heat of his body warming me. "If you go to Arizona, it won't be right," he says, his voice low and quiet as he looks down at me. "It's never right when you aren't with us."

My heart jumps up and down like a pogo stick when I feel his fingers brush mine.

"This is where you should be, Mara. Here." He pauses, studying my surprised face as his fingers lace through mine. "I know I don't have the right to ask you this but stay. Please. This is where you belong."

Where I belong?

My heart drums wildly in my chest as the golden flecks swimming in his eyes flash at me. For the first time, I wonder if he feels this, too. When he hugs me or touches me, does he feel that nudge, too? Was sleeping beside me last night just as peaceful for him as it was for me?

I fight to keep my hopes at bay because this could all be some misunderstanding. Just because he wants me here doesn't mean that he has feelings for me. Those weren't the words that came out of his mouth. He said I belong *here*. In Minnesota, next door to him and his family.

I swallow hard. His familiar sawdust scent and his close proximity makes me want to close my eyes and fall into him, but I can't let myself disappear into someone else who doesn't really want me. I'm sure he doesn't mean anything romantic by asking me to stay for Thanksgiving, even if maybe it sounds that way. He may not mean to be leading me on, but he is.

"Sean," I say softly, "when you say things like that, I—it makes me feel things that I don't think you mean to make me feel."

One brow wiggles slightly in confusion, so I continue.

"You've shown me so much kindness and so much concern that my heart wants to take it a different way, even though I know I shouldn't." I think to remove my fingers from his but can't get myself to. "I don't think you're *trying* to, but you're awakening my heart, so I need you to just...be careful with what you're saying and how it might come across." My mouth feels dry as I finish speaking, and I feel embarrassed to admit that to him, but I need to protect myself from getting hurt even if it's awkward.

Sean's mouth opens to speak but nothing comes out, and then he blinks several times like what I said to him makes no sense at all. "You think I'm leading you on?"

I shrug my good shoulder. "Aren't you?"

He looks at me for a long moment, and the longer the quiet stretches on, the more confused I become.

"No," he finally says. "I'm not leading you on."

Maybe it's the head injury, but I'm not following. What I wouldn't give for him to just spit out what he feels. I sigh softly.

Just ask him, Mara. Ask him how he feels.

My stomach churns painfully, and my breath goes choppy. "Sean, what am I to you?"

He hesitates, and for the first time, he looks away, down at his dusty boots, gathering himself as I wait under a mountain of nerves and vulnerability. When he looks up at me again, his brown eyes are glassy, and the breath catches in my throat.

"You're more to me than I'm ready to admit," he whispers. "Last night, in the waiting room, I was terrified that I might never see your beautiful face again, or hear you laugh, or sing, or smile that little smile I secretly hope is just for me." His free hand gently meets my cheek. "Life is so precious, Mara, and time isn't guaranteed. I thought I learned that lesson when Gabby died, but I didn't truly until last night when I thought —when I thought I might never get to find out what your lips taste like."

My face instantly goes red hot.

"When I thought I might never know what it would feel like for you to be mine." He shakes his head slightly, warm eyes staying on mine. "Whether you know it or not, Mara, I've been yours for a while now. Whether you meant for me to fall for you or not, I did." He studies my face with blushing cheeks, a blush that only makes his words mean that much more to me. "So, no, I'm not leading you on. If it sounds like I'm gone over you, it's because I am."

My heart drumrolls as I stare back at his cautiously hopeful face. And I return that same expression because I can barely believe the words he just gifted me.

I can't breathe. In the best possible way, I can't catch my breath. Without thinking, I lean into his sweet caress and close my eyes. My heart stutters as his thumb softly strokes across my cheek, and I open my eyes to find him studying me with an affectionate expression.

I can't believe he's really saying these things to me. I can't believe that he feels something deeper than friendship for me. I can't believe he wants *me*. I can't believe he's eye to eye with me, hoping that I'll want him, too.

Oh, my heart.

"I understand if it's too soon," he adds gently, holding my hand tighter and smoothing his thumb across my warm cheek one more time. "You just got out of a marriage, and I get it if you need more time to heal. But I'm here whenever you're ready." Something flashes over his face, just a flicker of some big emotion that imprints on me. It was fear. Fear to step into something new with me when he's been alone so long. Fear of putting himself out there like this.

I know that Mason has no hold on my heart anymore. I don't care that it hasn't been that long since the divorce. Because Sean's right. Life is short. And even though my little slip yesterday didn't do any long-lasting damage, I know that it could have. Linda said earlier if you find a good man, keep him. So that's what I'm going to do.

My hand moves of its own accord and lightly presses to his chest. His pulse jumps on my palm. I feel the strong pull to let myself fall for this man. I never thought he would look at me like this or say these things to me.

"Are you sure?" I whisper.

A sweet smile lights up his mouth as he looks down at me. "I'm sure, sweetheart."

Waves of emotion roll through me, hitting me square in the tear ducts. I nod slightly and give him a watery smile as I attempt to process all of this.

He wants me.

"Okay."

"Okay?"

I nod and lean into him, causing his hand to move over my cheek and back through my hair as our faces move closer.

"I'll stay."

A beautiful grin cracks instantly across his face.

"This is where I want to be anyway," I add gently, my good arm slipping around his middle. He releases my hand, and then his arm comes around me, too, the warmth of our bodies mingling into a glow I can feel inside of me as well.

A little sigh of relief slips out of him, and he moves in to rest his forehead against mine. "It is?" His voice is rough and deep and hopeful, so transparent and sweet.

"Yes," I whisper back. "Right here."

He gives a little hum of agreement. "Me, too." He raises his head and kisses my forehead and then exactly between my eyes and then my nose, the scruff of his stubbly chin scratching my skin as he moves.

My body thrums with nerves and desire for him as he looks between my eyes and my mouth. And then, he's tentatively moving in closer, a little uncertainty mixed in with his affectionate expression. The breath catches in my throat when his nose nuzzles mine and his head angles slightly to the side, pausing only inches from my lips.

He's going to kiss me. Sean is going to kiss me...

And then he does. Gentle, warm lips press to mine, his prickly chin meeting my own. I close my eyes and marvel at the intensity that explodes between us. I grip his shirt, forgetting all about my sore elbow, and everything else, and kiss him back.

It lasts only a few sweet seconds, but when he pulls back just slightly, both of our breathing patterns are ragged and unsteady, and I can't help feeling like everything has changed. My future is here, holding me like if he lets go, his knees might give out.

But when I look up at him, his expression isn't what it was before he kissed me. Where there were nerves and exhilaration before, there's pain and grief now. Before I can even react to it though, it's gone. A shy little smile transforms the mouth I just kissed, and his golden-brown eyes turn warm and soft.

He sighs with contentment and then puts one more quick kiss on my lips before he pulls me into his chest. I close my eyes tightly and feel that soul-kicking nudge once again. His fingers gently sift through my hair, and I know; I belong with him. I know it in my gut. And he feels it, too. Happiness fills me up from head to toe, so much happiness that I don't know what to do with it.

I grin into his shirt, feeling like my heart is about to explode. This is really happening. Me and Sean... Sean Dunbar wants to be with me, even though he's seen me at my absolute worst.

There's a peace that permeates me then. The kind of peace I've been searching for my whole life. And I'm convinced he's been searching for it, too.

He's been sneaking me looks and smiles all night, and each time, it sends a thrill up my spine. I know it isn't a coincidence that Sean seems happier than usual, but Linda doesn't comment on it, which surprises me. She usually calls him out no problem, but maybe she's too distracted by me being back at her dinner table after two nights.

My mom left yesterday morning, without offering me a hug or anything maternal. But her lack of hostility and commentary are a good sign that the common ground we've reached is something that will stick. I really, really hope so. It feels good to not be fighting, and finding out more information about her youth helps me understand her so much better. I can't imagine how much it would hurt to be denied the love of your life because you were judged as not being good enough.

I didn't tell her that I'm staying here for Thanksgiving, but I will. She probably won't mind since we just saw each other. She might even prefer to have some space now that she told me everything.

Even though my injuries are better, I don't feel any more mentally clear. Mostly because of the man sitting on the other side of Rosie. It doesn't feel real, and yet it felt perfectly natural to be around him yesterday when he and his family came over after lunch to hang out. I followed his lead, in that he said nothing about us in front of Rosie and Linda, and he made no attempt to touch me like he had Saturday night. But he did throw a smile my way when no one was looking that made me warm from the inside out.

I never expected that he would feel something for me, and because he does, it just seems all the more precious and sacred.

"So, Sean said you've changed your mind about going to

Arizona for Thanksgiving," Linda says as she passes Doug the butter dish. When I first came inside earlier, he hugged me like he was my own father and apologized for not being around this weekend. It meant a lot to me.

"I did," I answer quietly and aim a glance at Sean, who smiles a crooked little half smile at me before going back for another bite of pot roast. Even though we haven't said anything else to each other regarding whatever we are, I feel content just knowing how he feels. I'm not in a hurry to lock him into a relationship. He has Rosie to think about, and if he needs time to make sure he's ready to move on with me, then I have no problems with that.

"Probably a good idea," Doug pipes up as he liberally butters his wheat roll. "You had quite the scare there this weekend. You could use some time to just be home."

"Home with *us*, right?" says Rosie with her blue eyes open wide and pointing at me.

I smile at her and pat the hand she has resting on the table between our bowls. "Wherever you are, sweet girl, is where I want to be."

Rosie beams at me and bounces in her seat a little.

"Does that mean you'll be with us for Thanksgiving?" Linda asks hopefully, drawing my gaze away from her granddaughter.

"If you'll have me, I'd love to."

"Of course!" She claps her hands together with a big smile. "Oh, I can't wait. I bet you have some amazing recipes for Thanksgiving. I haven't cooked Thanksgiving dinner with anyone since—" Her mouth abruptly shuts, and her eyes go to Sean. He gives her an understanding sort of grimace.

Oh. The last time she had help cooking Thanksgiving

dinner was Gabby.

"Since when, Grandma?"

Linda clears her throat awkwardly and flicks her eyes to the ceiling like she's kicking herself. "Since I cooked with your mama," she answers gently.

"Oh." Rosie's little face clouds over with an unreadable expression. The adults exchange uncomfortable glances for a moment, each of us wondering what to say.

It kills me that she doesn't remember her mother. I'm sure it's strange to hear people talk about someone you have no memory of, especially when it's someone who's supposed to be such a big part of your life.

"I bet if she were here, she would love cooking with you," I say to her, hoping to redirect the conversation into a place that might cheer Rosie up.

She looks up at me blankly, like she doesn't know what to do with that idea.

"You know what? Maybe you can help me and your grandma cook this year, and we can make your mom's favorite foods," I offer, because it would be a nice way to have Gabby be a part of Thanksgiving that might not make her sad or uncomfortable.

"I don't know what she liked to eat," Rosie says with a thoughtful frown, and when I look up at Sean for help, his brown eyes are fixed on me. My stomach rolls anxiously. I shouldn't have said anything. I've overstepped and made everyone uncomfortable. I'm about to apologize or change the subject when Sean finally speaks up.

"Lasagna was her favorite food," he says to his daughter. "And she loved anything chocolate. Chocolate cake, chocolate ice cream, chocolate candy, chocolate milk, chocolate covered popcorn—"

"Chocolate covered *popcorn*?" Rosie gasps incredulously. He chuckles and affectionately tugs on her little blonde ponytail.

"That's right, Rosiecakes."

Rosie blinks up at him a couple of times, and then the cutest little laugh bubbles up out of her. "*Popcorn*? That's so silly."

I feel the whole room relax, like we were collectively holding our breath.

Sean grins at her. "Silly and delicious."

"We could make a chocolate cream pie," Linda suggests brightly. "She would've loved that."

"Honestly, Thanksgiving lasagna sounds amazing," Doug adds and takes a giant bite of his roll.

Rosie nods, still a little smile on her face, and then goes back to her food.

Feeling like the crisis was averted, I look at Sean in time to see him lean over and kiss his daughter on the top of her head. He smiles at me as he sits back, and I'm instantly relieved that he isn't upset.

But as we continue eating, it dawns on me that becoming something more to Sean inherently means that I'll always share him with Gabby. She might be gone, but her name will always be whispered between words and events and holidays.

She had him first, and the loss of her will still be there even if things go well between me and Sean. It's unsettling that Sean will always have a sadness in him that I can't take away. The pain of losing his wife won't stop just because he's moved on with me. Sharing him with Gabby doesn't feel like something that could get between us; it feels more like a willing duty. Especially because he doesn't want Rosie to forget her. If I end up with Sean, I would have to keep room in her heart for Gabby, and in his as well.

He'll never be completely mine, and even though I shared my husband with Sarah for a time, I know this is different. At the end of the day, I have to believe that Sean is capable of loving Gabby and all his memories of her, while still loving me, too. It would be wrong to ask him not to talk about her, and I would never do that. She is still a big part of who he is, and I'm very much attracted to who he is. His gentleness. His need to protect the people he cares about. His snarky comebacks when he's trying to rile up his mom. His ability to work hard and provide for his daughter. I'm captivated by all of it, and even if I have to share him, I know I could love him for the rest of my life.

CHAPTER TWENTY-NINE

Sean

S he fell asleep on me twenty minutes ago. To be fair, she warned me that wine makes her sleepy. I can't explain the contentment I feel with her sidled up next to me on her couch, my arm around her shoulders and her cheek on my chest. It's perfect.

The movie has ended, and I turned off the TV, so her little house is quiet and peaceful. We've taken to a sort of routine since last week. She's over for dinner every night as usual, but after Rosie goes to bed, I come over to her house to see her alone. These moments with her are priceless to me, and I find myself leaning toward the end of the day when I can have her all to myself.

I listen to her slow breaths and memorize the floral smell of her hair as she sleeps, feeling a deep sense of love for her that I don't think I could describe if I tried. All I know is, this is meant to last. Her and me. We're the real thing.

We made popcorn and watched a movie on Netflix as we sipped at the bottle of wine I brought over. And the last thing I want to do is wake her up or go back to my house. I just want to stay here with her, where everything feels right.

But she stirs a moment later, snuggling into me a little more, and I feel like I can't breathe. I kiss her forehead gently, hoping she'll drift off again, but instead, her head slowly lifts off my chest until she's looking me in the eyes, her own wide.

"Oh my gosh, did I fall asleep?" she whispers in embarrassment, her cheeks already growing pink.

I trace her cheek with my thumb. "Mhm."

She sits back a little and slaps a hand over her face. "Wow, I'm so sorry—I knew I shouldn't have had that second glass of wine."

I chuckle. "Don't be sorry for nodding off. Be sorry for what you said about me in your sleep," I tease.

Her hand drops, and her jaw does, too. "Oh my gosh! I was talking in my sleep?"

I bite my lip to keep from laughing and sift my fingers back through her long hair. "No, sweetheart; I'm just kidding."

She looks like she wants to be playfully outraged, but I know the hearts in my eyes are keeping her from going off.

"*Do* you talk in your sleep though?" I ask, continuing to stroke my fingers along the side of her head, her soft hair feeling like silk on my skin.

"No, I don't. Do you?"

I shake my head. "Sometimes Rosie does, but usually just if she has a fever and isn't sleeping well."

She smiles at the mention of my daughter. "Poor thing."

"My dad was a sleepwalker. One time when I was kid, he came into my room in the middle of the night and just stood there. I asked him what he was doing and then he just turned around and walked back out. It was super weird."

Mara giggles. "My mom sleeps with her eyes open."

"What?" I exclaim, my hand pausing at the back of her head.

She full on laughs now and leans toward me again, her hand resting on my chest. "She won't believe me, but I saw it plenty of times when I was a kid. It was horrifying."

I laugh, too. "My mom is a drooler."

That has Mara cackling.

"That reminds me—I need to tell Doug to get flood insurance for when she moves in with him."

She laughs from her belly, such a sweet, carefree sound that I feel swallowed up by it in the best possible way. I watch her laugh for another moment, grinning at how stupidly good it feels to make her laugh. When I met her, I had no idea how beautiful she was, inside and out. And seeing it now feels like a gift. Seeing her joy after seeing so much of her depression is a gift.

As her laughter dies down, I bring her back in close to me, and she easily obliges. Her cheek goes to my chest again, and I sigh like a lovesick teenager as I move my arms around her.

"Has she said when she's moving?" Mara asks gently, speaking around the smile still on her face from my joke.

"She was thinking after Christmas, but I don't think that's soon enough for Doug."

She hums. "That's sweet."

I move my hand up and down her arm, being extra gentle near her elbow. "I really couldn't ask for better for my mom."

Her fingers tentatively smooth across my chest, and I can't stop myself from kissing her forehead like it's the most natural thing in the world. Like this is just another Wednesday night for us. The peace I feel about that is unreal.

"I'm going to miss her being next door," Mara says quietly.

"Yeah, but she'll be over a lot still. And you'll still have me and Rosie."

She lifts her head and rests her chin on my chest as she looks at me, a sweet little smile and beautiful blue eyes directed at me. "I hope I always do."

"If I have anything to do with it, you will, sweetheart."

Her expression, which was already warm, softens and melts me like butter. A zing of exhilaration pulses through me as I move in closer, and an iridescent pleasure consumes me when my lips meet hers. And when we kiss a second time, slowly and tenderly, I'm more than a goner.

I pull back just enough to see her eyes, all out of focus and beautiful, our accelerated breaths mingling, and my heart aches to say it.

"Mara..." I whisper longingly. "I...I care about you so much. You're everything I..."

Her mouth touches mine again in a soothing way, like she can feel how much I'm holding back. I feel her fingers sift through the short hairs at the nape of my neck, and goosebumps erupt all over my body. Her touch is like a fire that doesn't incinerate or damage. Her fire is a gentle glow that comforts me. But when I part my lips and feel her tongue brush against mine, that gentle glow consumes me in such intense flames, I forget about every damn thing.

Her face is hot, and her breath is going in and out in bursts, just like mine, and I can't stop my hands as they move down her sides and to her lower back where her shirt has ridden up slightly. My heart hammers in my chest when I sneak my fingers under the hem and palm the small of her back with one hand and the curve of her spine with the other. She gives a little sigh that has my whole body lighting up for her in a way my body hasn't come alive in years.

"Mara..." I whisper between deep, satisfying kisses.

I love you, I say in my mind, pressing kisses along her neck and then back up towards her ear. She's panting now and moans softly when I tug her earlobe into my mouth with my teeth. I move my mouth across her jaw and back to her lips.

I love you, I think, as I revel in the feel of her soft, hot skin on my hands.

"Sean," she breathes, and her hands explore me, too, across my chest and then up and over my shoulders where she wraps her arms and pulls me flush against her.

Everything feels so right. This is...so much more than I expected it to be. This woman snuck into my heart, and by the time I realized it, it was too late to stop it. She's under my skin in the best way. She's become a part of my life in such an irreplaceable way. She's *my* Mara. And she always will be.

I love you, I think, holding her tightly to me.

But then she abruptly pulls back and stares at me. "What?" she asks, her eyes wide and her face flushed, her breath ragged.

"Huh?" is my confused response.

"You...you just said you loved me," she murmurs roughly.

My pulse, which was already elevated, skyrockets. "I said that *out loud*?"

Mara nods, her fingers clutching my shoulder blades.

I close my eyes and mentally kick myself.

"Did you...mean it?" she whispers when I open my eyes again.

I remove my hands from under her shirt and place them on her hips as I try to figure out how to handle this. I don't want to scare her off. But there's no denying that what I said is the truth.

"Yes, I meant it."

She swallows hard, her breathing leveling out slightly. The flush is still present on her face, but so are a dozen other emotions that send me into a panic.

"You don't have to say anything back, okay? It's—I didn't mean to say it so soon."

She nods distractedly and moves back so she can stand up. She walks around her coffee table on unsteady legs, and the lack of her close to me is one of the worst things I've ever felt. So, I get up, too, adjust my jeans, and move toward her. She turns toward me and then—"I love you, too," she says before I can take more than two steps.

I stop, my heart pounding all over again when I see the tears in her eyes and hear the honesty, and little bit of fear, in her voice.

"I—I didn't want to say it this soon either, but...I do," she says. "I do. And this between us is something I never expected, but I know that if I lost you, I...I don't know what I would do." Those tears tip over onto her pink cheeks, and I close the space between us. I wrap my arms around her, and she leans into me.

"I don't know what I would do either," I whisper, and when she gives me the tiny smile that made me fall in love with her, I smile too and drop my forehead to hers.

The relief I feel is palpable.

She loves me.

I breathe in this moment of vulnerability and commit everything I can to memory. I know that one day, I'll look back on my life and this will be one of those moments that I'd kill to go back and relive.

After a moment, she chuckles. "So much for taking this slow, huh?"

I chuckle too and kiss the tip of her nose. "I'm not that upset about it."

She beams up at me with a stunning smile that takes my breath away. And I know right then. I know that I'm going to marry her someday.

I'm distracted as hell at work the next day, and Rhys more than notices. He's been calling me "space cadet" and "zombie brains" all day. But I can't help it. Everything has changed. And as soon as I spilled the beans to Rhys and my mom, I haven't heard the end of it. They keep saying how good it is that I'm moving on after so long, and how proud of me they are for finally going all in with Mara. Their opinions don't really matter to me; I just want to dwell in the feeling of being wanted by her, in whatever capacity that is.

"You good, man?" Rhys calls to me from the other side of his truck. "Or are you just zoning out again?"

I realize I'm standing at my tailgate, not doing a damn thing but staring at the bright orange case of my chainsaw. When I scowl over at him, he chuckles.

"Mind your business," I say roughly, but it does nothing to change his amused expression.

The sun has already settled behind the horizon, dropping the temperature even more and casting us in shadows and dark shapes as we pack up our gear. But even the lack of lighting doesn't mask how bright Rhys's features are.

"All I know is, if I ever start daydreaming about a woman like that, you have my permission to smack me upside the head."

I huff and round the bumper, headed towards the driver's side door. "I could do it now to save time, if you want."

Rhys laughs and gives me a shrug that's meant to portray nonchalance. "Nah. If I have anything to do with it, I won't ever settle down."

"Ah, come on. You're just saying that because it's been a couple years since you had a girlfriend. I'm sure there's some lucky lady out there just waiting for you to sweep her off her feet."

He closes the tailgate of his truck a little harder than necessary. "No lady would be lucky to date me, man. I've got too much baggage." Rhys says it as lightheartedly as he can manage, but his tone is still dejected.

"I know you're not fishing for compliments, Rhys, but you're a good guy. The right one won't mind your baggage." The baggage we're referring to is his family, who pop in and out his life seemingly at random, only when they want something from him.

He looks at me for a long moment, like he can't decide

whether I'm right or wrong.

"Trust me. I know from experience."

He nods in the falling darkness but doesn't move toward the front of his truck to leave, so I wait to see if he'll clue me in on what he's thinking.

"You know I didn't want Bethany back, right?" His voice is low and broken as he brings up his last girlfriend. He never really went into specifics about why they broke up, just that it was over, and it was for the best.

"You didn't?"

He hesitates for a second, and I wait with interest. He hasn't talked about anyone, including his ex-girlfriend, in years.

"She...uh, she got spooked by my family," he admits so quietly I can barely hear him. "She wasn't supposed to meet them, but Dad just showed up one day and...that was it."

"That sucks, Rhys. I'm sorry."

"Yeah."

"And you didn't want her back because...?" I add, hoping he'll explain a little more about it.

He clears his throat. "She deserved better, Sean. I try my hardest, but there's no escaping biology. I'm bound to turn out just like him."

My eyes widen in surprise, but before I can argue with that, he keeps talking.

"Bethany was better off without this ticking time bomb."

I knew Rhys's family messed him up, but I didn't realize he still thought so little of himself after all this time. I thought he had realized how different he is from them, but apparently, he hasn't.

"You're nothing like him, Rhys," I tell him gravely. "And you never will be."

He says nothing, likely shutting down because his family has always been a sensitive subject for him.

I can't stand that he hates himself just as much as his parents do. Despite his upbringing, he's one of the most loyal people I've ever known. There hasn't been one tough situation in my life that he hasn't been there for me.

I stride over to him quickly and plant both my hands on his shoulders. "Say it," I demand.

Rhys looks up at me, his eyes shining with tears in the fading light of the sun. "I'm nothing like him," he whispers.

"Say it again."

He sniffs, his shoulders emitting just the tiniest shudder. "I'm nothing like him."

I know he doesn't believe it. The lack of conviction in his voice worries me. I've always been aware that his jovial disposition is used to hide his own pain, but I didn't realize his pain was this deep.

"Have you heard from him at all lately?"

Rhys shakes his head and steps back, my hands falling off his shoulders. "He's probably back in jail again."

I nod, watching him closely.

"Anyway," he mutters, and clears his throat. "I'm happy for you, man. Mara's good people."

His attempt to change the subject doesn't sit well with me, and I wonder if he's lying to me about not hearing from his dad. I decide to let it go for the time being, hoping that he'll seek me and my family out like he did when we were teenagers, back when our house was his safe haven.

"Thanks, Rhys."

"Let me know what to bring for Thanksgiving," he says, heading to the driver's side of his truck. Before I can tell him we're doing Gabby's favorite foods for Thanksgiving, the door closes, and then he's pulling his truck out onto the street.

CHAPTER THIRTY

Mara

It's the night before Thanksgiving, and I'm feeling particularly thankful at the moment. Sean and I are on my couch, my legs thrown over his, his arms around me, our faces close. He touches his nose lightly to mine, and I smile.

Whatever movie we watched is over, and we both know he should head back to his house for the night. He's already mentioned he's looking forward to his mom moving out so that I can hang out over there in the evenings. Either way, I get to see him, so I don't mind.

It's been nothing but bliss since he asked me not to go to Arizona, and now I know there's nothing that could've kept me away from him and his family. I keep thinking that what happened between me and Mason was meant to happen the way it did.

I touch the buttons of Sean's blue flannel shirt, my brow crinkling. But does that mean that what happened to Sean was meant to happen as well? Does that mean he was meant to lose his wife so he could find me? I don't like that. It feels...wrong. Like she had to be sacrificed so that I could be happy with him instead.

It would be so nice to tie up our lives with a cute little bow as we both move on together into a new life, but that isn't how it works. Our happiness now will never erase the pain he feels from her death. Love doesn't change what's broken; it just helps carry the pieces.

I took Mason's love, or whatever lame version of it he gave me, and tried to use it to glue my jagged edges together. I've learned that now. I know not to use Sean's love to hold me together. I can do it myself, and I should. And I don't want Sean to use my love to help him walk on the days he needs to kneel at his wife's grave. I want him to get up himself, knowing that I'm right beside him and always will be. Love gives you the strength to stand, not from the outside, but from within.

"I can feel your mind turning," Sean murmurs and leans his head to the side so he can kiss my temple. His mouth is warm and soft and everything I love about him. Gentle, purposeful, reliable.

"Love is no simple thing," I whisper, and he pulls back enough to see my face. I look up into his golden-brown eyes that are so closely watching me. "You're only the second man I've ever loved, and I guess I'm just hoping I have it right."

His nose scrunches up slightly. "Feels pretty right to me," he says. "Feels pretty damn perfect, actually."

My gaze falls to where my fingers rest on his shirt. "But love *isn't* perfect. I'll never be able to love you perfectly, Sean, and I'm sure you won't be able to love me perfectly either."

He lifts one hand from my back and tips my chin up so I meet his eyes. "That doesn't mean it isn't right. That doesn't mean I'll change my mind." His thumb smooths over my cheek. "You were the last thing I was looking for, but I sure as hell don't plan on giving you up."

I turn my face enough to kiss his hand and then look

back at him. "Me either."

A little smile lifts up one corner of his mouth. "You're very introspective," he comments lightly and kisses the tip of my nose. "I can't remember a single time Gabby and I talked about things like this."

I smooth my hand over his chest. "What did you talk about then?"

He shrugs, his hand moving from my face so he can sift his fingers through my long hair. He does this a lot, and every time, it makes me feel beautiful in a way I can't describe.

"We could talk about anything," he says, his expression shuttering. "She was an open book. I think that's why I fell for her so quickly. She let me love her exactly as she was, even if that included her being a little wild or a little too loud." His smile returns, but it's sad. "She was always giving me guff or laughing at something stupid I said. It's a wonder she was interested in me. I always thought so."

"Is it weird that I wish I could've met her? I feel like if I had known her, I would just be knowing you better. Does that make sense?"

"Yeah, sweetheart," he says gently, still touching my hair. "Rhys said she would've liked you."

That makes me smile, even though he spoke in a broken sort of way. He can feel just how complicated this all is, and it comforts me a little. But his body begins to tense under my palms. His fingers press into my hip, and his hand stops moving to cup the back of my head.

"I know you'll always love her," I whisper to him, and run my fingers through his dark hair. "I don't plan on competing with her. That goes for Rosie, too."

He puts his forehead against mine and lets out a sigh.

"You say you can't love me perfectly, but here you are doing it."

"I'm trying."

He pulls back, staring at me with both desire and pain. It causes tears to well up in my eyes as I remember him begging me to promise him that I would keep trying.

"I'll *always* keep trying," I whisper even quieter. Without another breath, kisses me.

It's a firm kiss, filled with a different kind of intensity than usual. It's a kiss that's seeking out comfort, and it breaks my heart for him. I offer him a second kiss, meant to give him strength, but his hands start to tremble anyway.

When he pulls away, his eyes are rimmed red. "Mara, I—" He stops and clears his throat, the hand on my hair dropping away from me. "I don't like to talk about the way Gabby died," he admits quietly, his voice sounding ragged and pained.

"Okay," I reply gently, patiently. I can respect that he doesn't like talking about it. I certainly can't imagine it would be an easy thing to do. But instead of taking the out I'm giving him, he takes a deep breath and then looks up at me.

"She..." he hesitates, every muscle in his body tight. "Mara, she committed suicide." The sentence stumbles out of his mouth, and then he shuts his eyes tightly, his chest rising and falling in a pattern approaching hyperventilation. "I found her in the bathtub."

I go perfectly still.

Suicide.

His wife died by *suicide*...

My heart lurches so hard in my chest that I feel the pain of it in my lungs, too. My mouth dries up and so do all the words I wish I could say to make it better.

It all makes sense now.

Everything he's ever said to me comes to mind.

Promise me you'll keep trying.

The very first time he touched me—looking at me so seriously, with so much passion, as he told me I needed to keep trying…it was because *she didn't.*

It's dangerous to look at the water under the bridge.

Oh, no. When he found me at the bridge… He was terrified that I would meet the same fate as his wife.

"Sean…" I choke out. I had no idea how much pain I've been causing him all this time… I had no idea that this is what he's been battling all these years while trying to raise Rosie on his own.

He sniffs and looks down again to where his hand rests on my thigh.

There's so much I want to say, and yet, I can't form a single sentence. All I can do is hold him and hope he somehow can understand how deeply I mourn for him.

I wish I could reach into his chest and hold his heart. I wish I could make it all just go away, but I can't. I can't fix what happened or change the choice Gabby made.

But I can stay by his side. I can hold him when he breaks down. I can show him the love he wasn't looking for when he found me.

Blinking back my own tears, I reach inside myself, to the depths where I remember how much I succumbed to my own depression.

"Sometimes it's hard to fight that darkness," I whisper,

my voice wobbling slightly. "I know that firsthand. And *because* I know it, I can tell you that her choice wasn't an easy one for her to make." Sean closes his eyes, and I reach up to smooth my thumb across his stubbly cheek. "I can tell you that I understand *why* she made that choice." His eyes open again, but his eyebrows scrunch together with emotion. "And I can tell you that the unfortunate feelings she and I have shared in common will only make me love you more." I sniff and bring his face just slightly closer. "I will love you on her behalf and my own." I kiss his chin. "I will love you when you miss her." I kiss his cheek. "I will love you when you talk about her." I kiss his other cheek. "I will love you when we include her in our family holidays." I kiss his forehead. "I will love you even as you love her, too."

He captures my lips with his and gives me another firm, pained kiss. My heart beats louder in my ears as I return it, as if I'm once again sitting in the cab of his truck after he took my hand and walked me back from the bridge, hearing the life pumping through me.

Well, he can have my life. There is no fear in me about belonging to him. There is no worry that if I let him have every last bit of me, he'll one day trade me in for someone better. *This* is trust. Faith. Love. I'm sure of it. And I will choose to give him everything I have because I know he's doing that very thing right now—giving me even the dark, broken, bleeding parts that he's been holding back from me all this time.

Love isn't some perfect, intact thing.

Love has edges, some of them soft, some of them rough.

Love is a moving, living thing, like the current under the surface.

And I choose to let myself get swept away.

———————————————

Sean's house is buzzing, and I feel the same buzz deep inside my soul.

Everywhere I look, I see someone I care about. Doug, trying to sneak his finger into the mixing bowl of chocolate creme pie filling. Linda smacking his hand away with the whisk. Rosie dipping her finger in while her grandma is distracted. Rhys's riotous laughter carrying through the doorway to the living room. The man I love's laughter mixing in, lower and more restrained, but just as carefree.

A buoyant sense of belonging and rightness fills me up.

I'm exactly where I'm meant to be.

Everything that's happened in the last year has brought me here. Each moment of heartache and desperation. Each moment pondering what happened to life I loved.

Well, the life I love is this one. With Doug, Linda, Rhys, Rosie, and Sean.

When everyone stops what they're doing and looks at me, I realize belatedly that I've started to sing to myself as I was mixing the whipped cream. I just smile and keep going because to me, everything is a song.

Sometimes it's an absent sort of song that emanates out of you and blends into whatever you're doing, wherever you are.

Sometimes it's the song of how it feels when his arms reach around you as you sing, pulling you back against his steady chest where his heartbeat syncs with yours.

Sometimes it's a mournful sort of song, the kind that

thrusts you into the past where you no longer fit so that you remember all you've soldiered through.

Sometimes it's the sound of water under the bridge, enticing you to jump, or the sound of running water in a bathtub, pulling you under.

Sean kisses my cheek, and I close my eyes. "I love you," he whispers in my ear.

Sometimes it's a love song born out of a broken heart.

And as we finish up cooking all of Gabby's favorite foods, I still sing softly. I sing for the pain she felt and for the people she left.

Then, Sean and Rhys spread the little kitchen table apart to put the leaf in and make it bigger for all of us to sit together. And as I look around at all these faces, I know that there isn't a single one of us who hasn't been touched in some way by something painful. Rhys and his complicated family. Doug and his kids, who are elsewhere for Thanksgiving. Linda and her husband's sudden death years ago. Rosie and her mother. Sean and his late wife. And me.

We're each enduring something. Each fighting with something that we don't want to let go of, even if it's just the idea of the perfect family or what should have happened instead of what actually did. I've never felt so safe, so steady anywhere in my entire life. I'm right where I belong here with these people who pass lasagna, spinach artichoke dip, and four kinds of chocolate dessert in the name of someone they loved.

And then Rhys lifts his glass and says with a saddened smile, "To Gabby."

EPILOGUE

Sean

The coffee shop is bustling as I take a seat with Rosie on my lap. We're sitting at the closest table we could get to where a stool and microphone sit. Mom and Doug are to my left, and Rhys is to my right, each of us here to support my girl. For whatever reason, I'm a ball of nerves as we wait for Mara to take the little stage tucked back into the corner and begin her very first gig in a year.

When I asked her if she was nervous on the way here, she said she was just excited. I admire her for having zero nerves, and I'm so proud of her for getting to this point. She's been through so much and fought so hard to get her passion for music back. It's been a privilege to see her grow from the quiet, depressed neighbor to my sweet, confident Mara.

"Daddy, I'm waiting so hard!" Rosie whines, and I chuckle as I switch her to my one knee. Instantly, my heel taps up and down on the floor.

"She'll start soon, Rosiecakes."

"Oh, I can't wait," Mom agrees with Rosie. "It's been so long since I've seen her perform."

I take a deep breath, irritated at myself for feeling nervous on Mara's behalf. There's no need to worry, especially because I know Mara is doing the thing she was made to do.

"She's going to do great," Rhys says in a lower voice, just loud enough to be heard over the hum of the coffee shop. I look over at him, my foot still bouncing.

"Why the hell am I nervous?"

He rolls his eyes. "Because you love her, you idiot, and you worry about people when you love them."

I heave out a sigh. "She deserves to have this back," I say, facing forward again. "I just want her to be happy."

Rhys visibly stiffens next to me. "Dude, of course she's happy. Even if she wasn't about to get back into the music world, she'd still be happy."

My stomach tightens into a knot. "Why?"

He groans. "You really are an idiot," he mutters to himself. "She'd still be happy because she has you, you moron, and Rosie and Mrs. D, and all of us."

Rosie wiggles off my lap and goes to sit with my mom instead, probably because my anxious energy is throwing her off. I push my hand through my hair and turn a little more towards my best friend.

He's right. I know we make Mara happy. I know we're enough for her. With us, she has everything.

Despite how difficult it was for me to tell her how Gabby died, Mara was incredibly supportive and empathetic...in a way I had hoped for and then some. I can't believe how well she understands what I need.

Mara appears then, moving confidently to the stool and microphone with a beautiful smile on her face and her guitar in one hand. She's wearing a flowy white dress and no shoes, with her long red hair curled in loose waves. She looks...

perfect. Angelic, almost. And when she turns that smile towards my family and me, my heart beats hard in my chest.

I'm going to love this woman for the rest of my life.

And there's a part of me then that feels a strange gut instinct that Mara moving in next door was no accident. It couldn't be.

No, Gabby sent me Mara.

There's no other explanation. Gabby helped Mara move into my life because I needed someone to lift me out of my own guilt and my own depression. By putting Mara in my path, she gave me what she was unable to give me when she was alive.

And when Mara begins to sing and strum her guitar, I feel a bit of peace wash over me. Because Gabby made her own peace, however final, and Mara's peace is evident in the passionate, natural way she sings and plays.

Between songs, I glance back at the rest of the coffee shop to find it packed with everyone anticipating her next song. It makes me so proud of her—for not giving up.

And as soon as this is over, I'll be sure to tell her that I'll never give up on us, no matter what comes. I'll be sure to tell her every day that I love her and am so glad she's by my side.

She's the kind of thing you don't mess up. The kind of thing you hold on to for as long as you possibly can. And with Gabby always in the back of my mind, I know I'll never take Mara for granted.

Mara begins her next song, and goosebumps rise all over my body as I hear the crowd singing along. And then she smiles at me, this brilliant, stunning smile, and I know. I know in my gut that the best is yet to come.

ACKNOWLEDGEMENTS

First of all, thank you for reading this book! Being a newbie author with a tiny reader base is intimidating, so thank you for giving me a try. You'll never know how grateful I am.

Thank you to Emily Ciochetto and Marti Galbraith for being such amazing beta readers! Your feedback has helped me turn this story into what it was meant to be, especially in regards to the ending. Thanks for putting up with all my unsolicited book nonsense.

This was my first time hiring an editor and I feel like I seriously lucked out! Thank you, Tiff, for all the help in editing this book. Your enthusiasm pumped me up so much, and your editing skills made this book shine.

As always, thank you to my family. I've received so much support from both close and extended relatives. I hope I make y'all proud.

Lastly, thank you to my husband. Thanks for distracting our children so I could get some words in. Without your encouragement and belief in me, I wouldn't be doing this. I love you.

ABOUT THE AUTHOR

Katie Stearns

Katie Stearns is a contemporary romance author from Clarkfield, MN. In addition to being an author, she is also a stay at home mama to two adorable little girls, aged 6 and 3. In what little spare time she has, she enjoys baking, photography, reading and rereading romance novels by her favorite authors, traveling with her husband, and watching The Office.

NATIONAL SUICIDE PREVENTION LIFELINE

800-273-8255

Made in the USA
Columbia, SC
26 December 2022